CONTENT

Cliff
Richard

There they all were. Names to set the pulses racing - Elvis,
The Everlys, Jerry Lee Lewis, Marty Wilde, Buddy Holly, the
Big Bopper. And there was I - Harry Webb! Fine for a
plumber. Ideal for a policeman. But for a pop singer, the
kiss of death.

So we sat round a table in a pub and threw out ideas. After
an hour we got near it. Russ Clifford ... Cliff Russord.
Ten minutes later, Cliff Richards. Then the brainwave.
'If you leave off the 's',' someone said, 'you'll be paying
tribute to Little Richard, and be out of the ordinary with
two christian names at the same time. When you're
interviewed on air (we were nothing if not confident!), the
interviewer's bound to get it wrong and call you 'Richards'.
You can correct him and that gets the name mentioned twice!'

That clinched it. Back home I announced the big news to my
parents and sisters. From now on I was Cliff Richard.
No-one must call me Harry again. 'OK, Cliff,' they said -
and they never did!

Elsewhere it wasn't so easy. Having two names caused no end
of hassles with passports and legal documents, and I remember
being stuck for hours at an Indian airport with immigration
officials trying to cope with my title 'Harry Webb alias
Cliff Richard'. To their minds that meant only one thing -
a professional criminal! Soon after that I had my name
officially changed by deed poll. Harry Webb was finally
laid to rest.

Today the only reminder of him is when fans use the name
thinking they're getting through to the real me. What a
give-away!

I wonder how many similar stories lie behind the many name
changes featured in this book.

CLIFF RICHARD
also known as Harry Webb

INTRODUCTION

The desire to assume a more glamorous, more commercially appealing and artistically appropriate identity is by no means exclusive to entertainers. Authors, politicians, criminals, sportsmen and even plumbers have abandoned their birth name for reasons without number. But the very combinations of ego, ambition and audacity which sends individuals in search of footlights and headlines seems to invariably encourage a total metamorphosis, from unknown ugly duckling to adored beautiful swan.

In the words of J. F. Clarke, author of *Pseudonymns*, "Ours is the age of celebrity, in which it is possible to achieve an almost instant, and frequently international reputation by appearing in one film, or a networked television series; by writing one best-selling novel, or enjoying a celebrated season on the football field. When, in Daniel J. Boorstin's phrase, you can be 'known for your well-knownness', having the *right* name is vital ingredient in maintaining your total image."

Dwight Jamison, the superbly drawn blind white jazz pianist in Evan Hunter's *Streets of Gold*, who begins life as Ignazio Silvio Di Palermo, essentially concurrs. "I changed my name just in the nick, as it turned out, because I was on the verge of becoming a big success, ma'am, and think what might have happened to Kirk Douglas if he'd still been Issur Danielovitch Demsky when he made *Champion* . . . I no longer wished to belong to that great brotherhood of *compaesani* whose sole occupation seemed to be searching out names ending in vowels."

Let there be no doubt that there is no intolerance greater than that of the 'New World' and its media, toward lengthy, complicated or simply unattractive names. Try to imagine how many banner headlines opera star Maria Callas would have featured in during her romantic fling with Greek shipping magnate Aristotle Onassis, had newspapers been required to deal with Maria Kalogeropoulos.

There have been instances of name changing for apparent career advancement since man learned to scratch his name in the dust with a stick. Classical composer Jacques Offenbach (1819-1880) was actually born Jakob Eberst, and a number of his peers effected similar changes. The instances were isolated until around the turn of this century, when Europe's huddled masses, pogrom bruised and hopeful of a new life under the shelter of the Statue of Liberty, began to stream into America. For many, the desire for a new beginning in the land where the streets were supposedly paved with gold, was so strong that the loss of a family name, no matter how precious, was a relatively small price to pay for acceptance.

Slavic, Mediterranean, Arabic, Polish and Spanish names, drenched in centuries of rich tradition and history, were cast aside willingly, like so many pairs of soiled socks. Fifteen letters were reduced to five, four syllables to one. Those who didn't actually forsake their family name were motivated sufficiently by a survival instinct to at least adopt a working nickname. Certainly it is easy to accept the enduring legend that, during the Swing Jazz and Big Band era, it wasn't possible to join the Musician's Union unless you had changed some part of your original handle. Stumpy, Wingie, Ziggy, Red, Sonny, Tex, Shorty, Doc, Papa, King, Buddy, Duke, Kid, Fats, Buster and Buck were sure passports to a place in the jazz realm.

Not all European names were corrupted or abandoned becuase of their complexity. If called upon to nominate the single most prevalent cause of name changing, one would have to cite it as the desire to hide a Jewish background. From George Gershwin (Jacob Gershovitz) to David Soul (David Solberg), there are thousands of examples within these pages of such process (made all the more puzzling by the strong degree of Jewish control of the entertainment industry). Bob Dylan may indeed have wanted to honour his favourite poet, Dylan Thomas, but all the same its hard it imagine Robert Allen Zimmerman being accepted as 'the voice of the generation'.

Political and sociological reasons aside, the reasons for name changes in music are as numerous as the names themselves and the means by which they are changed. Comics take names that sound funny, opera singers take names that sound Italian, punk rockers take names that sound angry. Performers from 'good families' take names to avoid embarrassing their parents. Insecure neophytes takes names that brim full of strength, even arrogance.

Original names are shortened, reversed, mis-spelt and combined. Mother's maiden names are adopted and childhood pet names are retained. For many who are dissatisfied with the name bestowed upon them by surely well intentioned parents, the search for a new identity is often conducted no further afield than their own middle name. Glenn Miller, Louis Armstrong, Gene Autry, Dionne Warwick, Steve Forbert and scores more have, by simply severing and discarding their first Christian name, achieved a more satisfying identity that appeared to them at least, more inviting to fame's fickle finger.

More than a few changes are understandable and entirely forgiveable: particularly in the case of those offspring whose parents' sense of gratitude for a new start in life landed them with the names of contemporary American presidents, particularly Woodrow Wilson (Woody Guthrie, Woody Herman) and Franklin Delano Roosevelt (Del Reeves). One unfortunate gentleman within these pages was actually saddled with the city and state of his birth — Hartford, Connecticut.

The end of the jazz era closed the door on almost-mandatory name changes. The first flush of rock'n'roll was almost organic, and Bill Haley, Elvis Presley, Carl Perkins, and Jerry Lee Lewis were real names (although Gene Vincent, Buddy Holly and Ritchie Valens were not). In the fifties, the Hollywood Dream Machine still had the monopoly on 'starmaking' and it seems likely that the ruthlessly efficient practices of the major studios were imitated by British entrepreneur Larry Parnes, known to his colleagues as Mr Parnes, Shillings & Pence. This charismatic svengali vitalised British entertainment in the immediate pre-Beatles years with his audacious assembly line system of teen idol manufacture. Indeed, Stan Freberg's *Old Payola Roll Blues* scenario ("Hey kid, can you sing?". "No". "Good, come with me . . . You got all the requirements, a pretty face and a pompadour") might well have been a tribute to Parnes' style of operation.

Entering the management field in 1956 to assist publicist John Kennedy in the promotion of merchant seaman Thomas Hicks, who soon became pioneering British rocker Tommy Steele, Parnes signed a stable of earnest, handsome young men to five year contracts with stipulated rising yearly wages. His deft grooming and positioning (in a land which had already taken a character called Dickie Valentine to its heart) transformed unknowns Reginald Smith, Ronald Wycherly, Clive Powell, Ray Howard, Roy Taylor and Malcolm Holland into scream sensations Marty Wilde, Billy Fury, Georgie Fame, Duffy Power, Vince Eager and Nelson Keene. Sadly, Parnes' magic kingdom of fame was bowled for six by The Beatles (who, ironically, were once employed by Parnes to back Johnny Gentle) and he eventually yielded up his throne to the less flamboyant Brian Epstein.

Although there was no real American equivalent of the incredible Mr. Parnes, the teen idol 'industry' in Philadelphia and New York employed similar methods at much the same time. Their clean cut, square-jawed young crooners were uniformly *Bobby* in name (Vee, Vinton, Rydell, Darin) and orientation (Fabian, Frankie Avalon, Troy Shondell). Equipped with a slick new name, press agent and echo-drenched singles, they were sent forth for their fifteen minutes of manipulated fame.

If the Beatles succeeded in giving pop music a degree more seriousness in the sixties, then they also managed to stem to flow of identi-kit pin up boys. Ringo may have been a nickname, but John, George and Paul really were John, George and Paul (well, actually James Paul). With the aid of the Fab Four, radical changes in music galvanised our collective attention far more than a string of fabricated teen idols.

By the turn of the decade, the cosmic, transcendental, macrobiotic, mother nature's son syndrome has fostered a general attitude so opposite to the traditional showbiz ethic that some established performers actually attempted to disown their stage names and 'come clean' about their fraud. Bobby Vee, Del Shannon, Lou Christie and Don Grady all released albums under their real names (or in Christie's case, a variation thereof); none of which were even remotely best sellers.

Woodstock Generation attitudes held sway in America throughout the greater part of the seventies, while in Britain the ghost of Larry Parnes had inspired a new troupe of masquerading marvels, the likes of Gary Glitter (Paul Gadd), Alvin Stardust (Bernard Jewry), Marc Bolan (Mark Feld) and David Essex (David Cook). When punk and new wave rock exploded across Europe and Australia and lightly touched America in the late seventies, any remaining guilt feelings about deceiving the public swiftly evaporated.

The New Music boom was as gloriously trashy, disposable and self-effacing as the beefcake teen idol era. Instead of being collectively called Bobby, the punks became caricatures of public enemies numbers 1 to 99; their mock menace no more absurd than their comic book identities — Johnny Rotten, Sid Vicious, Rat Scabies, Jeff Magnum, Johnny Blitz, Richard Hell, Johnny Dole, Poly Styrene.

The derivation of assumed names is as fascinating as the names themselves and, although there is simply not the space to footnote every entry, some of the most appealing annecdotes are related. It is also worthwhile to touch on a handful of instances here.

Brenton Wood, who scored a 1967 smash with *Gimme Little Sign*, was plain Alfred Jesse Smith until he adapted the name of plush Hollywood suburb Brentwood. Blues singer Little Esther Phillips was Esther Mae Jones until she spotted a roadside billboard advertising Phillips brand gasoline. Troggs drummer Ronnie Bond was Ronald Bultis until he developed a fascination for movie spy James Bond. Kiss leader Gene Simmons was languishing in obscurity as Gene Klein until he decided to imitate his favourite actress, Jean Simmons.

Philadelphia chicken plucker Ernest Evans was offering a tribute to his idol Fats Domino when he became Chubby Checker. Reginald Dwight, piano pumper with late sixties British blues outfit Steampacket, borrowed a word each from Soft Machine sax player Elton Dean and singer Long John Baldry to become Elton John. Harry Lillis Crosby picked up the name Bing during his childhood in Spokane as, a result of his liking for a character called Bingo in the comic book *The Bingville Bugle*.

The name Crosby gives us an interesting example of how one performer will covet what another seeks to discard. Byrds founder David Crosby was actually born David Van Cortland, while country-folk singer Ronald Crosby tossed away the very same name that David had adopted, by becoming Jerry Jeff Walker. Of course, there are some names that find unanimous rejection, such as Kaminsky, which was jettisoned by Neil Diamond (Noah Kaminsky), Danny Kaye (David Daniel Kaminsky) and film director-cum-pop singer Mel Brooks (Melvyn Kaminsky). Even an innocuous name like Webb has found considerable disfavour, being abandoned by Cliff Richard (Harry Rodger Webb) and Gary Numan (Gary Anthony James Webb). One name seemingly heaven sent for pop stardom, Steven Nice, was dropped by its owner in favour of Steve Harley.

The wrong colour can also propel young hopefuls toward concerned action. Thus did Priscilla White become Cilla Black and Barry Green become bubblegum star Barry Blue. Fleetwood Mac founder Peter Green was basically content with his colour, after lopping off a clumsy Jewish ending (Greenbaum).

Not all changes are necessarily intentional. Take the case of country singer Warner Mack, as related by writer Irwin Stambler, "At first Warner MacPherson performed under his original name. However, when he began recording, the person preparing the label copy mistook his nickname for his actual surname, hence Mack." Ray Charles might well have continued to face life as Ray Charles Robinson, had not American boxer Walker Smith styled himself Sugar Ray Robinson.

Meat Loaf blames a football coach for his new identity, which began as a school nickname and eventually edged out his birth name of Marvin Lee Aday. It seems that Marvin managed to lumber his awesome frame onto the coach's foot during a particular manoeuvre, eliciting a howl to the general effect of, "Get off me, you great hunk of meat loaf!"

This book is intended to serve as both a reference work and a source of amusement and interest for those with a penchant for the trivial and obscure. It would be reasonable to state that no work of this scope has been previously attempted. I believe it reveals much about the nature of entertainers and the industry that surrounds them.

A number of criteria were applied to the following listings. Firstly, the change from maiden name to married name on the part of females was not considered grounds for inclusion, although a few entries may have slipped through the lines. There is a modest Maiden Names section and a number of such names have been included as part of entries where other changes have been effected (e.g. Tina Turner — Annie Mae Turner nee Bullock, Cass Elliot — Ellen Naomi Elliot nee Cohen).

Secondly, general acceptance of standard Christian name contractions has been assumed throughout. Accordingly, no entries appear from the Henrys who became Hank, Williams who became Billy, Lawrences who became Larry, etc. There are some exceptions where there is a possible doubt regarding the original name. For instance, Bert can be Bertram, Herbert, Hubert, Cuthbert, or (as in the case of bandleader Bert Kaempfert) Berthold.

Finally, the first and major section of the book is an A-Z listing of rock, popular and contemporary performers, along with 'household names' from other genres. Although there are specialist listings for Jazz, Blues, Country & Western, Reggae, Opera, Songwriters etc, this section carries such major entities as Count Basie, Dizzy Gillespie, Hank Snow, Maria Callas, George Gershwin, Peter Tosh and Billie Holiday.

This pioneering work makes no claim to comprehensivity or complete accuracy. Although every effort has been made to secure multiple confirmations of each entry, it is inevitable, given the highly personal nature of true identities, that some inaccurate information has been repeated on these pages. Any observant reader chancing upon such errors is entitled to a smug sigh of satisfaction, although a polite notification will be somewhat more productive.

Glenn A. Baker

MEAT LOAF — Marvin Lee Aday

ADAM ANT — Stuart Leslie Goddard

CHARLES AZNAVOUR — Charles Aznavurjan

JANE AIRE — Jane Ashley

LOUIS ARMSTRONG -– Daniel Louis Armstrong

8

A

JOHNNY ACE .... John Marshall Alexander Jnr.
FAYE ADAMS .... Fay Scruggs
RITCHIE ADAMS (FIREFLIES)) .... Richard Adam Ziegler
GENE ADKINSON (DREAMWEAVERS) .... Harvey Adkinson
JANE AIRE (& BELVEDERES) .... Jane Ashley
AL ALBERTS (FOUR ACES) .... Albert Nicholas Albertini
BERNARD ALBRECHT (JOY DIVISION) .... Bernard Dicken
GEORGE ALEXANDER (GRAPEFRUIT) † .... Alex Young
JOHNNY ALLAN .... John Allan Guillot
JIGGS ALLBUT (ANGELS) .... Phyllis Allbut
CHAD ALLEN (GUESS WHO/BRAVE BELT) .... Allan Kowbel
CHRIS ALLEN (ALLEN BROTHERS) .... Christopher Bell
FRANK ALLEN (SEARCHERS) .... Francis McNiece
PETER ALLEN .... Peter Woolnough
RITCHIE ALLEN (& PACIFIC SURFERS) .... Richard Podolor
BOB ALLISON (ALLISONS) .... Robert Colin Day
JOHN ALLISON (ALLISONS) .... John Brian Alford
KEITH ALLISON (RAIDERS) .... Sydney Keith Allison
DUANE ALLMAN .... Howard Duane Allman
MARC ALMOND (SOFT CELL) .... Peter Mark Almond
LOUIS ALPHONSO (BAD MANNERS) .... Louis Cook
ED AMES .... Edward Yorick
PETE ANDERS (TRADEWINDS) .... Peter Andreoli
ANGRY ANDERSON (ROSE TATTOO) .... Gary Anderson
RUBY ANDREWS .... Ruby Stackhouse
BOBBY ANGELO (& TUXEDOS) .... Robert Hemmings
ADAM ANT .... Stuart Leslie Goddard
RONNIE ARBUCKLE (ARBUCKLE) .... Ronald K. Fierstein
TONI ARDEN .... Antionette Aroizzone
LOUIS ARMSTRONG .... Daniel Louis Armstrong
DESI ARNAZ JNR. (DINO, DESI & BILLY) .... Desiderio Alberto Arnaz IV
KEN ANDREW (MIDDLE OF THE ROAD) .... Ken Andrew Ballantyne
EDDY ARNOLD .... Richard Edward Arnold
PAUL ARNOLD (OVERLANDERS) .... Paul Friswell
P. P. ARNOLD .... Patricia Arnold
GENE AUTRY .... Orvon Gene Autry
FRANKIE AVALON .... Francis Avallone
PACKY AXTON (MAR-KEYS) .... Charles Axton
CHARLES AZNAVOUR .... Charles Aznavurjan

† The brother of Angus & Malcolm Young of AC/DC and George Young of Easybeats/Flash & The Pan.

FRANKIE AVALON — Francis Avallone

Sincerely,
Edd "Kook...

EDD 'KOOKIE' BYRNES — Ernest Breiten Berger

B

BOB BABITT† .... Robert Kreina
BUTCH BAKER (BARRON KNIGHTS) .... Leslie Baker
LAVERN BAKER .... Delores Williams
GEORGE BAKER (... SELECTION) .... Hans Bouwens
GINGER BAKER (CREAM/BLIND FAITH) .... Peter Baker
MICKEY 'GUITAR' BAKER (MICKEY & SYLVIA) .... McHouston Baker
RICK BAKER (OUTSIDERS) .... Richard Biagiola
MARTY BALIN .... Martyn Jere Buchwald
HONEY BANE .... Donna Tracey Boylan
PETER BANKS (YES) .... Peter Brockbank
CHRIS BARBER .... Donald Christopher Barber
SYD BARRETT (PINK FLOYD) .... Roger Keith Barrett
STEVE BARRI (FANTASTIC BAGGIES) .... Stephen Barry Lipkin
J. J. BARRIE .... Barry Authors
JOE BARRY .... Joseph Barios
JOHN BARRY (... SEVEN/ORCHESTRA) .... John Barry Prendergast
LEN BARRY .... Leonard Borisoff
COUNT BASIE†† .... William Basie
STIV BATORS (DEAD BOYS) .... Stivin Bator
ROBIN BATTEAU (BATTEAUX) .... Dwight Wayne Batteau Jnr.
SKIP BATTIN (BYRDS) .... Clyde Battin
SKUNK BAXTER (STEELY DAN) .... Jeff Baxter
RICHARD T. BEAR .... Richard Gerstein
JOHNNY BEE (DETROIT WHEELS) .... John Badanjek
MADELINE BELL (BLUE MINK) .... Madeline Phillips
PETER BELL (SULTANS) .... Peter Birch
WILLIAM BELL .... William Yarbough
TONY BENNETT .... Anthony Dominick Bendetto
RAY BENSON (ASLEEP AT THE WHEEL) .... Ray Benson Seifert
TERRY BENSON (NEW CHRISTY MINSTRELS) .... Terry Williams
BROOK BENTON .... Benjamin Franklin Peay
ARTIE BERK (IVY THREE) .... Arthur Berkowitz
IRVING BERLIN .... Israel Baline
CHUCK BERRY .... Charles Edward Anderson Berry
DAVE BERRY .... David Berry Grundy
JAN BERRY (JAN & DEAN) .... William Jan Berry
MIKE BERRY .... Michael Bourne
JELLO BIAFRA (DEAD KENNEDYS) .... Eric Boucher
ACKER BILK .... Bernard Bilk
CINDY BIRDSONG (SUPREMES) .... Cynthia Birdsong
BEEB BIRTLES (LITTLE RIVER BAND) .... Gerard Bertlekamp
CILLA BLACK .... Priscilla Maria Veronica White
JAY BLACK (JAY & AMERICANS) .... David Black
JET BLACK (STRANGLERS) .... Peter Black
BRUCE BLACKMAN (STARBUCK) .... Michael Bruce Blackman
ANDY BLADE (EATER) .... Andrew Blake
GINGER BLAKE (HONEYS) .... Saundra Glantz
JOHNNY BLITZ (DEAD BOYS) .... John Madansky
FATTY BUSTER BLOODVESSEL (BAD MANNERS) ...... Douglas Trendle
KURTIS BLOW .... Kurt Walker
BABBITY BLUE .... Barbara Chalk
BARRY BLUE .... Barry Green
DAVID BLUE .... S. David Cohen
VICKI BLUE (RUNAWAYS) .... Victoria Louise Teshler

MEL BROOKS — Melvyn Kaminsky

ELKIE BROOKS — Elaine Bookbinder

JELLO BIAFRA (DEAD KENNEDYS) — Eric Boucher

DAVID BOWIE — David Robert Jones

LEN BARRY — Leonard Borisoff

GARY U.S. BONDS — Gary Anderson

Charles Eugene Boone

'Twixt
Twelve
and
Twenty

PAT BOONE
talks to
teen-agers

A
CEDAR
SPECIAL
5/-

13

MARC BOLAN .... Mark Feld
JOHNNY BOND .... Cyrus Whitfield Bond
RONNIE BOND (TROGGS) .... Ronald Bultis
BEKI BONDAGE (VICE SQUAD) .... Rebecca Louise Bond
GARY U.S. BONDS††† .... Gary Anderson
MARS BONFIRE†††† .... Dennis Edmonton
TAKA BOOM (UNDISPUTED TRUTH)‡ .... Yvonne Stevens
DANIEL BOONE .... Peter Charles Greene
PAT BOONE .... Charles Eugene Boone
STEVE BOONE (LOVIN' SPOONFUL) .... John Stephen Boone
ANGIE BOWIE .... Mary Angela Bowie nee Barrety
DAVID BOWIE .... David Robert Jones
TOMMY BOYCE (BOYCE & HART) .... Sidney Thomas Boyce Jnr.
TINY BRADSHAW .... Myron Bradshaw
BRIAN BRAIN .... Martin Atkins
BOB BRAUN .... Robert Earl Brown
TERESA BREWER .... Theresa Brewer
FANNY BRICE‡‡ .... Fanny Borach
DEE DEE BRIDGEWATER .... Denise Bridgewater
LILLIAN BRIGGS .... Lillian Marie Biggs
BETTE BRIGHT (& ILLUMINATIONS) .... Anne Martin
LEE BRILLEAUX (DR. FEELGOOD) .... Lee Collinson
ELKIE BROOKS .... Elaine Bookbinder
HARVEY BROOKS (ELECTRIC FLAG) .... Harvey Goldstein
LA LA BROOKS (CRYSTALS) .... Delores Brooks
MEL BROOKS .... Melvyn Kaminsky
EDGAR BROUGHTON .... Robert Edgar Broughton
ARTHUR BROWN (CRAZY WORLD OF . . .)‡‡‡ .... Arthur Wilton
MICHAEL BROWN (LEFT BANKE) .... Michael Lookofsky
JACK BRUCE .... John Simon Asher Bruce
BEAU BRUMMELL ESQ. .... Mike Bush
BUDDY BUIE (ATLANTA RHYTHM SECTION) .... Perry C. Buie
CLEM BURKE (BLONDIE) .... Clement Anthony Bozewski
DAVE BURKE (STANDELLS) .... David Eugene Burker
SASCHA BURLAND (NUTTY SQUIRRELS) .... Granville Burland
T-BONE BURNETT‡‡‡‡ .... John Henry Burnett
BOZ BURRELL (BAD COMPANY) .... Raymond Burrell
GEEZER BUTLER (BLACK SABBATH) .... Terrence Butler
BIFF BYFORD (SAXON) .... Peter Byford
MAX BYGRAVES .... Walter William Bygraves
EDD 'KOOKIE' BYRNES .... Edward Breiten Berger

†Bob is a legendary American session bass player.
††"I hated the name 'Count'. I wanted to be called Buck or Hoot or even Arkansas Fats."
†††Legrand Records tried to convince the world that U.S. stood for Ulysses Samuel.
††††Brother of Steppenwolf's Jerry Edmonton. Recorded an album for Columbia.
‡Taka Boom is Chaka Khan's sister.
‡‡The all-singing, all-dancing Fanny, a leading light of the Ziegfeld Follies was the subject of the
  musicals/movies *Funny Girl* and *Funny Lady*.
‡‡‡Arthur's father invented the world's first fully automatic toothbrush.
‡‡‡‡T. Bone's first album, on Uni in 1972, was recorded as J. Henry Burnett.

CILLA BLACK — Priscilla
Maria Veronica White

COUNT BASIE — William Basie

TONY BENNETT — Anthony Dominick Bendetto

DAVE BERRY — David Berry Grundy

15

ERIC CLAPTON — Eric Patrick Clapp

16

C

MARTI CAINE	Lynda Denise Crapper
J. J. CALE	Johnny Cale
MARIA CALLAS	Maria Cecilia Sophia Kalogeropoulos
CAB CALLOWAY	Cabell Calloway
HAMILTON CAMP	Hamid Hamilton Camp
CHARLIE CANE (IVY THREE)	Charles Koppelman
RAY CANE (HONEYBUS)	Raymond Byart
JOHN CANN (ATOMIC ROOSTER/HARD STUFF)	John DuCann
FREDDY CANNON	Frederick Anthony Picariello
BUN E. CARLOS (CHEAP TRICK)	Brad Carlson
HOAGY CARMICHAEL	Howard Hoaglund Carmichael
JOE 'FINGERS' CARR	Lou Busch
JOHNNY CARR (& CADILLACS)	Con O'Sullivan
VIKKI CARR	Florencia Bisenta de Casillas Martinez Cardona
JOE 'KING' CARRASCO	Joseph Teutsch
ANDREA CARROL	Andrea Lee De Capite
RONNIE CARROLL	Ronald Cleghorn
RUTH CARROLL	Ruth Carroll Dodd
PHIL CARSON (LONDONERS/SPRINGFIELDS)	Philip Pratt
CARLENE CARTER†	Carlene Smith/Carter/Cash/Routh/Lowe
JOHN CARTER (IVY LEAGUE)	John Shakespeare
JOHNNY CASH††	J.R. Cash
TERRY CASHMAN (CASHMAN & WEST)	Dennis Michael Minogue
BUZZ CASON	James E. Cason
JOEY CASTLE	Joseph John Castaldo
EXENE CERVENKA (X)	Christine Cervenka
JAMES CHANCE/WHITE (CONTORTIONS)	James Siegfrid
LARRY CHANCE (EARLS)	Lawrence Figueiredo
CHAS CHANDLER (THE ANIMALS)	Bryan James Chandler
GENE CHANDLER	Eugene Dixon
BRUCE CHANNEL	Bruce McMeans
BOBBY CHARLES	Robert Charles Guidry
DON CHARLES (& SINGING DOGS)	Carl Weisman
RAY CHARLES	Ray Charles Robinson
RONNIE CHARLES (ATLAS)	Ronald Charles Boromeo
CHUBBY CHECKER	Ernest Evans
BRIAN CHEW-IT (BAD MANNERS)	Brian Tuitt
ALEX CHILTON (BOX TOPS)	William Alexander Chilton
LOU CHRISTIE	Lugee Alfredo Giovanni Sacco
CHEETAH CHROME (DEAD BOYS)	Gene Connor
ERIC CLAPTON	Eric Patrick Clapp
BOOMER CLARK (LEWIS & CLARK EXP.)	Owen Castleman
DEE CLARK	Delectus Clark
GENE CLARK (BYRDS)	Harold E. Clark
JUDY CLAY	Judy Guions
KEITH CLAYTONS (FEELIES)	Keith DeNuzio
CLEM CLEMPSON (HUMBLE PIE)	David Clempson
JIMMY CLIFF	James Chambers
BUZZ CLIFFORD	Rees Francis Clifford III
PATSY CLINE	Virginia Patterson-Hensley
JOE COCKER	John Robert Cocker
COZY COLE	William Randolph Cole
NAT 'KING' COLE	Nathaniel Adams Coles
BOOTSY COLLINS	William Collins
DAVE COLLINS (DAVE & ANSELL COLLINS)	David Barker

```
JESSI COLTER ............................................................................ Mirriam Johnson-Jennings
RUSS COLUMBO ........................................... Ruggerio Eugenio de Rudolpho Columbo
PERRY COMO ............................................................................................. Pierino Como
CAROL CONNORS ...................................................................... Annette Kleinbard
BOB CONRAD (MOJOS) ........................................................................ John Conrad
JESS CONRAD ............................................................................................ Gerald James
RUSS CONWAY ....................................................................................... Trevor Stanford
RY COODER ....................................................................................... Ryland Peter Cooder
ALICE COOPER .................................................................................. Vincent Furnier
JULIAN COPE (TEARDROP EXPLODES) ........................................... Kevin Stapleton
CHICK COREA .................................................................... Armando Anthony Corea
JILL COREY ............................................................................. Norma Jean Speranza
DON CORNELL ................................................................ Dominico Francisco Connello
LYN CORNELL††† ....................................................................... Audrey Ann Cornett
GENE CORNISH (RASCALS) ........................................................... Jean Paul Cornish
DAVE 'BABY' CORTEZ ................................................................ David Cortez Clowney
DAY COSTELLO ..................................................................................... Ross McManus
ELVIS COSTELLO†††† ............................................................ Declan Patrick McManus
PAUL COTTON (POCO) .................................................................. Norman Paul Cotton
JOHNNY COUGAR ................................................................................. John Mellencamp
CRASH CRADDOCK .................................................................. William James Craddock
VINCENT CRANE (ATOMIC ROOSTER) ................................ Vincent Rodney Cheesman
BOB CREWE (... GENERATION) .................................................. Stanley Robert Crewe
PETER CRISS (KISS) .................................................................................. Peter Crissciola
```

RAY CHARLES — Ray Charles Robinson

18

NAT 'KING' COLE — Nathaniel Adams Coles

LOU CHRISTIE — Lugee Alfredo Giovanni Sacco

DOROTHY COLLINS	Marjorie Chandler
SAM COOKE	Samuel Cook
BING CROSBY	Harry Lillis Crosby
DAVID CROSBY (BYRDS/CSNY)	David Van Cortland
CHRIS CROSS (ULTRAVOX)	Christopher St. John
CHRISTOPHER CROSS	Christopher Geppert
CY CURNIN (FIXX)	Cyril Curnin
CHRIS CURTIS (SEARCHERS)	Christopher Crummey
JIMMY CURTISS (BAG)	James Stulberger
JESSE CUTLER ('GODSPELL')	Louis Milo Gibaldi

†Carlene's father is country singer Carl Smith; her mother is June Carter; she grew up with Johnny
Cash (Rosanne Cash is her sister); her two married names are Routh and Lowe.

††As legend has it, Cash was born with the initials J.R. only (a not uncommon practice in America's rural
regions) and adopted the name Johnny when he joined the army.

†††For lovers of terminal trivia: this early sixties British pop singer married session drummer Andy White,
the man who played on the commonly heard version of The Beatles *Love Me Do*.

††††Elvis Costello adopted the same pseudonymn surname as his musician father Ross McManus, who
charted in some territories in 1970 with a rival recording of The Beatles *The Long And Winding Road*.

CHUBBY CHECKER LIMBO PARTY

THE DANCE CRAZE THAT'S SWEEPING THE COUNTRY!

NOW... HAVE YOUR OWN LIMBO PARTY!

PARKWAY P 7020

Ernest Evans

VIKKI CARR — Florentina Bisenta de Casillas Martinez Cardona with BUDDY RICH — Bernard Rich

ALICE COOPER — Vincent Furnier

MARIA CALLAS — Maria Cecilia Sophia Kalogeropoulos

21

Doris Day

Doris Kappelhoff

D

ALAN DALE .... Aldo Sigismondi
DICK DALE (& DELTONES) .... Richard Monsour
GLEN DALE (FORTUNES) .... Glen Garforth
LACY J. DALTON .... Jill Byrem
JOE DAMIANO .... Joseph DiAngelis
VIC DAMONE .... Vito Farinola
JIM DANDY (BLACK OAK ARKANSAS) .... James Mangrum
BOBBY DARIN .... Walden Robert Cassotto
AUGUST DARNELL (KID CREOLE) .... Darnell August Browder
JAMES/JIMMY DARREN .... James William Ercolani
F. R. DAVID .... Robert Fitussi
HOD DAVID .... Howard M. Schudson
IVA DAVIES (ICEHOUSE) .... Ivor Davies
BILLIE DAVIS .... Carol Hedges
MAC DAVIS .... Scott Davis
SANDY DAVIS .... Paul Davis
SKEETER DAVIS .... Mary Frances Penick
BOBBY DAY .... Robert Byrd
DORIS DAY .... Doris Kappelhoff
RUSTY DAY (CACTUS) .... Russell Edward Davidson
JIMMY DEAN .... Seth Ward
SANDY DEANE (JAY & AMERICANS) .... Sandy Yaguda
DAVE DEE .... David Harman
JOEY DEE .... Joseph DiNicolo
KIKI DEE .... Pauline Matthews
SYLVIA DEE .... Josephine Moore Proffitt nee de Sylvia
ZENON DE FLEUR (COUNT BISHOPS) .... Zenon Hierowski
DESMOND DEKKER .... Desmond Dacres
FITO DE LA PARRA (CANNED HEAT) .... Adolpho De La Parra
WAYNE DeLISLE (MENTAL AS ANYTHING) .... David Toohill
TOMMY DELL .... Thomas O'Fagan
PETE DELLO (HONEYBUS) .... Peter Blumson
RICHARD DELVY (CHALLENGERS) .... Richard Delvecchio
DUKE D'MOND (BARRON KNIGHTS) .... Richard Palmer
TERRY DENE .... Terrence Williams
FUZZ DENIZ (MAX MERRITT & METEORS) .... Howard Martin Deniz
SANDY DENNY .... Alexandra Elene Maclaine Denny
JOHN DENVER .... John Henry Deutschendorf
KARL DENVER .... Angus McKenzie
LYNSEY DE PAUL .... Lynsey Rubin
RICK DERRINGER .... Richard Zehringer
SUGAR PIE DeSANTO .... Peylia Balington
JACKIE DeSHANNON .... Sharon Lee Myers
JIMMY DESTRI (BLONDIE) .... James Mollica
WILLIE DeVILLE (MINK DeVILLE) .... William Borsey
HOWARD DEVOTO (MAGAZINE) .... Howard Trafford
NEIL DIAMOND .... Noah Kaminsky
DICK DIAMONDE (EASYBEATS) .... Dingeman Vandersluys
CHARLES DICKENS .... David Anthony
DUB DICKERSON .... Willis Dickerson
BO DIDDLEY† .... Otha Ellis Bates/Ellas McDaniel
RALPH DINO (DINO & SEMBELLO) .... Ralph Francis Palladino
RONNIE JAMES DIO .... Ronald Padavona
BUCK D'HARMA (BLUE OYSTER CULT) .... Donald Roeser
DICK DODD (STANDELLS) .... Joseph Richard Dodd
ERNIE K. DOE .... Ernest Kador Jnr.
THOMAS DOLBY .... Thomas Morgan Dolby Robertson

COCO DOLENZ††	German Marie Dolenz
MICKY DOLENZ (MONKEES)	George Michael Dolenz Jnr.
FATS DOMINO	Antoine Domino
LONNIE DONEGAN	Anthony James Donegan
DICKIE DOO (& DON'TS)†††	Dave Aldred
CHIP DOUGLAS (TURTLES)	Douglas Farthing Hatlelid
CRAIG DOUGLAS	Terence Perkins
CHARLIE DRAKE	Charles Springall
RUSTY DRAPER	R. D. Farrell
PATTY DUKE	Anna Marie Patricia Duke
LISA DULITTLE	Margaret Burns
DUCK DUNN (M.G.'s)	Donald Dunn
SIMON DUPREE (& BIG SOUND)	Derek Schulman
SLIM DUSTY††††	David Gordon Kirkpatrick
BOB DYLAN	Robert Allan Zimmerman

† Bo was adopted at an early age into the McDaniel family.
†† Sister of Monkee Micky Dolenz who dabbled a little in singing and acting.
††† Because Gerry Granahan was lead singer of the group, it is widely assumed that he was Dickie Doo.
    However, it was member Dave Aldred who adopted the name.
†††† Australia's country music king who made the British top three in 1959 with *A Pub With No Beer*.

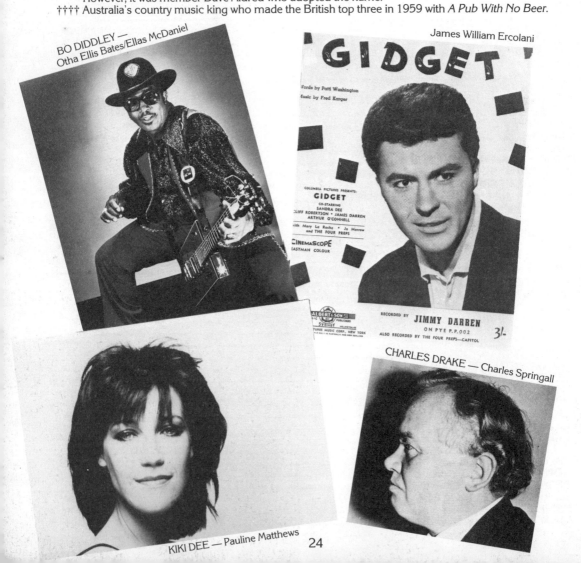

BO DIDDLEY —
Otha Ellis Bates/Ellas McDaniel

James William Ercolani

GIDGET

Words by Patti Washington
Music by Fred Karger

COLUMBIA PICTURES PRESENTS:
GIDGET
CO-STARRING
SANDRA DEE
CLIFF ROBERTSON • JAMES DARREN
ARTHUR O'CONNELL
with Mary La Roche • Jo Morrow
and THE FOUR PREPS
CINEMASCOPE
EASTMAN COLOUR

RECORDED BY **JIMMY DARREN**
ON PYE P.P. 002   3/-
ALSO RECORDED BY THE FOUR PREPS—CAPITOL

CHARLES DRAKE — Charles Springall

KIKI DEE — Pauline Matthews   24

NEIL DIAMOND — Noah Kaminsky

VIC DAMONE — Vito Farinola

JOHN DENVER — John Henry Deutschendorf

JIMMY DEAN — Seth Ward (left) with BUCK OWENS — Alvis Edgar Owens

Walden Robert Cassotto

THOMAS DOLBY — Thomas Morgan Dolby Robertson

SHEENA EASTON —
Sheena Shirley Orr

DUKE ELLINGTON — Edward Kennedy Ellington

CASS ELLIOT —
Ellen Naomi Elliot nee Cohen

BILLY ECKSTINE — William Eckstein

E

VINCE EAGER .... Roy Taylor
LINDA EASTMAN/McCARTNEY .... Linda Epstein
ELLIOTT EASTON (CARS) .... Elliott Shapiro
SHEENA EASTON .... Sheena Shirley Orr
BILLY ECKSTINE .... William Eckstein
JASON EDDIE† .... Edward Wycherly
BOBBY EDWARDS .... Robert Moncrief
RUSTY EGAN (VISAGE) .... Peter Anselm Egan
DUKE ELLINGTON .... Edward Kennedy Ellington
CASS ELLIOT (MAMAS & PAPAS) .... Ellen Naomi Elliot nee Cohen
BRAXTON ELLIOTT .... Stafford Marquette Floyd
DAVE ELLIOTT .... David Ellot Stingle
RAMBLIN' JACK ELLIOTT .... Elliott Charles Adnopoz
ROKY ERICKSON (13TH FLOOR ELEVATORS) .... Roger Erickson
COKE ESCOVEDO (SANTANA) .... Peter Escovedo
DAVID ESSEX .... David Albert Cook
VINCE EVERETT†† .... Marvin Benefield
  †Brother of Billy Fury.
††This rocker took his name from Elvis Presley's character in *Jailhouse Rock*.

DAVID ESSEX — David Albert Cook

CONNIE FRANCIS --- Concetta Rosemarie Franconero

F

SHELLEY FABARES†	Michelle Fabares
BENT FABRIC	Bent Fabricus Bjerre
ADAM FAITH	Terrence Nelhams
RODERICK FALCONER††	Roderick Taylor
B.P. FALLON	Bernard Patrick Fallon
GEORGIE FAME	Clive Powell
HERB FAME (PEACHES & HERB)	Herbert Freemster
DON FARDON	Donald Maughn
DONNA FARGO	Yvonne Vaughan
CHRIS FARLOWE	John Henry Deighton
GENE FARROW (& G.F.BAND)	Norman Hitchcock
NARVEL FELTS	Albert Narvel Felts
FREDDY FENDER	Baldemar Huerta
EDDIE FIELDS (JOHNNY & HURRICANES)	Edward James Waganfield III
GRACIE FIELDS	Grace Stansfield
ANTON FIER (FEELIES)	Andrew Fisher
LARRY FINNEGAN	John Lawrence Finnegan
SNOWY FLEET (EASYBEATS)	Gordon Fleet
KLAUS FLOURIDE (DEAD KENNEDYS)	Geoff Lyall
HERBIE FLOWERS (BLUE MINK/SKY)	Brian Flowers
EDDIE FONTAINE	Edward Reardon
D.J. FONTANA†††	Dominic Joseph Fontana
WAYNE FONTANA	Glyn Ellis
STEVE FORBERT	Samuel Stephen Forbert
BRUTE FORCE	Arthur Friedlander
DEAN FORD (MARMALADE)	William McAleese
EMILE FORD (& CHECKMATES)	Emile Sweetnam
FRANKIE FORD	Frank Guzzo
MARY FORD	Colleen Sumner
PERRY FORD (IVY LEAGUE)	Brian Pugh
GEORGE FORMBY	George Hoy Booth
FLAME FORTUNE	Heather Shane
JOHNNY FORTUNE	John Sudetta
LANCE FORTUNE	Colin Jones
NICK FORTUNE (BUCKINGHAMS)	Nicholas Fortuna
CLIFF FOX (MODELS-UK)	Cliff Harris
JACKIE FOX (RUNAWAYS)	Jacqueline Fuchs
JOHN FOXX	Dennis Leigh
CONNIE FRANCIS	Concetta Rosemarie Franconero
MELVYN FRANKLIN (TEMPTATIONS)	David English
JOHN FRED (& HIS PLAYBOY BAND)	John Frederick Gourrier
ACE FREHLEY (KISS)	Paul Frehley
KINKY FRIEDMAN	Richard Friedman
WYNDER K. FROG	Mick Weaver
MAX FROST (& TROOPERS)	Chris Jones
JERRY FULLER	Jerrell Lee Fuller
BILLY FURY	Ronald Wycherly

†Shelley is the niece of actress Nanette Fabray, who changed her surname after Ed Sullivan managed
to rhyme it with 'arse'. Shelley apparently had no fears of similar treatment.
††This artist cut two albums for U.A. in 1976/77 as Roderick Falconer and one album for Metronome
in 1980 as Roderick Taylor.
†††D.J. Fontana was Elvis Presley's drummer from 1955 to 1968.

Clive Powell

John Henry Deighton

WAYNE FONTANA — Glyn Ellis

JOHN FOXX — Dennis Leigh

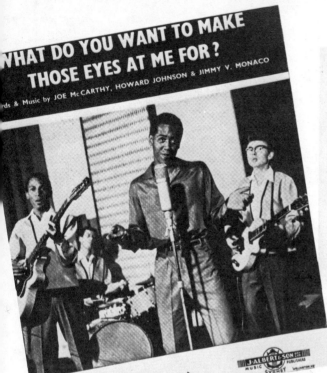

WHAT DO YOU WANT TO MAKE THOSE EYES AT ME FOR?

Words & Music by JOE McCARTHY, HOWARD JOHNSON & JIMMY V. MONACO

J. ALBERT & SON
MUSIC PUBLISHERS
SYDNEY
MELBOURNE   WELLINGTON N.Z.

3/-

RECORDED BY
EMILE FORD and the CHECKMATES
EMILE FORD — Emile Sweetnam

HERBIE FLOWERS — Brian Flowers

ADAM FAITH — Terrence Nelhams,
with SANDIE SHAW — Sandra Ann Goodrich

Edith Gormezano and Steven Leibowitz

DIZZY GILLESPIE — John Birks Gillespie
DOBIE GRAY – Leonard Victor Ainsworth

BOBBIE GENTRY — Roberta Streeter

GEORGE GERSHWIN — Jacob Gershovitz

G

MARGE GANSER (SHANGRI-LAS) .... Marguerite Ganser
JERRY GARCIA (GRATEFUL DEAD) .... Jerome John Garcia
BUNK GARDNER (MOTHERS OF INVENTION) .... John Leon Gardner
BOBBY GARRETT (BOB & EARL) .... Robert Relf
CRYSTAL GAYLE .... Brenda Gail Webb
ANDY GEE (ELLIS) .... Andreas Groeber
J. GEILS (. . . BAND) .... Jerome Geils
SIR HORACE GENTLEMAN (SPECIALS) .... Horace Panter
BOBBIE GENTRY .... Roberta Streeter
JIMMY GEORGE .... Jimmy P. Georgantones
GEORGE GERSHWIN .... Jacob Gershovitz
BARRY GIBB† .... Barry Crompton-Gibb
GEORGIA GIBBS†† .... Freda Lipson
FRANK GIBSON .... Helmuth Franks
TERRY GILKYSON .... Hamilton Henry Gilkyson
DIZZY GILLESPIE .... John Birks Gillespie
GARY GLITTER .... Paul Francis Gadd
PABLO GOMEZ (LOS BRAVOS) .... Pablo Sanllehi
EYDIE GORME .... Edith Gormezano
CHARLIE GRACIE .... Charles Graci
DON GRADY††† .... Donald Agrati
GOGI GRANT .... Myrtle Audrey Arinsberg
STEPHANE GRAPPELLI .... Stephane Grappelly
DOBIE GRAY .... Leonard Victor Ainsworth III
R.B. GREAVES .... Ronald Bertram Aloysius Greaves
BUDDY GRECO .... Armando Greco
PETER GREEN (FLEETWOOD MAC) .... Peter Greenbaum
DENNIS GREENE (SHA NA NA) .... Frederick Greene
GANDOLF T. GREY (RAINBOW GROUP) .... Christopher Richard Wilson
SONNY GRIFFIN (NUTMEGS) .... James Griffin
JOHNNY GUITAR (R. STORM & HURRICANES) .... John Byrne
WOODY GUTHRIE .... Woodrow Wilson Guthrie

†This is Barry's legal name. Sir Isaac Crompton, inventor of the mule spinner (which revolutionised the
   cotton industry in England in the last century) is an ancestor of the Gibb family.
††Some sources indicate Freda Gibson.
†††Don Grady, apart from recording solo for Capitol and Canterbury, portrayed Robbie Douglas in the
   My Three Sons TV series and was a member of the Palace Guard, and of the Yellow Balloon as Luke
   R. Yoo. In 1973 he recorded an Elektra album under his real name.

GOGI GRANT — Myrtle Audrey Arinsberg

ENGLEBERT HUMPERDINCK — Arnold George Dorsey

JOHNNY HALLYDAY — Jean-Philippe Smet

MEDIUM 434.955 Bk

JOHNNY
LE PÉNITENCIER
TOUJOURS PLUS LOIN ● ONE MORE TIME, ENCORE UNE FOIS
JE TE REVERRAI

PHILIPS

BOBBY HART— Robert Luke Harshman (left), with TOMMY BOYCE — Sidney Boyce Jnr (right) and comedian
SOUPY SALES — Milton Hines Supman

H

JENNY HAAN (BABE RUTH) .... Janita Haan
JOHNNY HALLYDAY .... Jean-Philippe Smet
OLLIE HALSALL (TIMEBOX) .... Peter Halsall
RUSS HAMILTON .... Ron Hulme
JACK HAMMER .... Earl S. Burroughs
PEARL HARBOUR (& EXPLOSIONS) .... Pearl Gates
STEVE HARLEY (COCKNEY REBEL) .... Steven Nice
BE-BOP HARRELL (BLUE CAPS) .... Richard Harrell
JET HARRIS (SHADOWS) .... Terrence Hawkins
MICKI HARRIS (SHIRELLES) .... Adelle Harris
BOBBY HART (BOYCE & HART) .... Robert Luke Harshman
RITCHIE HART .... Richard Gearheart
CHIP HAWKES (TREMELOES) .... Len Hawkes
DALE HAWKINS .... Delmar Allen Hawkins
SCREAMING JAY HAWKINS .... Jalacy Hawkins
KATE HAYSI (HAYSI FANTAYZEE) .... Katherina Maria Garner
TOPPER HEADON (CLASH) .... Nicholas Headon
RICHARD HELL .... Richard Myers
JIMI HENDRIX† .... Johnny Allen/James Marshall Hendrix
NONA HENDRYX (LABELLE) .... Wynona Hendryx
HONEYTREE HENIGBAUM .... Nancy Henigbaum
FRANCISCUS HENRY .... Frank Antheunis
WOODY HERMAN .... Woodrow Wilson Herman
BUNKER HILL .... David Walker
Z.Z. HILL .... Arzel Hill
CHICKEN HIRSCH (THE FISH) .... Gershon Hirsch
NODDY HOLDER (SLADE) .... Neville John Holder
BILLIE HOLIDAY†† .... Elenora Gough/Holiday/Fagen
MICHAEL HOLLIDAY††† .... Michael Miller/Milne
BUDDY HOLLY .... Charles Hardin Holley
JELLY HOLT (FOUR BLAZES) .... Paul Lindsley Holt
STIX HOOPER (CRUSADERS) .... Nesbert Hooper
CISCO HOUSTON .... Gilbert Vandine Houston
CISSY HOUSTON†††† .... Emily Houston nee Drinkard
DON HOWARD .... Donald Howard Koplow
ENGELBERT HUMPERDINCK††††† .... Arnold George Dorsey
IAN HUNTER (MOTT THE HOOPLE) .... Ian Hunter Patterson
WILLIE HUTCH .... William McKinley Hutchinson
TYGER HUTCHINGS (FAIRPORT CONVENTION) .... Ashley Hutchings

†Jimi's name was altered at age 4 by his father.
††Born the illegitimate daughter of jazz guitarist Clarence Holiday, to a mother named Gough who
married a gentleman named Fagen, Elenora borrowed her first name from actress Billie Dove.
†††This early sixties British chart idol was born Miller, changed his name by deed poll to Milne and
eventually used his mother's maiden name, Holliday.
††††Cissy is Dionne Warwick's cousin.
†††††Mr Dorsey 'borrowed' this name from a very real classical composer, born in 1854.

BUDDY HOLLY— Charles Hardin Holley

JIMI HENDRIX — Johnny Allen/James Marshall Hendrix (centre) with MITCH MITCHELL — John. Mitchell (right)

BILLIE HOLIDAY — Elenora Gough/Holiday/Fagen

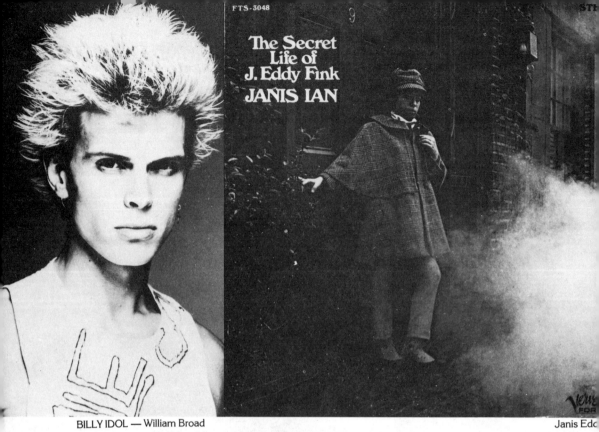

FTS-3048

The Secret
Life of
J. Eddy Fink
JANIS IAN

BILLY IDOL — William Broad

Janis Edd

PAUL JONES — Paul Pond (second from right), with MANFRED MANN — Michael Lubowitz (second from left)

I

JANIS IAN .... Janis Eddy Fink
BILLY IDOL .... William Broad
LUX INTERIOR (CRAMPS) .... Eric Perkheiser
DONNIE IRIS .... Dominic Ierace
BIG DEE IRWIN .... Defosca Ervin

J

ZENDA JACKS (SILVER CONVENTION) .... Susan McClosky
GATORTAIL JACKSON .... Willis Jackson
JACKIE JACKSON (JACKSONS) .... Sigmund Esco Jackson
J. J. JACKSON† .... Jerome L. Jackson
RANDY JACKSON (JACKSONS) .... Steven Randell Jackson
TITO JACKSON (JACKSONS) .... Toriano Adaryll Jackson
BRIAN JAMES (DAMNED) .... Brian Robertson
ETTA JAMES .... Jamesetta Hawkins
HARVEY JAMES (SHERBET) .... Harvey James Harrup
JONI JAMES .... Joan Carmella Babbo
MICHAEL JAMES†† .... Michael James Heinrich
RICK JAMES .... James Johnson Jnr.
SONNY JAMES .... James Loden
STU JAMES (MOJOS) .... Stuart Leslie Slater
TOMMY JAMES (& SHONDELLS) .... Thomas Gregory Jackson
JOE JAMMER .... Joseph Edward William Wright
STEVE JANSEN (JAPAN) .... Steve Batt
JOHNNY JAY .... John J. Huhta
JOAN JETT .... Joan Larkin
JAI JOHANNY JOHANSON (ALLMAN BROS.) .... John Lee Johnson
DAVID JOHN (& THE MOOD) .... Miffy Charnley
ELTON JOHN .... Reginald Kenneth Dwight
LEEE JOHN (IMAGINATION) .... Leslie McGregor John
LITTLE WILLIE JOHN .... William John Woods
ROBERT JOHN .... Robert Pedrick Jnr.
HOWARD JONES .... John Howard Jones
KRIPP JOHNSON (DEL VIKINGS) .... Corinthian Johnson
WILKO JOHNSON (DR. FEELGOOD) .... John Wilkinson
AL JOLSON .... Asa Yoelson
BRIAN JONES (ROLLING STONES) .... Lewis Brian Hopkins-Jones
CASEY JONES (& ENGINEERS) .... Brian Casser
DONNA JONES (PUSSYFOOT) .... Doreen Jones
JOHN PAUL JONES (LED ZEPPELIN) .... John Baldwin
PAUL JONES (MANFRED MANN/BLUES BAND) .... Paul Pond
SAMANTHA JONES .... Jean Owen
TOM JONES .... Thomas James Woodward
LONNIE JORDAN (WAR) .... Leroy Jordan
JIMMY JUSTICE .... James Anthony Bernard Little

†Not to be confused with the jazz performer of the same name.
††Michael was a much-touted but dismally unsuccessful American teen idol creation of the mid sixties.

JIMMY JUSTICE chan...
en Franç...

LA PARADE DES COEURS PERDUS The parade of broken hearts
LE PETIT AMOUREUX Ain't that funny
QUELQU'UN VEUT-IL DE MON AMOUR The world of lonely people
QUAND UN AIR VOUS POSSÈDE When my little girl is smiling

disques vogue
PNV. 24.1...

James Little

THE RUNAWAYS (from left):
CHERIE CURRIE, JOAN JETT — Joan Larkin,
SANDY WEST — Sandra Resavento, LITA FORD
and JACKIE FOX — Jacqueline Fuchs

TOM JONES — Thomas James Woodward

BRIAN JONES — Lewis Brian Hopkins-Jones

RICK JAMES — James Johnson Jnr.

ELTON JOHN —
Reginald Kenneth Dwight

EDEN KANE— Richard Sarstedt (left) with Australian pop
sensation JOHNNY YOUNG — John De Jong
RUFUS with CHAKA KHAN — Yvette Marie Stevens

JONATHAN KING— Kenneth King
THE MOVE with ACE KEFFORD — Christopher Kefford
(far right), and ROY WOOD — Adrian Ulysses Wood (top)

K

SHE KAHN (TEMPTERS)	Kenichi Hagiwara
EDEN KANE	Richard Sarstedt
HOWIE KANE (JAY & THE AMERICANS)	Howard Kirschenbaum
KEITH KARLSON (MOJOS)	Keith Alcock
MICK KARN (JAPAN)	Anthony Michaelides
KENNY KARTER/HILL (SENTINALS)	Kenneth Hinkle
JOHN KAY (STEPPENWOLF)	Joachim F. Krauledat
CAROL KAYE†	Carol Louise Smith
GEORGE KAYE (ROYALTONES)	George Katsakis
LARRY KAYE (QUOTATIONS)	Lawrence Kassman
NORMAN KAYE (REVELS)	Norman George Knowles
BOB KAYLI††	Robert Gordy
LAINIE KAZAN	Lainie Lavine
SPEEDY KEEN (THUNDERCLAP NEWMAN)	John Keen
NELSON KEENE	Malcolm Holland
ACE KEFFORD (THE MOVE)	Christopher Kefford
BRIAN KEITH (PLASTIC PENNY)	Brian O'Shea
CASEY KELLY	Daniel Cohen
JONATHON KELLY	John Ledingham
DEE DEE KENNIBREW/HENRY (CRYSTALS)†††	Dolores Kennibrew
AL KENT	Albert Hamilton
GARY KENT (DRUIDS)	Gearie Jay Kenworthy
ANITA KERR	Anita Jean Grob
CHAKA KHAN (RUFUS)	Yvette Marie Stevens
JOHNNY KIDD (& PIRATES)	Frederick Heath
B. B. KING	Riley King
BEN E. KING	Benjamin Earl Nelson
CAROLE KING	Carole Klein
EARL KING	Solomon Johnson
FREDDIE KING	Billy Myles
JONATHAN KING	Kenneth King
SID KING (& THE FIVE STRINGS)	Sidney Erwin
BAKER KNIGHT	Thomas Baker Knight
CURTIS KNIGHT	Curtis McNear
BUDDY KNOX	Wayne Knox
SKIP KONTE (BLUES IMAGE)	Frank Earl Konte
DANNY KOOTCH (FLYING MACHINE/SECTION)	Daniel Kortchmar
KATE KORUS (MO-DETTES)	Kate Corris
BILLY J. KRAMER (& DAKOTAS)	William Howard Ashton
BILLY KRISTIAN (NIGHT)	William Kariatiana
MARTY KRISTIAN (NEW SEEKERS)	Mark Vanags
KARI KROME	Kari Lee Mitchell

†One of rock's most famous session bass players.
††Bob is the brother of Motown founder Berry Gordy and the uncle of Rockwell (Kennedy Gordy).
†††Henry was Dee Dee's stepfather's surname. Though it appears often in rock encyclopaedias, she virtually never used it.

JULIAN LENNON — John Charles Julian Lennon

LENE LOVICH — Marlene Premilovich

BRENDA LEE — Brenda Mae Tarpley

LORETTA LYNN — Loretta Webb, with sister
CRYSTAL GAYLE — Brenda Gail Webb

L

SLEEPY LaBEEF	Thomas Paulsley LaBeef
PATTI LABELLE	Patricia Louise Holt-Edwards
CHERYL LADD	Cheryl Stoppelmoor
CLEO LAINE	Clementina Dinah Dankworth nee Campbell
DENNY LAINE (WINGS)	Brian Arthur Haynes
FRANKIE LAINE	Frank Paul LoVecchio
NEIL LANDON (FLOWERPOT MEN)	Patrick Cahill
GARY LANE (STANDELLS)	Gary McMillan
DON LANG	Gordon Langhorn
HONEY LANTREY (HONEYCOMBS)	Ann Lantrey
MARIO LANZA	Alfred Arnold Cocozza
D. C. LARUE	David L'Heureux
DENISE LaSALLE	Denise Craig
JAMES LAST	Hans Last
CYNDI LAUPER	Cynthia Ann Stephanie Lauper
LINDA LAURIE	Linda Gertz
ROGER LaVERN (TORNADOS)	Roger Jackson
GERTRUDE LAWRENCE	Alexandre Dagmar Lawrence-Klasen
STEVE LAWRENCE	Steven Leibowitz
GEORDIE LEACH (ROSE TATTOO)	Gordon Everett Leach
CURLY LEADS (& THE SWITCHES)	Maxmillian DeFrost
LEK LECKENBY (HERMAN'S HERMITS)	Derek Leckenby
BRENDA LEE	Brenda Mae Tarpley
CHARLES LEE	Charles Leath
DICKEY LEE	Richard Lipscomb
FREDDY 'FINGERS' LEE	Frederick Chessman
JACKIE LEE	Earl Nelson
MYRON LEE	Myron Wachendorf
PEGGY LEE	Norma Deloris Eggstrom
TOMMY LEE (MOTLEY CRUE)	Thomas Lee Bass
ST. CLAIR LEE (HUES CORPORATION)	Bernard St. Clair Lee Calhoun Henderson
BILL LEGEND (T. REX)	William Fyfield

JULIE LONDON — June Webb nee Peck

Norma Deloris Eggstrom

45

MARK LEEMAN (MARK LEEMAN FIVE) .... John Ardrey
JOHNNY LEGEND .... Martin Margulies
JULIAN LENNON .... John Charles Julian Lennon
DEKE LEONARD (MAN) .... Roger Leonard
PHIL LESH (GRATEFUL DEAD) .... Philip Chapman
KETTY LESTER .... Revoyda Frierson
HUEY LEWIS (& THE NEWS) .... Huey Louis Clegg
JAY LEWIS (MORNING) .... Jay Donnellan
KEN LEWIS (IVY LEAGUE) .... Kenneth Hawker
LICORICE LOCKING (SHADOWS) .... Brian Locking
JOHNNY LOGAN .... Sean Sherrard
JULIE LONDON† .... June Webb nee Peck
SHORTY LONG .... Frederick Long
TRINI LOPEZ .... Trinidad Lopez III
DONNA LOREN .... Donna Zukor
DICK LORY .... Richard Glasser
DARLENE LOVE .... Darlene Wright
LENE LOVICH .... Marlene Premilovich
LEM LUBIN (UNIT 4+2) .... Howard Lubin
NICK LUCAS .... Dominic Nicholas Anthony Lucanese
LYDIA LUNCH .... Lydia Cocks
ANNABELLA LWIN (BOW WOW WOW)†† .... Myant Myante Aye Dunn-Lwin
CISCO LYDE .... Cecil Orlando Lyde
BARBARA LYNN .... Barbara Lynn Ozen
DAME VERA LYNN .... Vera Margaret Welsh
LORETTA LYNN .... Loretta Webb

†Julie married actor Jack Webb of *Dragnet* fame.
††Allegedly born in Burma to an aristocratic family and taken to Britain as a 'refugee' at age 5.

FRANKIE LAINE — Frank Paul LoVecchio

CLEO LAINE - Clementina Dinah Dankworth nee Campbell

JONA LEWIE — John Lewis

DEAN MARTIN— Dino Crocetti

TONY MARTIN — Alvin Morris Jnr.

JONI MITCHELL — Roberta Joan Anderson

M

JACK MACK (& HEART ATTACK)	Claude Pepper
LONNIE MACK	Lonnie McIntosh
GISELE MacKENZIE	Gisele LaFleche
SHEL MACREA (FORTUNES)	Andrew Semple
JOHNNY MAESTRO (CRESTS)	John Mastrangelo
JEFF MAGNUM (DEAD BOYS)	Jeffery Halmezy
MIRIAM MAKEBA	Zenzile Makeba Qgwashu Nguvama Yiketheli Nxgowa Bantana Balomzi Xa Ufan Ubajabulisa Ubaphekeli Mbiza Yotshwala Sithi Xa Qgiba Ukutja Sithathe Izitsha Sizi Kabe Singama Lawu Singama Qgwashu Singama Ngamla Nqgithi
SIV MALMQUIST	Siw Malmkvist
DICK MANITOBA (DICTATORS)	Richard Blum
HERBIE MANN	Herbert Jay Solomon
MANFRED MANN	Michael Lubowitz
TONY MANSFIELD (DAKOTAS)	Anthony Bookbinder
PHIL MANZANERA (ROXY MUSIC)	Philip Targett-Adams
KELLY MARIE	Jacqueline McKinnon
TEENA MARIE	Mary Christine Brockert
MICK MARS (MOTLEY CRUE)	Robert Deal
BERYL MARSDEN (STEAMPACKET)	Beryl Hogg
MICHAEL MARTIAL (BITTER SWEET)	Michael John Bonagura
BOBBI MARTIN	Barbara Anne Martin
DEAN MARTIN	Dino Crocetti
DEWEY MARTIN (BUFFALO SPRINGFIELD)	Dewayne Midkiff
DINO MARTIN (DINO, DESI & BILLY)	Dean Paul Anthony Martin Jnr.
MOON MARTIN	John Martin
RICK MARTIN (SOCIETY'S CHILDREN))	Richard Victor Capellan
TONY MARTIN	Alvin Morris Jnr.
TRADE MARTIN (GORGONI, MARTIN & TAYLOR)	John Lione
AL MARTINO	Alfred Cini
HANK MARVIN (SHADOWS)	Brian Robson Rankin
HARPO MARX	Adolph Marx
NICK MASSI (FOUR SEASONS)	Nicholas Macioci
DEAN MATHIS (NEWBEATS)	Louis Al Mathias
MARK MATHIS (NEWBEATS)	Marcus F. Mathias
IAN MATTHEWS	Ian Matthew McDonald
SUSAN MAUGHAN	Marian Maughan
C. W. McCALL	William Fries
PAUL McCARTNEY	James Paul McCartney
SPANKY McFARLANE (SPANKY & OUR GANG)	Elaine McFarlane
MIKE McGEAR (SCAFFOLD)	Michael McCartney
ROGER McGUINN (BYRDS)†	James Joseph McGuinn
GOLDY McJOHN (STEPPENWOLF)	John Raymond Goadsby
BOB McKENZIE (McKENZIE BROS)	Rick Moranis
DOUG McKENZIE (McKENZIE BROS)	David Thomas
MAGGIE McNEAL (MOUTH & McNEAL)	Sjouke Van't Spijken
BIG JAY McNEELY	Cecil McNeely
DOLLY McRAE (COOKIES/RAELETS)	Ethel McCrea
RALPH McTELL	Ralph May
TONY MEEHAN (SHADOWS)	Daniel Joseph Anthony Meehan
FREDDIE MERCURY (QUEEN)	Frederick Bulsara
ETHEL MERMAN	Ethel Agnes Zimmerman
TERRY LEE MIALL (ADAM & ANTS)	Terry DeMiall Harron
GEORGE MICHAEL (WHAM!)	George Michael Panos
BUDDY MILES (... EXPRESS)	George Miles

JOHN MILES	John Errington
GLENN MILLER	Alton Glenn Miller
MRS. MILLER	Elva Miller
BILL MILLION (FEELIES)	William Clayton
BARBARA MILLS	Barbara Henley
GARNETT MIMMS	Garrett Mimms
BOB MIRANDA (HAPPENINGS)	Ralph F. Mirando
BLUE MITCHELL	Richard Allen Mitchell
GUY MITCHELL	Al Cernik
JONI MITCHELL	Roberta Joan Anderson
MITCH MITCHELL (HENDRIX EXPERIENCE)	John Mitchell
HANK MIZELL	William Mizell
ESSRA MOHAWK	Sandy Hurvitz
REG MOMBASSA (MENTAL AS ANYTHING)	Christopher O'Dougherty
EDDIE MONEY	Edward Mahoney
ZOOT MONEY	George Bruno Money
MATT MONRO	Terrence Parsons
CHRIS MONTEZ	Christopher Montanez
WES MONTGOMERY	John Leslie Montgomery
PETE MOORE (SMOKEY ROBINSON & MIRACLES)	Warren Thomas Moore
SCOTTY MOORE (ELVIS, SCOTTY & BILL)	Winfield Scott Moore
JOHNNY MOPED	Paul Halford
JANE MORGAN	Jane Courrier
JAYE P. MORGAN	Mary Morgan
JOHN MORGAN (STEPPENWOLF)	Rushton John Moreve
VAN MORRISON	George Ivan Morrison
JELLY ROLL MORTON	Ferdinande Joseph La Menthe
JOHN MULLIGAN (FASHION)	Salvatore Jonathon Mulligan
BILL MUMY (BARNES & BARNES)	Charles William Mumy Jnr.
COATI MUNDI	Andrew Hernandez
JIM MORRISON (DOORS)	James Morrisson

†McGuinn began his recording career as Jim, changing to Roger in 1967 when he took up the Subud faith. "They offer an optional name change, which is in correspondence to the verbal sound that your soul has, as a vibration . . . I sent to Indonesia for it and the Guru picked it."

Ferdinande Joseph LaMenthe

Mary Christine Brockert

HARPO

CUSTOM HIGH FIDELITY

ASTOR

BLUE STAR SERIES

Adolph Marx

GUY MITCHELL— Al Cernik

Ian Matthews Journeys from Gospel Oak

Ian Matthew McDonald

VAN MORRISON — George Ivan Morrison

PHIL MANZANERA — Philip Targett-Adams

RALPH McTELL — Ralph May

Ethel Agnes Zimmerman

Christopher Montanez

FREDDIE MERCURY — Frederick Bulsara

TED NUGENT
Theodore Anthony Nugent

VINCE NEIL (MOTLEY CRUE)
Vincent Neil Wharton

GARY NUMAN
Gary Anthony James Webb

RICK NELSON — Eric Hilliard Nelson

ESTHER & ABI OFARIM: Esther Ofarim nee Zaled and Abraham Reichstadt

N

TINA NATURAL (DAN HICKS' HOT LICKS) .... Christina Gancher
WAZMO NARIZ .... Lawrence Grennan
DOC NEESON (ANGEL CITY) .... Bernard Neeson
VINCE NEIL (MOTLEY CRUE) .... Vincent Neil Wharton
RICKY NELSON .... Eric Hilliard Nelson
SANDY NELSON .... Sander L. Nelson
LISA NEMZO .... Lisa Nemtzow
MIKE NESMITH (MONKEES) .... Robert Michael Nesmith
MICKEY NEWBURY .... Milton S. Newbury Jnr.
STEVIE NICKS .... Stephanie Nicks
TONY NINETEEN (DILS) .... Anthony Kinman
STEVE NIEVE (E. COSTELLO & ATTRACTIONS) .... Steve Mason
HANK NOBLE .... William H. Noble
TRISHA NOBLE .... Patsy Ann Noble
SONNY NORTON (CROWS) .... Daniel Norton
GEOFF NUGENT (UNDERTAKERS) .... Gordon Geoffrey Nugent
TED NUGENT .... Theodore Anthony Nugent
GARY NUMAN (TUBEWAY ARMY) .... Gary Anthony James Webb
P.NUT (BARRON KNIGHTS) .... Peter Langford
JUDY NYLON .... Judith Nyland

O

CUBBY O'BRIEN (M. M. CLUB/CARPENTERS) .... Carl Patrick O'Brien
RIC OCASEK (CARS) .... Richard Otcasek
LUCKY OCEANS (ASLEEP AT THE WHEEL) .... Reuben Gosfield
KENNY O'DELL .... Kenneth Gist Jnr.
ABI OFARIM .... Abraham Reichstadt
SPOONER OLDHAM† .... Dewey Lindon Oldham
VIC OLIVER .... Victor Von Samek
TONY ORLANDO .... Michael Anthony Orlando Cassivitis
BEN ORR (CARS) .... Benjamin Orzechowski
OZZY OSBOURNE .... John Osbourne
LEE OSKAR (WAR) .... Oskar Levetio Hansen
MARIE OSMOND .... Olive Marie Osmond
WAYNE OSMOND (OSMONDS) .... Melvin Wayne Osmond
GILBERT O'SULLIVAN .... Raymond O'Sullivan
JOHNNY OTIS .... John Veliotes
SHUGGIE OTIS†† .... John Otis Jnr.
BUCK OWENS .... Alvis Edgar Owens

†Although well known as a Memphis songwriter, Spooner has recorded his own albums.
††Shuggie is the son of Johnny Otis.

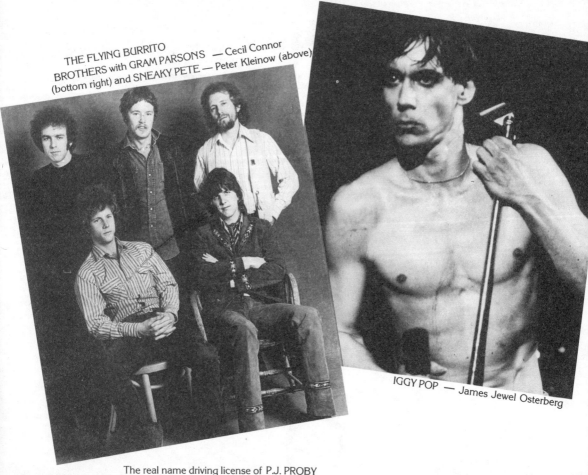

THE FLYING BURRITO BROTHERS with GRAM PARSONS — Cecil Connor (bottom right) and SNEAKY PETE — Peter Kleinow (above)

IGGY POP — James Jewel Osterberg

The real name driving license of P.J. PROBY

EDITH PIAF — Edith Giovanna...

P

PATTI PAGE .... Clara Ann Fowler
ELAINE PAIGE .... Elaine Bikerstaff
POLI PALMER (FAMILY) .... John Palmer
GRAM PARSONS † .... Cecil Connor
JOE PASS .... Joseph Anthony Passalaque
JACO PASTORIUS (WEATHER REPORT) .... John Francis Pastorius
MIKE PATTO (BOXER) .... Michael McCarthy
LES PAUL .... Lester William Polfus
LYN PAUL (NEW SEEKERS) .... Lynda Susan Belcher
RAY PAUL .... Ray Paul Klimek
JOHNNY PAYCHECK .... Don Lytle
MIKE PENDER (SEARCHERS) .... Michael Pendergast
DANNY PEPPERMINT (& JUMPING JACKS) .... Daniel Lamego
MARK PETERS (& SILHOUETTES) .... Peter Fleming
PAUL PETERSEN .... William Paul Petersen
SNOOPY PFISTERER (LOVE) .... Alban Pfisterer
SLIM JIM PHANTOM (STRAY CATS) .... Jim McDonell
LITTLE ESTHER PHILLIPS .... Esther Mae Jones
MICHELLE PHILLIPS (MAMAS & PAPAS) .... Holly Michelle Phillips nee Gilliam
PHIL PHILLIPS .... John Philip Baptiste
EDITH PIAF†† .... Edith Giovanna Gassion
MARTIN PLAZA (MENTAL AS ANYTHING) .... Martin Edward Murphy
BONNIE POINTER .... Patricia Pointer
DEE POP (BUSH TETRAS) .... Dimitri Papadopoulous
IGGY POP .... James Jewel Osterberg
SANDY POSEY .... Martha Sharp
COZY POWELL .... Colin Flooks
DUFFY POWER .... Ray Howard
KID CONGO POWERS (CRAMPS/GUN CLUB) .... Brian Tristan
REG PRESLEY (TROGGS) .... Reginald Maurice Ball
EARL PRESTON (& THE T.T.'s) .... George Spruce
ANDRE PREVIN .... Andre Prewin
P.J. PROBY .... James Marcus Smith
PRETTY PURDIE .... Bernard Purdie
BOBBY PURIFY (JAMES & BOBBY PURIFY) .... Robert Dickey

†Coon Dog Connor shot himself when Gram was 13 and his wife married New Orleans businessman
  Robert Parsons, who changed the boy's name to Gram, a Southern corruption of Graham.
††Piaf roughly translates to 'The Little Sparrow'.

Q

TOMMY QUICKLY .... Thomas Quigley
CHRISTOPHER QUINN .... John Francis Quinn III
FREDDY QUINN .... Manfred Petz

R

EDDIE RABBITT	Edward Thomas
MARVIN RAINWATER†	Marvin Percy
DEE DEE RAMONE (RAMONES)	Douglas Colvin
JOEY RAMONE (RAMONES)	Jeffrey Hyman
JOHNNY RAMONE (RAMONES)	John Cummings
MARKY RAMONE (RAMONES)	Mark Bell
TOMMY RAMONE (RAMONES)	Thomas Erdelyi
LARRY RAMOS (ASSOCIATION)	Hilario D. Ramos Jnr.
DON RANDI	Donald Schwartz
DODIE RANDLE	Roberta Jean Flournoy
BOOTS RANDOLPH	Homer Louis Randolph lll
GENYA RAVAN	Genya Goldie Zelkowitz
MARTHA RAYE	Margaret Teresa Yvonne O'Reed
TEDDY REDDELL	Edward Delano Reidel
JERRY REED	Jerry Reid Hubbard
JIMMY REED	Mathis James Reed Geland
LOU REED	Louis Firbank
DELLA REESE	Dellareese Taliaferro
BOB REGAN (CANADIAN SWEETHEARTS)	Robert Frederickson
DJANGO REINHARDT	Jean Reinhardt
PAUL REVERE (& THE RAIDERS)	Paul Revere Dick
DEBBIE REYNOLDS	Mary Frances Reynolds
NICK RHODES (DURAN DURAN)	Nicholas James Bates
RED RHODES (FIRST NATIONAL BAND)	Orville J. Rhodes
MANDY RICE-DAVIES††	Marilyn Rice-Davies
BUDDY RICH	Bernard Rich
CLIFF RICHARD	Harry Rodger Webb
KEITH RICHARD (ROLLING STONES)†††	Keith Richards
TERRY RICHARDS (CHASE)	Terrence Richard Marinan
CHUCK RIO (CHAMPS)	Danny Flores
MAX RIPPLE (DEAF SCHOOL)	John Wood
TEX RITTER	Woodward Maurice Ritter
JOHNNY RIVERS	John Ramistella
MARTY ROBBINS	Martin D. Robinson

CLIFF RICHARD — (Harry Rodger Webb) & THE SHADOWS with HANK MARVIN — Brian Robson Rankin

PIG ROBBINS	Hargus Robbins
AUSTIN ROBERTS	George Austin Robertson Jnr.
B. A. ROBERTSON	Brian Alexander Robertson
ROBBIE ROBERTSON (THE BAND)	Jaime Robert Robertson
IVO ROBIC	Eevo Robish
SMOKEY ROBINSON	William Robinson Jnr.
MONTI ROCK III/DISCO TEX	Joseph Moses Martinez Jnr.
TOMMY ROCK	Thomas Evan Johnson
LEE ROCKER (STRAY CATS)	Lee Drucker
TIMMIE RODGERS	Timothy Louis Aiverum
JOHNNY RODRIGUEZ	Juan Raul Davis Rodriguez
MOD ROGAN (ROULETTES)	John Rogan
JULIE ROGERS	Julie Rolls
ROY ROGERS	Leonard Slye
WAYNE ROGERS	Wayne Garwood Bacon Jnr.
CHAN ROMERO	Robert Romero
ANNIE ROSS (LAMBERT, HENDRICKS & ROSS)	Annabelle Lynch nee Short
DIANA ROSS	Diane Ross
NINO ROSSO	Celeste Rosso
JOHNNY ROTTEN (SEX PISTOLS)	John Lydon
PHIL RUDD (AC/DC)	Philip Rudzevecuis
RIKKY RUSH (& RIALTONES)	Richard Gagnon
LEON RUSSELL	Russell Bridges
BARRY RYAN	Barry Sapherson
MARION RYAN††††	Marion Sapherson
PAUL RYAN	Paul Sapherson
BOBBY RYDELL	Robert Lewis Ridarelli
MITCH RYDER	Billy Levise

†Marvin is of Cherokee Indian descent, Rainwater being his mother's maiden name.
††Although best remembered as a call girl in Britain's Profumo Affair, Mandy also tried her hand at pop recording for Ember Records.
†††Keith was inspired to drop the 's' from his surname by Cliff Richard.
††††Marion Ryan, who scored a 1958 top five British hit with *Love Me Forever*, is the mother of twins Paul and Barry Ryan.

JERRY REED — Jerry Reid Hubbard

EDDIE RABBITT — Edward Thomas
BOBBY RYDELL — Robert Lewis Ridarelli

LOU REED — Louis Firbank
Edward Delano Reidel

ORIGINAL 50'S RECORDINGS

THE TEDDY REDELL SOUND

JOHNNY ROTTEN — John Lydon   MITCH RYDER — William Levise

JULIE ROGERS — Julie Rolls

BOOTS RANDOLPH — Homer Louis Randolph III

NICK RHODES (DURAN DURAN) — Nicholas James Bates

ARTIE SHAW — Abraham Isaac Arshawsky, with wife LANA TURNER — Julia Jean Mildred Frances Turner

S

LEO SAYER – Gerrard Hugh Sayer

GENE SIMMONS (KISS) .... Gene Klein
NINA SIMONE .... Eunice Kathleen Waymon
RICKY SLAUGHTER (MOTORS/CAMERA CLUB) .... Richard Wernham
P. F. SLOAN (FANTASTIC BAGGIES) .... Phillip 'Flip' Sloan
MICKEY SLUTZKY (RENEGADES) .... Melvin Slutzky
N.D. SMART II (KANGAROO/BO GRUMPUS) .... Norman Dow Smart II
CHAS SMASH (MADNESS) .... Cathal Smyth
GREEDY SMITH (MENTAL AS ANYTHING) .... Andrew Smith
HURRICANE SMITH .... Norman Smith
KEELY SMITH .... Dorothy Jacqueline Keely Prima nee Smith
O. C. SMITH .... Ocie Lee Smith
WHISTLING JACK SMITH††† .... Billy Moeller
DEE SNIDER (TWISTED SISTER) .... David Daniel Snider
HANK SNOW .... Clarence Eugene Snow
PHOEBE SNOW .... Phoebe Laub
SAL SOLO (CLASSIX NOUVEAUX) .... Charles Carlos Smith

RAY STEVENS — Harold Raymond Ragsdale   SHAKIN' STEVENS — Michael Barrett

JOE STRUMMER (THE CLASH) — John Mellor

THE POLICE (from left): STEWART COPELAND (aka Klark Kent),
ANDY SUMMERS — Andrew James Somers, and
STING — Gordon Matthew Sumner

DAVID SYLVIAN (JAPAN) — David Batt

DAVID SOUL — David Solberg

TOMMY STEELE — Thomas Hicks

RICK SPRINGFIELD — Richard Lewis Springthorpe

DAVID SOUL .... David Richard Solberg
JIMMY SOUL .... James McCleese
JOE SOUTH .... Joseph Alfred Souter
BOB B. SOXX (& BLUE JEANS) .... Robert Sheen
RONNIE SPECTOR .... Veronica Spector nee Bennett
SKIP SPENCE (MOBY GRAPE) .... Alexander Spencer
SAM SPOONS (BONZO DOG BAND) .... Martin Stafford
DUSTY SPRINGFIELD .... Mary Isobel Catherine O'Brien
RICK SPRINGFIELD .... Richard Lewis Springthorpe
TOM SPRINGFIELD (SPRINGFIELDS) .... Thomas O'Brien
ALICE SPRINGS (SLACK ALICE/DARLING) .... Sandra Barry
PAUL STANLEY (KISS) .... Stanley Eisen
POP STAPLES (STAPLE SINGERS) .... Roebuck Staples
ALVIN STARDUST .... Bernard William Jewry
BONGO STARR (SKYHOOKS) .... Robert Starkie
EDWIN STARR .... Charles Hatcher
FREDDIE STARR (& MIDNIGHTERS) .... Frederick Powell
KAY STARR .... Katherine LaVerne Starks
LUCILLE STARR .... Fern Frederickson
RINGO STARR .... Richard Starkey
TOMMY STEELE .... Thomas Hicks
DANE STEPHENS (FAIRIES) .... Douglas Orde
CAT STEVENS .... Stephen Demetri Georgiou
CONNIE STEVENS .... Concetta Ann Ingolia
DODIE STEVENS .... Geraldine Ann Pasquale
RAY STEVENS .... Harold Raymond Ragsdale
SHAKIN' STEVENS .... Michael Barrett
B. W. STEVENSON .... Louis C. Stevenson
BILLY STEWART .... Lawrence William Stewart
SANDY STEWART .... Sandra Esther Galitz
DICK ST. JOHN (DICK & DEE DEE) .... Richard Frank Gosting
JODY ST. NICHOLAS (NRBQ) .... Joseph Spampinato
JOHN STOKES (BACHELORS) .... Sean Stokes
SLY STONE .... Sylvester Stewart
PAUL STOOKEY (P. P. & M.) .... Noel Paul Stookey
GALE STORM .... Josephine Owaissa Cottle
RORY STORME (& HURRICANES) .... Alan Caldwell
CRISPIAN ST. PETERS .... Peter Smith
SHIRLEY STRACHAN (SKYHOOKS) .... Graeme Strachan
NICK STRAKER .... Nick Bailey
STEVE STRANGE (VISAGE) .... Steve Harrigan
RICHARD STREET (TEMPTATIONS) .... Richard Strick
BARBRA STREISAND .... Barbara Joan Streisand
JEZ STRODE (KAJAGOOGOO) .... Jeremy Strode
JOE STRUMMER (CLASH) .... John Mellor
POLY STYRENE (X-RAY-SPEX) .... Marion Elliott
NASTY SUICIDE (HANOI ROCKS) .... Jan Stenfors
YMA SUMAC†††† .... Emperatriz Chavarri
DONNA SUMMER .... Donna Andrea Sommer nee Gaines
ANDY SUMMERS (POLICE) .... Andrew James Somers
RICHARD SUPA .... Richard John Goodman
SCREAMING LORD SUTCH .... David Edward Sutch
BETTYE SWANN .... Betty Jean Champion
SYLVAIN SYLVAIN (NEW YORK DOLLS) .... Ronald Mizrahi
DAVID SYLVIAN (JAPAN) .... David Batt

†Tony, leader of 60s outfit Tony & The Tigers, is the son of comedian Soupy Sales.
††This chrome-dome cops'n'robbers actor actually made #1 in Britain and Australia in 1975 with
a cover of Bread's *If*.
†††It is rumoured that Billy, brother of Tommy Moeller of Unit 4 + 2, did not actually whistle on his sole
hit, *I Was Kaiser Bill's Batman*.
††††Yma Sumac is a reversal of Amy Camus, her first attempt at a stage name.

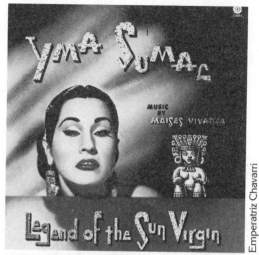

Emperatriz Chavarri

Josephine Owaissa Cottle

Concetta Ann Ingolia

Gary Shelton

JACK SCOTT — Jack Scaffone Jnr.

Eunice Kathleen Waymon

THE MONKEES (from top left): PETER TORK — Peter Thorkelson, MICKEY DOLENZ — George Michael Dolenz Jnr., DAVY JONES, and MIKE NESMITH (aka Michael Blessing)

T

CHIP TAYLOR†	James Wesley Voight
CONRAD TAYLOR (GENYA RAVAN BAND)	Conrad John Danowski
GARY TAYLOR (HERD)	Graham Taylor
JOHN TAYLOR (DURAN DURAN)	Nigel John Taylor
KINGSIZE TAYLOR (& DOMINOES)	Edward Taylor
LITTLE JOHNNY TAYLOR	John Young
ROGER TAYLOR (QUEEN)	Roger Meadows-Taylor
BRAM TCHAIKOVSKY	Peter Brammel
WILLIE TEE	Wilson Turbinton
NINO TEMPO	Antonio LoTempio
TAMMI TERRELL	Tammy Montgomery
JOE TEX	Joseph Arrington Jnr.
PEPPY THIELHEIM (BLUES MAGOOS)	Emil Castro
B.J. THOMAS	Billie Joe Thomas
SUE THOMPSON	Eva Sue McKee
JOHNNY THUNDERS (NEW YORK DOLLS)	John Genzalli
SONNY TIL (& ORIOLES)	Earlington Tilghman
OLIVER TOBIAS (WHY NOT)††	Oliver Tobias Tureitag
NICK TODD†††	Nicholas Boone
GERONIMO TOLBERT (UNIVERSAL ROBOT BAND)	Gregory Jerome Tolbert
STEVE PEREGRINE TOOK (TYRANNOSAURUS REX)††††	Stephen Porter
TOP TOPHAM (YARDBIRDS)	Anthony Topham
PETER TORK (MONKEES)	Peter Thorkelson
PETER TOSH	Winston Hubert McIntosh
VAUGHAN TOULOUSE (DEPARTMENT S)	Vaughan Cotillard
JAY TRAYNOR (JAY & AMERICANS)	John Traynor
DORIS TROY	Doris Payne
SOPHIE TUCKER †††††	Sophie Kalish/Abuza/Tuck
TOMMY TUCKER	Robert Higginbotham
SCOTTY TURNBULL (SHARKS)	Graham Morrison Turnbull
IKE TURNER	Isaiah Turner
SAMMY TURNER	Samuel Black
TINA TURNER	Annie Mae Turner nee Bullock
BOBBY TWINE	Robert C. Morphis
CONWAY TWITTY	Harold Lloyd Jenkins
BONNIE TYLER	Gaynor Sullivan nee Hopkins
KIP TYLER	Jimmy Daley
STEVE TYLER (AEROSMITH)	Steven Tallarico

† Chip (who happened to write *Wild Thing* and *Angel Of The Morning*) is the brother of actor Jon Voight.

†† After fronting the Swiss/British hard rock outfit Why Not in the sixties, Oliver turned to TV and film acting, his most visible role being in the movie *The Stud*.

††† Nick Todd is Pat Boone's brother. Todd was derived from the backward spelling of record label Dot.

†††† A change inspired by reading Tolkien.

††††† Sophie's birth name is Kalish. However, when she was 4, her father fled Russia with a stolen passport in the name of Abuza, which the family retained upon arrival in America. In 1900 she married Louis Tuck.

CONWAY TWITTY — Harold Lloyd Jenkins

CHIP TAYLOR — James Wesley Voight

Sophie Kalish/Abuza/Tuck

72

SONNY TIL (& ORIOLES) — Earlington Tilghman

TAMMI TERRELL — Tammy Montgomery

Eva Sue McKee

PETER TOSH — Winston Hubert McIntosh

Frank Abelson

RITCHIE VALENS — Richard Valenzuela

Richard Bryce

MIDGE URE (JJI TRAVOX) — James Ure

THE EASYBEATS: HARRY VANDA — Johannes Jacob Hendrickus Vandenberg (centre), SNOWY FLEET — Gordon

U

ARI UP (SLITS) .... Arianna Forster
MIDGE URE (ULTRAVOX) .... James Ure

V

RICKY VALANCE .... David Spencer
JERRY VALE .... Genaro Louis Vitaliano
RITCHIE VALENS .... Richard Valenzuela
DINO VALENTI (QUICKSILVER) .... Chester Powers
DICKIE VALENTINE .... Richard Bryce
MARK VALENTINO .... Anthony Busillo
SAL VALENTINO (BEAU BRUMMELS) .... Salvatore Spampinato
TONY VALENTINO (STANDELLS) .... Emilio Tony Bellissimo
RUDI VALLEE .... Hubert Prior Vallee
FRANKIE VALLI (FOUR SEASONS) .... Frank Castelluccio
BILLY VANCE .... William Gallenti
KENNY VANCE (JAY & THE AMERICANS) .... Kenny Rosenberg
HARRY VANDA (EASYBEATS) .... Johannes Jacob Hendrickus Vandenberg
DAVE VANIAN (DAMNED) .... David Letts
CHERRY VANILLA .... Kathy Dorrittie
JOEY VANN (DUPREES) .... Joseph Canzana
TEDDY VANN .... Theodore Williams
BILLY VAUGHAN (HILLTOPPERS) .... Richard Smith Vaughan
FRANKIE VAUGHN .... Frank Abelson
BOBBY VEE .... Robert Thomas Velline
TATA VEGA .... Carmen Rose Vega
FRANKIE VENOM (TEENAGE HEAD) .... Frank Kerr
BILLY VERA .... William Patrick McCord
TOM VERLAINE (TELEVISION) .... Thomas Miller
ROBERT VERNE (COLUMBUS) .... Robert Arnold Vernoff
RAY VERNON .... Vernon Wray
SID VICIOUS (SEX PISTOLS) .... John Simon Ritchie
MONTE VIDEO (& CASSETTES) .... Murray Grindlay
GENE VINCENT .... Vincent Eugene Craddock
BOBBY VINTON .... Stanley Robert Vinton
BONO VOX (U2) .... Paul Hewson

MUDDY WATERS — McKinley Morganfield

KIM WILDE — Kim Smith

STEVIE WONDER — Steveland Morris/Judkins/Harda

W

WADDY WACHTEL	Robert Wachtel
GARY WALKER (WALKER BROS)	Gary Leeds
JERRY JEFF WALKER	Ronald Crosby
JOHN WALKER (WALKER BROS)	John Maus
JUNIOR WALKER (& ALL STARS)	Autry DeWalt Jnr.
SCOTT WALKER (WALKER BROS)	Noel Scott Engel
FATS WALLER	Thomas Wright Waller
CLARA WARD (. . . SINGERS)	Gertrude Ward
ROBIN WARD†	Jackie Ward
BRENT WARREN (THE ACTION)	Brent Kubasta
CLINT WARWICK (MOODY BLUES)	Clinton Eccles
DIONNE WARWICK	Marie Dionne Warwick
JIMMY WARWICK (NITE PEOPLE)	James Warwick Shipstone
DAVID WAS (WAS NOT WAS)	David Weiss
DON WAS (WAS NOT WAS)	Donald Fagenson
BABY WASHINGTON	Jeanette Washington
DINAH WASHINGTON	Ruth Lee Jones
MUDDY WATERS	McKinley Morganfield
ROGER WATERS (PINK FLOYD)	George Roger Waters
DOC WATSON	Arthel Watson
FEE WAYBILL (TUBES)	John Waldo
ALAN WAYNE	Albertus Wayne Johnson
DIG WAYNE (JO BOXERS)	Timothy Wayne
THOMAS WAYNE††	Thomas Wayne Perkins
BLUE WEAVER (AMEN CORNER)	Derek Weaver
SONNY WEBB (& CASCADES)	Kenny Johnson
BOB WEIR (GRATEFUL DEAD)	Robert Hall
FREDDIE WELLER (RAIDERS)	Wilton Frederick Weller
KEITH WEST	Keith Hopkins
MAX WERNER (KAYAK)	Max Werlerofzoiets
LESLIE WEST (MOUNTAIN)	Lesley Weinstein
RICKY WEST (TREMELOES)	Richard Weston
SANDY WEST (RUNAWAYS)	Sandra Resavento
TOMMY WEST (CASHMAN & WEST)	Thomas R. Picardo
KIM WESTON	Agatha Natalie Weston
TINA WEYMOUTH (TALKING HEADS)	Martina Michelle Weymouth
DAVE WHITE (DANNY & THE JUNIORS)†††	David White Tricker
JAMES WHITE/CHANCE (CONTORTIONS)	James Seigfried
SNOWY WHITE	Terrence White
SLIM WHITMAN	Otis Dewey Whitman Jnr.
CHARLIE WHITNEY (FAMILY)	John Whitney
BARRY WHITWAM (HERMAN'S HERMITS)	Jan Barry Whitwam
KIM WILDE	Kim Smith
MARTY WILDE	Reginald Smith
HANK WILLIAMS	Hirah Williams
HANK WILLIAMS JNR.	Randall Hank Williams
JERRY WILLIAMS (& VIOLENTS)	Erik Fernstrom
JOE WILLIAMS	Joseph Goreed
OTIS WILLIAMS (TEMPTATIONS)	Otis Miles
ROGER WILLIAMS	Louis Jacob Wertz
CHUCK WILLIS	Harold Willis
B.J. WILSON (PROCOL HARUM)	Barrie Wilson
MARI WILSON (& WILSATIONS)	Mairrhii MacMillan Ramsey Wilson
MUFF WINWOOD (SPENCER DAVIS GROUP)	Mervyn Winwood

JAH WOBBLE (PIL)	John Wordle
PETER WOLF (J. GEIL'S BAND)	Peter Blankenfield
STEVIE WONDER††††	Steveland Morris/Judkins/Hardaway
BRENTON WOOD	Alfred Jesse Smith
ROY WOOD (MOVE/WIZZARD)	Ulysses Adrian Wood
WOODY WOOD (BAY CITY ROLLERS)	Stuart Wood
WOODY WOODMANSEY (SPIDERS FROM MARS)	Michael Woodmansey
SHEB WOOLEY	Shelby Wooley
O.V. WRIGHT	Overton Vertis Wright
ROBERT WYATT (SOFT MACHINE)	Robert Ellidge
WILBUR WYLDE (JO JO ZEP & FALCONS)	Nicholas Aitken
BILL WYMAN (ROLLING STONES)	William Perks
TAMMY WYNETTE	Virginia Wynette Pugh
MARK WYNTER	Terry Lewis

† Session singer Jackie Ward, who ofted dubbed in singing voices for the likes of Natalie Wood and Janet Leigh, took the name of her baby daughter Robin to cut the hit single *Wonderful Summer*.

†† Thomas Wayne, who had a 1959 top five hit with *Tragedy*, is the brother of Luther Perkins from Johnny Cash's Tennessee Two.

††† White recorded a 1971 album on Bell under his full name.

†††† One of rock's most puzzling name games. His father's surname was Judkins but Stevie insists that Morris is on his birth certificate. Hardaway apparently came from a stepfather. Early Motown songwriting credits list him as S. Judkins.

MARK WYNTER — Terry Lewis

Thomas Wright Waller

WALKER BROTHERS (from left): GARY WALKER — Gary Leeds, SCOTT WALKER — Noel Scott Engel, JOHN WALKER -John Mau
JERRY JEFF WALKER — Ronald Crosby   TAMMY WYNETTE — Virginia Wynette Pugh

RUSTY YOUNG — Norman Russell Young

TIMI YURO — Rosemarie Yuro

JESSE COLIN YOUNG — Perry Miller

Y

SAM YAFFA (HANOI ROCKS)	Sam Tamaki
YOGI YORGESSON	Harry Stewart
JESSE COLIN YOUNG (YOUNGBLOODS)	Perry Miller
RUSTY YOUNG (POCO)	Norman Russell Young
TIMI YURO	Rosemarie Yuro

Z

ROGER ZAPP	Roger Troutman
JO JO ZEP	Joseph Camilleri
JIMMY ZERO (DEAD BOYS)	William Wildon
BILLY ZOOM (X)	Tyson Kindale

THE DEAD BOYS (from left): JIMMY ZERO — William Wildon, JOHNNY BLITZ — John Madansky, STIV BATORS — Stivin Bator, CHEETAH CHROME — Gene Connor, and JEFF MAGNUM — Jeffrey Halmezy

ANN-MARGRET (Olson)

CHRISTIAN NAME ONLY ARTISTS

AIRTO	Airto Guimorva Moreira
ANNETTE†	Annette Funicello
ANN-MARGRET	Ann Margret Olson
APOLLONIA	Appolonia Kotero
AURA (aka AURA LEE)	Aura Urziceanu
BRENDON	Brendon Dunning
CANDIDO	Candido Camero
CARLO	Carlo Mastrangelo
CARMEL	Carmel McCourt
CHARLENE	Charlene Duncan
CORY	Cory Braverman
CRISTINA	Cristine Monet
DAMITA JO	Damita Jo DuBlanc
DANNIEBELLE (ANDRAE CROUCH & DISCIPLES)	Danniebelle Hall
DARLENE†	Darlene Gillespie
DION	Dion Dimucci
DIVA	Diva Gray
DONOVAN	Donovan Phillip Leitch
DOTTSY	Dottsy Brodt
DRAFI	Drafi Deutscher
EARL-JEAN	Earl-Jean McCree
EVIE	Evie Tornquist
FABIAN	Fabiano Forte Bonoparte
FIONA	Fiona Flanagan
FREDDY	Freddy Quinn*
GIORGIO	Giorgio Moroder
GITTE	Gitte Haenning
GRAZINA	Grazina Frame
GREEN (SCRITTI POLITTI)	Green Strohmeyer-Gartside
HASAAN	Hasaan Ibn. Ali
HEINTJE	Heintje Simons
HEINZ	Heinz Burt
HILDEGARDE	Hildegarde Loretta Sell
HOLLY (FRANKIE GOES TO HOLLYWOOD)	William Holly Johnson
JENNIFER	Jennifer Warren
JOBRIATH	Jobriath Boone
JULIE	Julie Budd
JUNIOR	Junior Giscombe
LaCOSTA	La Costa Tucker
LETTA	Letta Mbulu
LOLITA	Lolita Ditta
MADONNA††	Madonna Louise Veronica Penn nee Ciccone
MARCY JOE	Marcy Joe Sockel
MECO	Meco Monardo
MELANIE	Melanie Safka
MILLIE	Millie (Millicent) Small
MYLON	Mylon LaFerve
NATASHA	Natasha England
NICOLE	Nicole Hohloch
NORMA JEAN	Norma Jean Beasler
O'BRYAN	O'Bryan Burnette III
ODETTA†††	Odetta Holmes/Felious/Gordon
OLIVER	William Oliver Swofford
PRINCE	Prince Roger Nelson
PRISCILLA	Priscilla Jones nee Coolidge

TOYAH (Wilcox)   DONOVAN (Phillip Leitch)

RAMONA	Ramona Myers/Davies
REX	Rex Smith
RICO	Rico Rodriguez
SHANNON	Shannon Green
SHARALEE	Sharalee Lucas
SHARON MARIE	Sharon Marie Exparza
SYLVESTER	Sylvester James
SYLVIA	Sylvia Kirby Allen
SYLVIA	Sylvia Robinson nee Vanderpool
SYLVIA	Sylvia Verthammar
SYREETA	Syreeta Wonder nee Wright
TACO	Taco Ockerse
TETSU	Tetsu Yamauchi
TOMPALL	Tompall Glaser
TOYAH	Toyah Ann Wilcox
TRACIE	Tracie Young
VALJEAN	Valjean Johns
VANGELIS	Vangelis Papathanassiou
YUTAKA	Yutaka Yokokura
ZULEMA	Zulema Cusseaux

* Refer to index for exact real name.

   † Annette and Darlene are both former Mouseketeers who went on to make records.

   †† "I didn't have a hard time growing up with the name Madonna because I went to a Catholic school."

††† Born Holmes, adopted stepfather's name of Felious, married Dan Gordon.

Heinz Burt

HEINZ
THE SINGLES

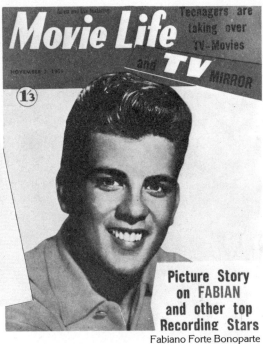

Gulrod and Eve featuring

Movie Life
and **TV** MIRROR

Teenagers are taking over TV-Movies

NOVEMBER 3, 1959

1/3

**Picture Story
on FABIAN
and other top
Recording Stars**

Fabiano Forte Bonoparte

Annette Funicello

DELL 10¢

NO. 905

Mouse Club

Walt Disney's
Annette

A clue...
to the mystery
of the
MISSING
NECKLACE!

BORN TO CRY
(JE SUIS NE POUR PLEURER)

LOVERS WHO WANDER Twist

LONELY WORLD Twist

DREAM LOVER Twist

**Mr. Hit Parade
DION**

vogue

DION (DiMucci)

TACO (Ockerse)

MELANIE (Safka)

PRINCE (Roger Nelson)

ETTA (Holmes/Felious/Gordon)

MECO (Monardo)

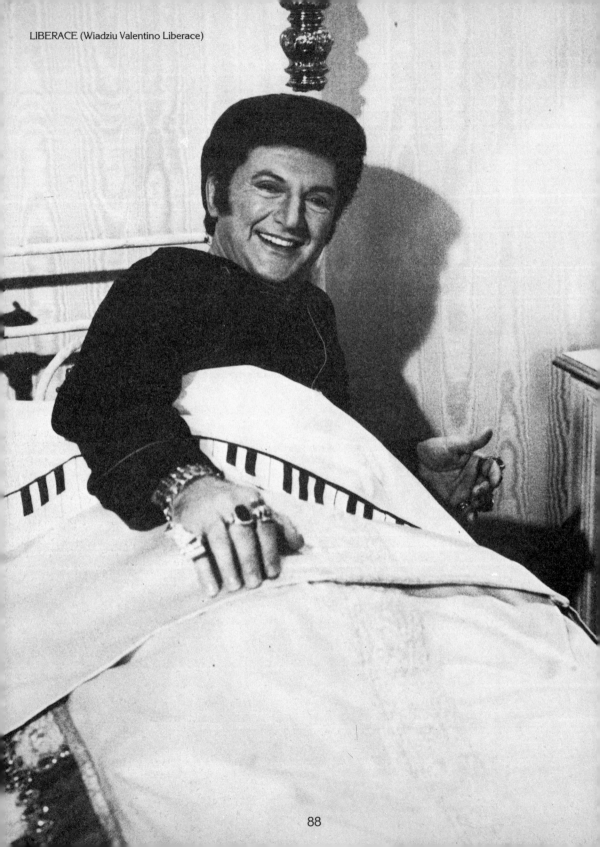

LIBERACE (Wiadziu Valentino Liberace)

SURNAME ONLY ARTISTS

ADAMO	Salvatore Adamo
BIDDU	Su Biddu
BOHANNON	Hamilton Bohannon
CAMERON	Rafael Cameron
CARUSO	Enrico Caruso
CERRONE	Jean-Marc Cerrone
CUGINI	Don Cugini
DEODATO	Eumir De Almeida Deodata
ENO	Brian Peter George St. John Le Baptiste De La Salle Eno
FALCO	Hans Falco
KENNY	Tony Kenny
LATIMORE	Benny Latimore
LIBERACE	Wiadziu Valentino Liberace
MANTOVANI	Annunzio Paolo Mantovani
MORRISSEY (THE SMITHS)	Stephen Morrissey
NILSSON	Harry Edward Nilsson lll
RODRIGUEZ	Sixto (aka Jesus) Rodriguez
SEGARINI	Bob Segarini
SEGOVIA	Andres Segovia
SILVETTI	Bebu Silvetti
TOMITA	Isao Tomita
ZACHERLE	John Zacherle

DEODATO (Eumir De Almeida Deodata)

SSON (Harry Edward Nilsson lll)   SEGOVIA (Andres Segovia)

BOY GEORGE — George Alan O'Dowd

STAGE NAMES
(WITHOUT SURNAMES)

ALF (YAZOO) .... Genevieve Alison Moyet
ALPO (REAL KIDS) .... Alan Paulino
ANEKA .... Mary Sandeman
ANGIE† .... Angela Porter
ARCHIBALD .... Leon T. Gross
ARKIE, THE ARKANSAS WOODCHOPPER .... Luther Ossenbrink
ASTRO (UB40) .... Terrence Wilson
BABY HUEY .... James Thomas Ramey
BABY LOVE (ROCK STEADY CREW) .... Daisy Castro
BABY RAY .... Raymond Eddleman
BALTIMORA .... James McShane
BANANA (YOUNGBLOODS) .... Lowell Vincent Levinger
BARON ANTHONY (BARRON KNIGHTS) .... Anthony Osmond
BASHFUL BROTHER OSWALD .... Beecher 'Pete' Kirby
BIG BANK HANK (SUGAR HILL GANG) .... Henry Jackson
BIG BLACK .... Danny Ray
BIG BOPPER, THE .... Jiles Perry (J.P.) Richardson
BLINKY (& EDWIN STARR) .... Sandra Williams
BRAT .... Roger Kitter
BONNIE LOU .... Sally Carson
BOWSER (SHA NA NA) .... Jon Bauman
BOXCAR WILLIE .... Cecil Travis Martin
BOY GEORGE (CULTURE CLUB) .... George Alan O'Dowd
BRICKTOP .... Ada Beatrice Queen Victoria Louise Virgina Smith Duconge
BUDGIE (SLITS, BANSHEES, etc) .... Peter Clark
BUZZ (SOUTHERN DEATH CULT) .... David John Burrows
CAPTAIN BEEFHEART .... Don Van Vliet
CAPTAIN SENSIBLE (DAMNED) .... Ray Burns
CAZZ .... Robert C. Lewis
CHAQUITETE (& QUEDO BRASS) .... Johnny Gregory
CHERRELLE .... Cheryl Norton
CHRISTIANE F. .... Christiane Felscherinow
COBRA .... Gyorgyi Mezovari
COMMANDER CODY .... George Frayne
COSMO GREEK (SEX CHANGE BAND) .... Walter Andrews
COUNT FLOYD .... Joseph Flaherty
COUSIN JODY .... James Clell Summey
COWBOY (FURIOUS FIVE) .... Keith Wiggins
CRAZY OTTO .... Fritz Schulz-Reichel
CUDDLY DUDLEY .... Dudley Heslop
CURTISS A .... Curtiss Almsted
DADDY DEWDROP .... Richard Monda
DADDY G.†† .... Gene Barge
DANA .... Rosemary Brown
DAN-I .... Selmore Lewison
DISCO TEX (& SEX-O-LETTES) .... Joseph Moses Montarez Jnr.
DIVINE .... Glen Harris Milston
DOCTOR BUZZARD .... Cory Dale
DOCTOR JOHN .... Malcolm 'Mac' John Creaux Rebennack Jnr.
DOCTOR K ('s BLUES BAND) .... Richard Kay
DOZY, BEAKY, MICK & TICH .... Trevor Davies, John Dymond, Michael Wilson and Ian Amey
DUCHESS, THE .... Norma G. Woford
DUFFO .... Geoff Duff
DUKE OF PADUCAH .... Benjamin Francis 'Whitey' Ford
EAST BAY RAY (DEAD KENNEDYS) .... Ray Pepperell
ELVIRA .... Cassandra Peterson
ENGLAND DAN .... Daniel Seals
ESQUERITA .... Eskew Reeder
FANTASTIC JOHNNY C., THE .... John Corley

FARINELLI	Carlo Broschi
FARON (FARON'S FLAMINGOS)	Bill Ruffley
FATHER YOD	'Yod' Aquarian
FISH (MARILLION)	Derek William Dick
FRIDA (ABBA)	Anni-Frid Lyngstad-Fredriksson
FROSTY (LEE MICHAELS' BAND)	Bartholomew Eugene Smith-Frost
GARBO	Christopher Evans
GRANDMASTER FLASH	Joseph Saddler
HARPO	Jan Svensson
HENRY VIII (FAMOUS JUG BAND)	Michael Bartlett
HERMAN (HERMAN'S HERMITS)	Peter Blair Dennis Bernard Noone
HONEY DUKE (& HIS UKE)	Johnny Marvin
ISHMAEL	Peter Smale
JADE	Arlene Williams
JAKKO	'Jakko' M. Jakszyk
JERRYO	Jerry Murray
JILL (FOUR JACKS & A...)	Glenys Lynn
JILTED JOHN	Graham Fellows
JON BON JOVI	John Bongiovi
JUNIOR (TOMORROW)	John Wood
KAI-RAY	Richard A. Caire
KAMAHL†††	Kamalesvaran, son of Kandiah
KASANDRA	John W. Anderson
KEITH	James Barry Keefer
KENTUCKY	Rodd Willings

HERMAN — Peter Blair Dennis Bernard Noone, with SHELLEY FABARES — Michelle Fabares

PLASTIC BERTRAND — Roger Jovet

LEADBELLY — Huddie William Ledbetter (right) with Woody (Woodrow Wilson) Guthrie

92

KID CREOLE	*August Darnell
KING BUSCUIT BOY	Richard Newell
KING CURTIS	Curtis Ousley
KING ERRISON	Errison Pallman Johnson
KING PLEASURE	Clarence Beeks
KING RADIO	Norman Span
KING ZANY	Jack Dill
KOKOMO	Jerry Wisner
LEADBELLY	Huddie William Ledbetter
LEAPY LEE	Lee Morgan or Lenny Graham
LEFTY LOU	Louise Crissman
LEGENDARY STARDUST COWBOY, THE	Norman Carl Odam
LEMMY (MOTORHEAD)	Ian Fraser Kilminster
LIL' QUEENIE	Leigh Harris
LIMAHL (KAJAGOOGOO)	Christopher Hamill
LITTLE BEAVER	William Hale
LITTLE EVA	Eva Narcissus Boyd
LITTLE JO ANN	Jo Ann Morse
LITTLE MILLIE	Millicent Small
LITTLE MILTON #1	Milton Campbell
LITTLE MILTON #2	Milton Anderson
LITTLE NELL	Nell Campbell
LITTLE RICHARD	Richard Wayne Penniman
LITTLE SISTER	Vanetta Stewart
LITTLE TONY	Antonio Ciacci
LOBO	Kent Lavoie
LONESOME JOHN (HOT DADA BAND)	John Lewis Ammirati
LULU	Marie McDonald McLaughlin Lawrie
MAGIC DICK (J. GEILS BAND)	Richard Salwitz
MAHA DEV (QUINTESSENCE)	Dave Codling
MAMA CASS	*Cass Elliot
MAMA LEE (GATEWAY SINGERS)	Elmerlee Thomas
MAMA LION	Lynn Carey
MARILYN	Peter Robinson
MASSIE	Maria de Los Angeles Santamaria
MASTER GEE (SUGAR HILL GANG)	Guy O'Brien
MAYUTO	Mailto Correa
MEATLOAF	Marvin Lee Aday
MELLE MEL	Melvin Glover
MERRICK (ADAM & THE ANTS)	Christopher Hughes
MIGHTY FLEA	Gene Connors

NAPOLEON XIV — Jerry Samuels

DO NOT DISTURB

TWINKLE — Lynn Ripley

LIMAHL — Christopher Hamill

TAJ MAHAL — Henry Sainte Claire Fredericks-
Williams

MISS X.	Joyce Blair
MOMOYO (LIZARD)	Yosuke Sugawara
MOULTY (BARBARIANS)	Victor Maltoa
MR. BLOE	Harry Pitch or Zack Laurence
MR. BONGO	Jack J. Costanzo
MR. NESS (FURIOUS FIVE)	Eddie Morris
NAPOLEON XIV	Jerry Samuels
NASH THE SLASH	Ben Mink
NDUGU	Leon Chancler
NEIL (WEEDON WATKINS PIE)	Nigel Planer
NENA	Gabrielle Susanna Kerner
NERVOUS NORVUS	Jimmy Drake
NICO (VELVET UNDERGROUND)	Christa Paffgen
OAKIE PAUL	Paul Westmoreland
OBSIDIKTION BLACKBYRD (HEADHUNTERS)	Dwayne McKnight
OLD PHILOSOPHER, THE	Eddie (Eisler) Lawrence
ORION	Jimmy Ellis
OSCAR	Paul Dean
PANTERA (THOR)	Rusty Hamilton
PAPA BUE (& VIKING JAZZ BAND)	Arne Bue Jensen
PHANTOM OF ROCK, THE	Wayne Stierle
PHAST EDDIE	Edward Arnold Fischer
PIGPEN (GRATEFUL DEAD)	Ronald McKernan
PIUTE PETE (Square Dance Caller)	Morris Kaufman
PLASTIC BERTRAND	Roger Jovet
PREACHER JACK	Jack Lincoln Coughlin
PROFESSOR LONGHAIR	Henry Roeland Byrd
RABBIT (FACES)	John Bundrick
RAHIEM (FURIOUS FIVE)	Guy Williams
RAJA RAM (QUINTESSENCE)	Ron Rothfield
RANKING ROGER (GENERAL PUBLIC)	Roger Charlery
RATTLESNAKE RATTLES (SEX CHANGE BAND)	Bob Greenlee
RAZZLE (HANOI ROCKS)	Nicholas Dingley
RED RIVER DAVE	David Largus McEnery
RICCI	Richard Rubin
RIKKI	Regina Blunk
ROCKIN' DOPSIE (& CAJUN TWISTERS)	Dopsie Rubin
ROCKIN' JIMMY (& THE BROTHERS OF NIGHT)	Jim Byfield
ROCKWELL‡	Kennedy Gordy
ROOT BOY SLIM (& SEX CHANGE BAND)	Foster MacKenzie III
ROSEBUD	Gloria Black
ROY C.	Roy Charles Hammond
SADE	Helen Folasade Adu
SAM THE SHAM	Domingo Samudio
SATORI	Dennis Warkentin
SENATOR BOBBY	Bill Minkin
SHAKEY VICK	Graham Vickery
SHEILA (B. DEVOTION)	Anny Chancel
SHEILA E.	Sheila Escovedo
SHIVA (QUINTESSENCE)	Phillip Jones
SINGING NUN, THE	Sister Luc-Gabrielle (Janine Deckers)
SIOUXSIE SIOUX (& THE BANSHEES)	Susan Dallion
SIRONE	Norris Jones
SISTER SMILE (aka SOEUR SOURIRE)	(see The Singing Nun)
SIVUCA	Seveino D'Olivera
SKETCH (LINX)	Peter Martin
SNAKEFINGER	Philip Lithman
SNEAKY PETE	Peter Kleinow
SNOUFER (MAGIC BAND)	Alex St. Claire
SOUTHSIDE JOHNNY	John Lyon
SPECIAL K (SEX CHANGE BAND)	Kathe Russell
STEVEN T. (VENUS & RAZORBLADES)	Steven Tetsch
STEWKEY (NAZZ)	Robert Antoni

STING (POLICE)	Gordon Matthew Sumner
STRINGBEAN	David Akeman
SUGGS (MADNESS)	Graham McPherson
SUN RA	Herman 'Sonny' Blount
SWAMP DOGG	Jerry Williams Jnr.
TAJ MAHAL	Henry Sainte Claire Fredericks-Williams
TEXAS JOHNNY	John Brown
THE EDGE (U2)	David Evans
THE THE	Matt Johnson
THOR	John Mikl
TINA B.	Tina Baker
TINY TIM	Herbert Buckingham Khaury
TONIO K.	Steve Krikorian
TOP TEN (DICTATORS)	Scott Kempner
TWIGGY‡‡	Lesley Hornby
TWINK (PRETTY THINGS)	John Alder
TWINKLE	Lynn Ripley
UKULELE IKE	Cliff Edwards
VANGELIS	Evangelos Papathanassiou
VIOLINSKY	Sol Ginsberg
WINGED EEL FINGERLING (MAGIC BAND)	Eliot Ingber
WOLF	Bill Wolfer
WONDER MIKE (SUGAR HILL GANG)	Michael Wright
WRECKLESS ERIC	Eric Goulden
YOUNG JESSIE (COASTERS)‡‡‡	Obediah Jessie
ZOOT HORN ROLLO (MAGIC BAND)	Bill Harkleroad

*Refer to index for (exact) real names.
†A schoolgirl 'discovery' of Who leader Pete Townshend, who made one stiff single for Stiff.
††Daddy G was the sax player for Frank Guida's Legrand label who was immortalised in Gary U.S. Bonds' *Quarter To Three* and the Church Street Five single *Nite With Daddy G.*
†††This real name appears on the recording contract of the Australian-based Sri Lankan warbler.
‡Rockwell is the son of Motown Records founder Berry Gordy.
‡‡Swinging London's fashion trendsetter of the sixties also made a number of singles.
‡‡‡All sources would lead one to believe that Jessie is in fact his surname, though it seems doubtful.

Christa Paffgen

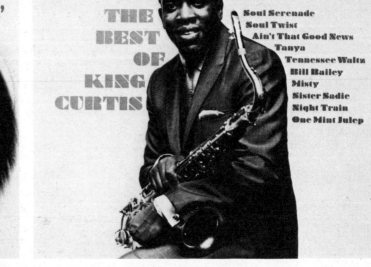

Curtis Ousley

96

Jiles Perry (J.P.) Richardson

Domingo Samudio

ILU — Marie McDonald McLaughlin Lawrie

HARPO — Jan Svensson

LITTLE ANTHONY & THE IMPERIALS — Anthony Gourdin

GROUP LEADERS

ANGIE & THE CHICLETTES .... Jean Thomas
ANITA & THE SO & SO's .... Anita Kerr*
ANNA & THE A-TRAIN .... Anna Rizzo
ANTHONY & THE SOPHOMORES .... Tony Maresco
BABY HUEY & THE BABYSITTERS .... James Raney
BANANA & THE BUNCH .... Lowell Vincent Levinger
BARBARA & THE UNIQUES .... Barbara Livsey
BARRY & THE TAMERLANES .... Barry DeVorzon
B. BUMBLE & THE STINGERS .... Billy Bumble*
BELLE & THE DEVOTIONS .... Kit 'Belle' Rolfe
BILLY & THE BEATERS .... Billy Vera*
BONNIE & THE CLYDES .... Bonnie Lee Sanders*
BILLY JOE & THE CHECKMATES .... Billy Joe Hunter
BILLY LEE & THE RIVIERAS .... Mitch Ryder*
BONNIWELL'S MUSIC MACHINE .... Thomas Sean Bonniwell
BOOGALOO & HIS GALLANT CREW .... Kent Harris
BOOKER T. & THE M.G's .... Booker T. Jones
BOOTSY'S RUBBER BAND .... William 'Bootsy' Collins
BRENDA & THE TABULATIONS .... Brenda Payton
CANNIBAL & THE HEADHUNTERS .... Frankie Garcia
CARL & THE CHEETAHS .... Carl Wayne
CARL & THE PASSIONS† .... Carl Wilson
CASS & THE CASSANOVAS .... Brian Casser
CHARLIE & THE WIDE BOYS .... Charles Ainley
CHICO & THE CHILE SISTERS .... Peter Thomson
C.L. & THE PICTURES .... Curtis Lee
COOKIE & HIS CUPCAKES .... Cookie Clinton
COUNTRY JOE & THE FISH .... Joseph McDonald
CRAZY CAVAN & THE RHYTHM ROCKERS .... Cavan Grogan
CUBY & THE BLIZZARDS .... Harry Muskee
DANNY & THE JUNIORS .... Danny Rapp
DANTE & THE INFERNOS .... Troy Dante
DAVE & THE CUSTOMS .... David Zdunich
DAVE & THE DERROS .... David Jones
DAVE & SUGAR .... Dave Rowland
DENNY & THE DIPLOMATS .... Denny Laine*
DEREK & THE DOMINOS .... Eric Clapton*
DERRY & THE SENIORS .... Derry Wilkie
DIAN & THE GREENBRIAR BOYS .... James Dian
DICKIE & THE GEES .... Dick Lory*
DION & THE BELMONTS/TIMBERLANES .... Dion DiMucci
DON & THE GOODTIMES .... Don Gallucci
DONNIE & THE DEL CHORDS .... Donald Huffman
DOUG & THE SLUGS .... Douglas Bennett
DR. WEST'S MEDICINE SHOW & JUNK BAND .... Norman Greenbaum
EDDIE & THE HOT RODS .... Barrie Masters
EDDIE & THE SHOWMEN .... Eddie Bertrand
FARON'S FLAMINGOS .... Bill 'Faron' Ruffley
FAT LARRY'S BAND (aka F.L.B.) .... Larry James
FELIX & THE ESCORTS†† .... Felix Cavaliere
FRANKIE & THE KNOCKOUTS .... Frankie Previte
FREDDIE & THE DREAMERS .... Frederick Garrity
GARY & THE NITE LIGHTS††† .... Gary Loizzo
GEFILTE JOE & THE FISH .... Chayam Lipschitz
GERRY & THE PACEMAKERS .... Gerald Marsden
GUS & THE NOMADS/HOUSE .... Angus McNeill
HAMILTON & THE MOVEMENT .... Gary Hamilton

```
HARVEY & THE MOONGLOWS ........................................................................... Harvey Fuqua
HOLLY & THE ITALIANS ....................................................................... Holly Beth Vincent
IAN & THE ZODIACS ........................................................................................ Ian Edwards
JACKIE & THE STARLIGHTS ......................................................................... Jackie Rue
JAKE & THE FAMILY JEWELS ..................................................................... Allan Jacobs
JAMES & THE GOOD BROTHERS ........................................................ James Ackroyd
JAY & THE AMERICANS ..................................... Jay Traynor* (1962), Jay Black* (1963-70)
JAY & THE TECHNIQUES ................................................................................ Jay Proctor
JENNIE & THE JOY STIX ................................................................... Jennie Beaumont
JEREMY & THE SATYRS ...................................................................... Jeremy Steig
JIMMY & THE BOYS ................................................................................ Ignatius Jones*
JIVIN' GENE & THE JOKERS ............................................................. Gene Bourgeious
JOHNNY & THE DISTRACTIONS ................................................... Johnny Koonce
JOHNNY & THE DRIVERS .................................................................. John Thomas
JOHNNY & THE EXPRESSIONS ................................................... Johnny Mathews
JOHNNY & THE G-RAYS ..................................................................... Johnny McLeod
JOHNNY & THE HURRICANES ......................................................... Johnny Paris
JOHNNY & THE JAMMERS .................................................................. Johnny Winter
JOHNNY & THE MOONDOGS ............................................................ John Lennon
JOHN'S CHILDREN ............................................................................... John Hewlett
JON & THE NIGHTRIDERS ...................................................................... Jon Blair
JOSIE & THE PUSSYCATS ............................................................... Cheryl Ladd *
JULES & THE POLAR BEARS ................................................................ Jules Shear
KATRINA & THE WAVES .............................................................. Katrina Leskanich
K.C. & THE SUNSHINE BAND ..................................................... Harry Wayne Casey
KENNY & THE KASUALS .................................................................... Ken Daniel
KID CREOLE & THE COCONUTS ................................................. August Darnell*
KILBURN & THE HIGH ROADS ............................................................... Ian Dury
KOOL & THE GANG .................................................................. Robert 'Kool' Bell
LARRY'S REBELS ............................................................................... Larry Morris
LAURIE & THE SIGHS .................................................................. Laurie Beecham
```

JAY & THE AMERICANS — Jay (David) Black

JOHNNY & THE HURRICANES — Johnny Paris

CANNIBAL & THE HEADHUNTERS — Frankie Garcia

RANDY & THE RAINBOWS — Dominick 'Randy' Safuto

RUBY & THE ROMANTICS — Ruby Nash

MICHAEL & THE MESSENGERS	Michael Morgan
MIKE & THE SENSATIONS	Michael James 'Bo' Kirkland
MIKE & THE UTOPIANS	Mike Lasman
MOUSE & THE TRAPS	Ronnie Weiss
MR. GASSER & THE WEIRDOS	Ed 'Big Daddy' Roth
MR. LEE & THE CADDIES	Myron Lee*
NERO & GLADIATORS	Michael O'Neil
NIKKI & THE CORVETTES	Dominique Lorenz
NINO & THE EBB TIDES	Antonio Aiello
OLA & THE JANGLERS	Ola Hakansson
OLLIE & THE NIGHTINGALES	Ollie Hoskins
PASHA & THE PROPHETS	Lou Reed*
PATTI & THE LOVELITES	Patti Hamilton
PEE WEE & THE SPECIALS	Rini Oudhuis
PETER B's LOONERS	Pete Bardens
PINKERTON'S ASSORTED COLOURS	Samuel 'Pinkerton' Kemp
QUESTION MARK & THE MYSTERIANS	Rudy Martinez
RAJAH & THE RAH PEOPLE	Roger A. Harworth
RANDY & THE RAINBOWS	Dominick 'Randy' Safuto
REPARATA & THE DELRONS	Mary 'Reparata' Aiese
RICHARD & THE YOUNG LIONS	Richard Bloodworth
RICK & THE RAIDERS	Rick Zehringer (Derringer)
RIKKI & THE LAST DAYS OF EARTH	Rikki Sylvan
ROCHELL & THE CANDLES	Rochell Henderson
ROCKIN' RONALD & THE REBELS	Ronnie Hawkins
RODNEY & THE BRUNETTES	Rodney Bingenheimer
ROGER & THE A TONES	Roger Bailon
ROGER & THE TRAVELERS	Roger Koob
RONNIE & THE DIRT RIDERS	Ron Dante
RONNIE & THE HI-LITES	Ronnie Goodson
RONNIE & THE RELATIVES	Ronnie Bennett/Spector
RONNY & THE DAYTONAS	John Buck Wilkin
ROSIE & THE ORIGINALS	Rosie Hamlin
RUBEN & THE JETS††††	Frank Zappa
RUBY & THE ROMANTICS†††††	Ruby Nash
SANDII & THE SUNSETZ	Sandii Kubota
SHEP & THE LIMELITES	James Sheppard
SHIRLEY & COMPANY	Shirley Goodman
SIOUXSIE & THE BANSHEES	Siouxsie Sioux*
SIR DOUGLAS QUINTET, THE	Doug Sahm
SOUTHSIDE JOHNNY & THE ASHBURY DUKES	John Lyon
SPANKY & OUR GANG	Elaine 'Spanky' McFarlane
STEVE & THE BOARD	Steve Kipner
SUNNY & THE SUNGLOWS/SUNLINERS	Sunny Ozuna
SUZY & THE RED STRIPES	Linda McCartney*
SYLVIA & THE SAPPHIRES	Sylvia Mason
TERRY & THE PIRATES	Terry Dolan
TEX & THE SADDLETRAMPS	Thomas Jay 'Tex' Edwards
TICO & THE TRIUMPHS	Paul Simon
TONY & THE TIGERS	Tony Sales*
TOOTS & THE MAYTALS	Fred Hibbert
VITO & THE SALUTATIONS	Vito Balsamo
WILLIE & THE WHEELS	P. F. Sloan*
WINSTON'S FUMBS	Jimmy Winston

* Refer to index for real name.
† Later The Beach Boys
†† Later The Young Rascals
††† Later The American Breed
†††† An alter-ego of The Mothers of Invention
††††† Ruby's name is variously given as Nash and Walsh

FREDDIE & THE DREAMERS — Frederick Garrity

FRANKIE & THE KNOCKOUTS   Frankie Previte

GERRY & THE PACEMAKERS — Gerald Marsden

STEREO
ELECTRONICALLY REPROCESSED

RCA CAMDEN

LOVE IS STRANGE

MICKEY & SYLVIA

NO GOOD LOVER
WALKIN' IN THE RAIN
TWO SHADOWS ON YOUR WINDOW
LOVE IS STRANGE
I'M GOING HOME
IN MY HEART
LOVE IS A TREASURE
LOVE WILL MAKE YOU FAIL IN SCHOOL
DEAREST
MOMMY OUT THE LIGHT

Mickey Baker* and Sylvia Vanderpool

Robert Garrett* and Earl N

BOB & EARL

CRAFTONE RECORDS CRS 3055

PETER & GORDON — Peter Asher and Gordon Waller

DUO IDENTITIES

ALLEN BROTHERS, THE .... Peter* and Chris* Allen
ALLISONS, THE .... Bob* and John* Allison
ALTHIA & DONNA .... Althia Forest and Donna Reid
ASHMAN & REYNOLDS .... Aliki Ashman and Harry Reynolds
BARNES & BARNES .... Art (Billy Mumy) and Artie (Robert Haimer) Barnes
BATDORF & RODNEY .... John Batdorf and Mark Rodney
BEAVER & KRAUSE .... Paul Beaver and Bernard Krause
BELL & JAMES .... Leroy Bell and Casey James
BILL & BOYD .... Bill Cate and Boyd Robertson
BILLY & LILLIE .... Billy Ford and Lillie Bryant
BILLY & SUE .... 'Oliver'* and Lesley Gore
BJORN & BENNY .... Bjorn Ulvaeus and Benny Andersson
BLUES BROTHERS, THE .... Jake (John Belushi) and Elwood (Dan Ackroyd) Blues
BO & PEEP .... Mick Jagger and Andrew Loog Oldham
BOB & EARL .... Robert Garrett* and Earl Nelson
BOB & JERRY .... Bob Feldman and Jerry Goldstein
BOB & MARCIA .... Bob Andy* and Marcia Griffiths
BOB & SHERI .... Bob Norberg/Norman and Cheryl Pomeroy
BOBBY & LAURIE† .... Bobby Bright and Laurie Allen
BOBBY & SYLVIA .... Bobby Hebb and Sylvia Shemwell
BOYCE & HART .... Tommy Boyce* and Bobby Hart*
BREWER & SHIPLEY .... Michael Brewer and Thomas Shipley
BRIAN & MICHAEL .... Kevin Parrott and Michael Coleman
BRUCE & TERRY .... Bruce Johnston and Terry Melcher
BUCHANAN & ANCELL .... Bill Buchanan and Bob Ancell
BUCHANAN & GOODMAN .... Bill Buchanan and Dickie Goodman
BUCKINGHAM & NICKS .... Lindsay Buckingham and Stevie Nicks
BUCKNER & GARCIA .... Jerry Buckner and Gary Garcia
BUD & TRAVIS .... Bud Dashiel and Travis Edmonson
CALVIN & CLARENCE (aka C&C BOYS) .... Calvin Scott and Clarence Carter
CARNABY & SHAKESPEARE .... Michael Burke and John Spirit
CAROLE & SHERRY .... Carole Bayer and Sherry Harway
CASHMAN & WEST .... Terry Cashman* and Tommy West*
CHAD & JEREMY .... Chad Stewart and Jeremy Clyde
CHAPMAN & WHITNEY .... Roger Chapman and Charlie Whitney
CHAS & DAVE .... Charles Hodges and David Peacock
CINDY & LINDY .... Cindy Lord and Linda Doherty
CHRIS & KATHY .... Chris Montez* and Kathy Young
CLARENCE & CALVIN .... Clarence Carter and Calvin Scott
CLARK-HUTCHINSON .... Andy Clark and Michael Hutchinson
COCKRELL & SANTOS .... Bud Cockrell and Pattie Santos
CRIB & BEN .... Eddie Simon and Paul Gelbar
CURLY FOX & TEXAS RUBY .... Arnim Leroy Fox and Ruby Owens
CYMBAL & CLINGER .... Johnny Cymbal and Peggy Clinger
DALE & GRACE .... Dale Houston and Grace Broussard
DAVID & JONATHAN .... Roger Cook and Roger Greenaway
DAVIS SISTERS, THE .... Betty Jack and Skeeter Davis *
DEAN & JEAN .... Welton Young and Brenda Lee Jones
DELANEY VENN .... Michael Delaney and Chris Venn
DELBERT & GLEN .... Delbert McClinton and Glen Clark
DEY & KNIGHT .... Tracey Dey and Gary Knight
DICK & DEE DEE .... Richard St. John* and Dee Sperling
DIFFORD & TILBROOK .... Chris Difford and Glen Tilbrook
DILLARD & CLARK .... Doug Dillard and Gene Clark*
DINO & SEMBELLO .... Ralph Dino* and John Sembello
DON & DEWEY .... Don 'Sugarcane' Harris and Dewey Terry
DON & JERRY .... Donald Griffin and Jerry Strickland
DON & JUAN .... Roland Trone and Claude 'Sonny' Johnson
DUNN & McCASHEN .... Donald Dunn and Troy McCashen
FAME & PRICE .... Georgie Fame* and Alan Price
FERRANTE & TEICHER .... Arthur Ferrante and Louis Teicher
FINNIGAN & WOOD .... Mike Finnigan and Jerry Wood
FLASH & THE PAN .... Harry Vanda* and George Young
FLATT & SCRUGGS .... Lester Raymond Flatt and Earl Eugene Scruggs
FLETCHER – GURL .... Gary Fletcher and Steve Gurl
FLO & EDDIE .... Mark Volman and Howard Kaylan
FLOTSAM & JETSAM .... B. C. Hilliam and Malcolm McEachern

```
FOSTER & ALLEN ..................................................................... Michael Foster and Tony Allen
GALLAGHER & LYLE ......................................................... Benny Gallagher and Graham Lyle
GARY & DAVE ...................................................................... Gary Beckett and David Weeks
GENE & DEBBIE ............................................................... Gene Thomas and Debbie Nevills
GENE & EUNICE ..................................................................... Gene Forrest and Eunice Levy
GEORGE & EARL ......................................................... George McCormick and Earl Aycock
GODLEY & CREME ............................................................... Kevin Godley and Lol Creme
GOOD & PLENTY .......................................................... Douglas Good and Ginny Plenty
HALL & OATES ..................................................................... Daryl Hall and John Oates
HANK & DEAN ......................................................................... Hank Jones and Dean Kay
HOMER & JETHRO ........................................... Henry D. Haynes and Kenneth C. Burns
HOMI & JARVIS ........................................................... Amanda Homi and Brian Jarvis
HUDSON & FORD (aka THE MONKS) ........................... Richard Hudson and John Ford
HUGHES & THRALL ........................................................ Glenn Hughes and Pat Thrall
HUGO & LUIGI ................................................................ Hugo Peretti and Luigi Creatore
JAN & ARNIE ........................................................................ Jan Berry* and Arnie Ginsberg
JAN & DEAN ........................................................................... Jan Berry* and Dean Torrance
JEWEL & EDDIE ........................................................... Jewel Akens and Eddie Cochran
JIMMY & JOHNNY .............................. Jimmy Lee Fautheree and Country Johnny Mathis
JOE & EDDIE ............................................................. Joseph Gilbert and Edward Brown
JOEY & DANNY ............................................................ Joe Reynolds and Daniel Neavertix
JOHN & ERNEST ................................................................... John Free and Ernest Smith
JOHNNY & JACKEY ................................................. Johnny Bristol and Jackey Beavers
JON & ROBIN (& THE IN CROWD) ................................... Jon Abnor and Robin Wright
KARL & HARTY ...................................... Karl Victor Davis and Hartford Connecticut Taylor
LAMBERT & NUTTYCOMBE ................................... Dennis Lambert and Craig Nuttycombe
LAVERN & SHIRLEY ................................................ Penny Marshall and Cindy Williams
LeBLANC & CARR .............................................................. Lenny LeBlanc and Peter Carr
LEE & PAUL ............................................................... Lee Pockriss and Paul Vance
LINK-EDDY COMBO ............................................................ Lincoln Mayorga and Ed Cobb
LOGGINS & MESSINA ............................................. Kenny Loggins and Jim Messina
MARIE & REX ...................................................................... Marie Knight and Rex Garvin
MAL & VAL .............................................................. Malcolm Funchon and Valentine Hart
MARK-ALMOND ............................................................... .. Jon Mark and Johnny Almond
MARSHALL HAIN .................................................................. Julian Marshall and Kit Hain
MARVIN & JOHNNY .......................................................... Marvin Phillips and Joseph Josea
MAURICE & MAC .......................................... Maurice McAlister and McLaurin Green
McGUINNESS-FLINT ......................................................... Tom McGuinness and Hugie Flint
McKENZIE BROTHERS, THE ....................................................... Bob* and Doug* McKenzie
MEL & TIM ................................................................ Melvin Harden and Tim McPherson
MICKEY & SYLVIA ........................................... Mickey Baker* and Sylvia Vanderpool
MILLICAN & NESBITT .......................................................... Alan Millican and Tom Nesbitt
MONTGOMERY & STONE ......................................... David Montgomery and Fred Stone
MORISSEY-MULLEN ........................................................ Dick Morrissey and Jim Mullen
MOUTH & MacNEAL ........................................... William Duyn and Maggie MacNeal*
```

Richard St. John* and Dee Sperling   Ray Hildebrand and Jill Jackson

DALE & GRACE — Dale Houston and Grace Broussard   PEACHES & HERB #3 — Linda Greene and Herb Fame*

MUSTARD & GRAVY	Frank Rue and Ernest Stokes
MYLES & LENNY	Myles Cohen and Lenny Solomon
NEIL & JACK	Neil Diamond* and Jack Parker
NIELSEN-PEARSON	Reid Neilsen and Mark Pearson
PACHECO & ALEXANDER	Tom Pacheco and Sharon Alexander
PAT & OLIVIA	Pat Carroll and Olivia Newton John
PAUL & PAULA††	Ray Hildebrand and Jill Jackson
PEACHES & HERB #1	Marlene Mack and Herb Fame*
PEACHES & HERB #2	Francine Barker nee Hurd and Herb Fame*
PEACHES & HERB #3	Linda Greene and Herb Fame*
PETER & GORDON	Peter Asher and Gordon Waller
PETERS & LEE	Lennie Peters and Diane Lee
PINKARD & BOWDEN	Sandy Pinkard and Richard Bowden
PRATT & McCLAIN	Truett Pratt and Jerry McClain
RENE & RENE	Rene Ornelas and Rene Herrera
RENEE & RENATO	Hilary Lester and Renato Paglaire
RIGHTEOUS BROTHERS, THE	Bill Medley and Bobby Hatfield
ROBERT & JOHNNY	Robert Carr and John Mitchell
SAM & DAVE	Samuel Moore and David Prater
SAUTER-FINEGAN	Eddie Sauter and Bill Finegan
SEALS & CROFTS	Jim Seals and Dash Crofts
SHIRLEY & LEE	Shirley Pixley and Leonard Lee
SIEGAL & SCHWALL	Corky Siegal and Jim Schwall
SKIP & FLIP (aka THE PLEDGES)	Clyde 'Skip' Battin and Gary Paxton
SKIPWORTH & TURNER	Rodney Skipworth and Phil Turner
SLIM & SLAM	Bulee 'Slim' Gaillard and Leroy 'Slam' Stewart
SMITH & D'ABO	Mike Smith and Mick D'Abo
ST. GEORGE & TANA	John Campolongo and Christina Law
STEVE & STEVIE	Steve Groves and Steve Kipner
STONEY & MEATLOAF	Shaun Murphy and Marvin Lee Aday
SUGAR 'N' DANDY	Sugar Simone* and Dandy Livingston
TARNEY SPENCER	Alan Tarney and Trevor Spencer
TEEGARDEN & VANWINKLE	David Teegarden and Skip Knape
TENNENT MORRISON (aka JOE SOAP)	John Tennent and David Morrison
TOM & JERRY	Arthur Garfunkel and Paul Simon
TONY & JOE	Anthony Savonne and Joseph Sarageno
TRAVIS & BOB	Travis Pritchett and Robert Weaver
TUFANO & GIAMARESE	Dennis Tufano and Carl Giammarese
TZUKE & PAXO	Judie Tzuke and Mike Paxman
VENUTI-LANG	Joe Venuti and Eddie Lang
VIGRASS & OSBORNE	Paul Vigrass and Gary Osborne
WILMA LEE & STONEY COOPER	Wilma Lee Leary and Dale T. Cooper
YARBROUGH & PEOPLES	Cavin Yarbrough and Alisa Peoples
YIN & YAN	Chris Sanford and Bill Mitchell
ZAGER & EVANS	Denny Zager and Rick Evans

† This Australian beat duo wrote songs under the collective name of Alan Brite.
†† Originally called Jill & Ray, the billing used on the LeCam release of *Hey Paula*.   *Refer to index for real name.

107

DINO DESI & BILLY — Dean Martin Jnr., Desi Arnez Jnr.* and Billy Hinsche

EMERSON LAKE & PALMER — Keith Emerson, Greg Lake and Carl Palmer

TRIO IDENTITIES

ADAM, MIKE & TIM .... Peter Sedgwick, Mike Sedgwick and Tim Sainders
ASHTON, GARDNER & DYKE .... Tony Ashton, Kim Gardner and Roy Dyke
BECK, BOGERT & APPLICE .... Jeff Beck, Tim Bogert and Carmine Appice
BRUNNING HALL SUNFLOWER BLUES BAND .... Bob Brunning, Mick Halls and Big Sunflower (Bob Hall)
CASHMAN, PISTILLI & WEST .... Terry Cashman*, Gene Pistilli and Tommy West*
COTTON, LLOYD & CHRISTIAN .... Darryl Cotton, Michael Lloyd and Chris Christian
CROSBY, STILLS & NASH .... David Crosby*, Stephen Stills and Graham Nash
DFK BAND .... Les Dudek, Mike Finnigan and Jim Krueger
DINO, DESI & BILLY .... Dean Martin Jnr., Desi Arnaz Jnr.* and Billy Hinsche
DON, DICK 'N' JIMMY .... Don Ralke, Dick Crowe and Jimmy Styne
EMERSON, LAKE & PALMER .... Keith Emerson, Greg Lake and Carl Palmer
ETHRIDGE, BARBATA & HILL .... Chris Ethridge, Johnny Barbata and Joel Scott Hill
FISHBAUGH, FISHBAUGH & ZORN .... Gary & Paula Fishbaugh and Peter Zorn
GILES, GILES & FRIPP .... Michael Giles, Peter Giles and Robert Fripp
GORGONI, MARTIN & TAYLOR .... Al Gorgoni, Trade Martin* and Chip Taylor*
HAMILTON, JOE FRANK & REYNOLDS .... Dan Hamilton, Joe Frank Carollo and Tom Reynolds
HANFORD, BLOOM & MAZZACANE .... Tony Hanford, Kath Bloom and Loren Mazzacane
HODGES, JAMES & SMITH .... Pat Hodges, Denita James and Jessica Smith
KGB BAND .... Ray Kennedy, Ric Grech and Mike Bloomfield
KOERNER, RAY & GLOVER .... 'Spider' John Koerner, Dave Ray and Tony Glover
LAMBERT, HENDRICKS & ROSS .... Dave Lambert, Jon Hendricks and Annie Ross*
MARVIN, WELCH & FARRAR .... Hank Marvin*, Bruce Welch and John Farrar
McGUINN, CLARK & HILLMAN .... Roger McGuinn*, Gene Clark* and Chris Hillman
PETER, PAUL & MARY .... Peter Yarrow, Noel Paul Stookey and Mary Travers
PADDY, KLAUS & GIBSON .... Paddy Chambers, Klaus Voorman and Gibson Kemp
RAY, GOODMAN & BROWN .... Harry Ray, Al Goodman and William Brown
ROBEY, FALK & BOD .... Bill Robey, Don Falk and Bod Noubarian
S.F.F. .... Edward Schicke, Gerhard Fuhrs and Heinz Frohling
SOUTHER, HILLMAN, FURAY BAND .... John David Souther, Chris Hillman and Richie Furay
STOCKLEY, SEE & MASON .... Chris Stockley, Sam See and Ian Mason
TALTON, STEWART & SANDLIN .... Tommy Talton, Bill Stewart and John Sandlin
WEST, BRUCE & LAING .... Leslie West*, Jack Bruce* and Corky Laing

PETER PAUL & MARY — Peter Yarrow, Noel Paul Stookey and Mary Travers

QUARTETS

HSAS .... Sammy Hagar, Neal Schon, Kenny Aaronson and Michael Shrieve.
KOSSOFF, KIRKE, TETSU & RABBIT .... Paul Kossoff, Simon Kirke, Tetsu Yamauchi and John 'Rabbit' Bundrick
MASON, WOOD, CAPALDI & FROG .... Dave Mason, Chris Wood, Jim Capaldi and Wynder K. Frog*

* Refer to index for real name.

FAMILY GROUPS
Duos

AUBRY TWINS, THE	Jerome and Tyrone Aubry
ALESSI	William and Robert Alessi
ALLEN BROTHERS	Austin Ambrose and Lee William Allen
ALLMAN & WOMAN	Gregg and Cher Allman
ALLMAN BROTHERS, THE	Duane and Gregg Allman
AMERICAN SPRING	Diane Rovell and Marilyn Wilson nee Rovell
ASHFORD & SIMPSON (aka VALERIE & NICK)	Nicholas Ashford and Valerie Simpson (h/w)
AVANTIS, THE	Pat and Lolly Vegas
AVONS, THE	Ellen and Ray Avon
BARRY SISTERS, THE	Dorothy and Lorna Barry
BARBARA & GWEN	Barbara and Gwen Livsey
BECKMEIER BROTHERS, THE	Fred and Steve Beckmeier
BELLAMY BROTHERS, THE	David and Howard Bellamy
BILL & TAFFY (aka FAT CITY)	Bill Danoff and Mary Catherine 'Taffy' Nivert (h/w)
BLUE DIAMONDS, THE	Rudi and Riem de Wolff
BLUE SKY BOYS	Bill and Earl Bolick
BRECKER BROTHERS, THE	Michael and Randy Brecker
BROOKS BROTHERS, THE	Ricky and Geoff Brooks
BROTHERS JOHNSON, THE	George and Louis Johnson
BROUGHTONS, THE	Edgar and Steve Broughton
BUTTERBEANS & SUSIE	Jody Edwards and Susie Hawthorn (h/w)
CALLAHAN BROTHERS, THE	Walter T. and Homer C. Callahan
CANADIAN SWEETHEARTS, THE	Fern and Bob Regan*
CAPTAIN & TENNILLE, THE	Daryl Dragon and Toni Tennille (h/w)
CARLISLES, THE	William and Clifford Carlisle
CARMEL SISTERS. THE (aka CAROL & CHERYL)	Carol and Cheryl Connors
CARPENTERS, THE	Richard and Karen Carpenter
CATE BROTHERS, THE	Earl and Ernie Cate
CHANTER SISTERS, THE	Doreen and Irene Chanter
CHAPIN BROTHERS, THE	Harry and Tom Chapin
CHEETAH	Chrissie and Lindsey Hammond
COCHRAN BROTHERS, THE	Eddie and Hank Cochran
COLLINS KIDS, THE	Lawrence Albert (Larry) and Lawencine Mae (Lorrie) Collins
COOPER BROTHERS, THE	Richard and Brian Cooper
CRAWFORD BROTHERS, THE	Johnny and Bobby Crawford
DEAN & MARK†	Dean and Mark Mathis*
DE JOHN SISTERS, THE	Julia and Dux DeGiovanni
DELANEY & BONNIE (aka LANI & BONNIE)	Delaney Bramlett and Bonnie Bramlett nee Lynn
DeZURICH SISTERS, THE (aka CACKLE SISTERS)	Mary and Caroline DeZurich
DELMORE BROTHERS, THE	Alton and Rabon Delmore
DINO & DEBBIE	Dino and Debbie Kartsonakis
DIXON BROTHERS, THE	Dorsey and Howard Dixon
DOLLY SISTERS, THE	Jenny (Janszieka) and Rosie (Roszicka) Deutsch
DUNCAN SISTERS	Rosetta and Vivian Duncan
EDDIE & BETTY	Edward and Betty Cole
ELMO & PATSY	Elmo and Patsy Shropshire
EMMANUEL BROTHERS, THE	Tommy and Phil Emmanuel
EVERLY BROTHERS, THE	Don and Phil Everly
FARINAS, THE	Richard and Mimi Farina
FRIEND & LOVER	James and Cathy Post
GENO & GINA	Geno and Gina Giosasi
GIRLS OF THE GOLDEN WEST, THE	Dorothy Lavern (Dolly) and Mildred (Millie) Ferngood (Good)
HAGERS, THE	Jim and John Hager
HANSEN BROTHERS, THE	Paul and Dale Hansen
HARNER	Charles and James Harner
HAYES BROTHERS, THE	Mike and Peter Hayes
HEDGE & DONNA	Hedge Capers and Donna Marie Carson (h/w)
HENSKE & YESTER	Judy Henske and Jerry Yester (h/w)
IAN & SYLVIA	Ian Tyson and Sylvia Fricker (h/w)
JACKIE & ROY	Jackie Cain and Roy Kral (h/w)
JIM & INGRID	Jim and Ingrid Croce

JIM & JEAN	James and Jean Glover
JIM & JESSE	James and Jessie McReynolds
JO ANN & TROY	Jo Ann Campbell and Troy Seals (h/w)
JUDDS, THE	Wynonna and Naomi Judd
KALIN TWINS, THE	Hal and Herbert Kalin
KEANE BROTHERS, THE	John and Tom Keane
KEITH & DONNA	Keith and Donna Godchaux
KENDALLS, THE	Royce and Jeanie Kendall
LANNY & GINGER	Lanny Grey and Ginger (Joan Beatrice) Grey nee Stewart
LEGARDE TWINS, THE	Tom and Ted Legarde
LIME	Denis and Denyse LePage
LONZO & OSCAR	John and Rollin Sullivan
LOS INDIOS TABAJAROS	Natalicio and Antenor Moreyra-Lima
LOUVIN BROTHERS, THE	Charles and Ira Louvin
LOVE UNLIMITED	Glodean and Linda James
LULU BELLE & SCOTTY	Myrtle Eleanor Wiseman nee Cooper and Scott Wiseman (Skyland Scotty)
McGEE BROTHERS, THE	Sam and Kirk McGee
MIKI & GRIFF	Emyr and Barbara Griffith
MORGAN-JAMES DUO	Pete Morgan and Colin James
MURRIS BROTHERS, THE	Wiley and Zeke Morris
NICHOLAS BROTHERS, THE	Harold and Fayard Nicholas
NINA & FREDERICK	Baron & Baroness Frederik van Pallandt
OSBORNE BROTHERS, THE	Bob and Sonny Osborne
PALEY BROTHERS, THE	Andy and Jonathon Paley
PATIENCE & PRUDENCE	Patience and Prudence McIntyre
POWELL TWINS, THE	Penni and Patti Powell
RUFUS & CARLA	Rufus and Carla Thomas
RUSTY & DOUG	Rusty and Doug Kershaw
SALLYANGIE	Mike and Sally Oldfield
SANTO & JOHNNY	Santo and John Farina
SIMON SISTERS, THE	Lucy and Carly Simon
SINCLAIR BROTHERS, THE	Wayne and John Sinclair
SINGING BELLES, THE	Anne and Angeia Berry
SONNY & CHER (aka CAESAR & CLEO)	Salvatore Bono and Cherilyn Sarkasian La Pier (h/w)
SPARKS	Ron and Russell Mael
STANLEY BROTHERS, THE	Carter Glen and Ralph Edmond Stanley
STEVE & EYDIE	Steve Lawrence* and Eydie Gorme* (h/w)
STONE, R&J	Russell and Joanna Stone
SUNNY & SUE	'Sunny' and Susan Leslie
SUTHERLAND BROTHERS, THE	Iain and Gavin Sutherland
SUTTONS, THE	Michael and Brenda Sutton
TALBOT BROTHERS, THE	Terry and John Michael Talbot
TEEN QUEENS, THE	Betty and Rosie Collins
UNIPOP	Phyllis and Manny Loiacono
WILBURN BROTHERS, THE	Doyle and Teddy (Thurman Theodore) Wilburn
WOMACK BROTHERS, THE	Bobby and Curtis Womack
YORK BROTHERS, THE	Leslie and George York

Ian Tyson and Sylvia Fricker

Mike and Sally Oldfield

THE JUDDS — Wyonna and Naomi Judd

THE BROTHERS JOHNSON — George and Louis Johnson

THE KALIN TWINS — Hal and Herbert Kalin

THE EVERLY BROTHERS — Don and Phil Everly

Trios

ANDREWS SISTERS, THE	Patti, Lavern and Maxine Andrews
ARCHERS, THE	Tim, Steven and Janice Archer
ART IN AMERICA	Christopher, Daniel and Shishonee Flynn
AVION	John, Randall and Kendall Waller
BANTAMS, THE	Mike, Jeff and Fritz Kirchner
BEE GEES, THE	Barry, Robin and Maurice Gibb
BEERS FAMILY, THE	Robert Harlan, Evelyne and Martha Beers
BEVERLY SISTERS, THE	Joyce, Babette and 'Teddy' Beverly
BLACKWOOD BROTHERS, THE	James, Cecil and Jimmy Blackwell
BONNIE SISTERS, THE	Pat, Jean and Sylvia Bonnie
BOSWELL SISTERS, THE	Helvetia (Vet), Martha and Connie Foore'Boswell
BREAK MACHINE	Lyndsay and Lindell Blake with cousin Cortez Jordan
BROWNS, THE	Maxine, Bonnie and Jim Ed Brown
CARTER FAMILY, THE #1	A. P.,* Sara and Maybelle Carter
CLANCY BROTHERS, THE #1	Pat, Liam and Tom Clancy
COON CREEK GIRLS, THE	Lily Mae, Rosie and 'Black Eyed' Susan Ledford
CORNELIUS BROTHERS & SISTER ROSE	Edward, Carter and Rose Cornelius
DeCASTRO SISTERS, THE	Peggy, Babette and Cherie DeCastro
DINNING SISTERS, THE††	Louise, Ginger and Jean Dinning
DRAGONS, THE	Daryl, Dennis and Doug Dragon
EDWIN HAWKINS SINGERS, THE	Edwin, Walter and Tremaine Hawkins
EMOTIONS, THE	Sheila, Wanda and Jeanette Hutchinson
FONTANE SISTERS, THE	Bea, Geri and Marge Rosse
GAP BAND, THE	Ronnie, Charles and Robert Wilson
GARY & THE HORNETS	Gary, Greg and Steve Calvert
GIBSON BROTHERS, THE	Alex, Patrick and Christopher Gibson
GLASER BROTHERS, THE	Tompall, Chuck and Jim Glaser
HARDEN TRIO, THE	Arleen, Bobby and Robbie Harden
HONEYS, THE	Marilyn and Diane Rovell with cousin Ginger Blake
HUDSON BROTHERS, THE	Bill, Brett and Mark Hudson
JONES GIRLS, THE	Shirley, Brenda and Valorie Jones
KAYE SISTERS	Carol, Lindsey & Sheila Jones, and Shan Palmer
KITTY & THE HAYWOODS	Kitty, Mary Ann and Vivian Haywood
LAST, THE	David, Joe and Mike Nolte
LIMMIE & THE FAMILY COOKING	Limmie, Jimmy and Martha Snell
MANDRELL SISTERS, THE	Barbara, Louise and Irlene Mandrell
McGUIRE SISTERS, THE	Phyliss, Dorothy and Christine McGuire
MOIR SISTERS, THE	Jean, Margo and Lesley Moir
O'DONNELLS, THE†††	Michael, Triona and Padraig O'Domnhaill
ORMSBY BROTHERS, THE	Neville, Michael and Adrian Ormsby
PICKENS SISTERS, THE	Patti, Jane and Helen Pickens
PARIS SISTERS, THE	Priscilla, Sherrell and Albeth Paris
PERSONALITY TRIO, THE (later MERRY MACS)	Joe, Ted and Judd McMichael
PETERS SISTERS, THE	Mattye, Ann and Virginia Peters
REDDINGS, THE	Otis III and Dexter Redding with cousin Mark Locket
ROCHES, THE	Suzzy, Maggie and Terre Roche
RONETTES, THE	Veronica and Estelle Bennett with cousin Nedra Talley
ROONEY BROTHERS, THE	Micky Jnr., Teddy and Timothy Rooney
ROWANS, THE	Lorin, Christopher and Peter Rowan
SARSTEDT BROTHERS, THE	Richard, Peter and Robin (Clive) Sarstedt
SHAGGS, THE	Betty, Helen and Dorothy Wiggin
SHARRETTS, THE	Fred, Edward and Robert Sharrett
SOUL STIRRERS, THE	Dillard, Rufus and Arthur Crume
STOVALL SISTERS, THE	Lillian, Netta and Joyce Stovall
SUZI SOUL & PLEASURE SEEKERS	Suzi, Patti and Nancy Quatro
SYLVIA & THE SAPPHIRES	Sylvia, Ruby and Vicki Mason
THERON HALE & DAUGHTERS	Theron, Elizabeth and Mamie Ruth Hale
THRASHER, BROTHERS, THE	Jim, Joe and Buddy Thrasher
WEBB BROTHERS, THE	Fabian, Marius and Berard Webb
WHITES, THE	Buck, Sharon and Cheryl White
WILLIS BROTHERS, THE	Guy, Skeeter and Vic Willis
WRAY BROTHERS, THE	Link, Vernon and Douglas Wray

THE SHAGGS
Philosophy of The World

Betty, Helen and Dorothy
Wiggin

THE ANDREWS SISTERS
AIR

Patti, Lavern and Maxine
Andrews

THE BEE GEES —
Barry, Maurice and Robin Gibb

Phyliss, Dorothy and Christine McGuire
THE McGUIRE SISTERS

GIBSON BROTHERS — Alex, Patrick
and Christoper Gibson

115

Quartets, Plus

AMES BROTHERS, THE .... Edward, Gene, Joeseph and Victor Yorick
BAILES BROTHERS, THE .... Kyle, Johnny, Walter and Homer Bailes
BEACH BOYS, THE .... Brian, Dennis and Carl Wilson with cousin Mike Love
BOONE GIRLS, THE .... Cherry (Cheryl), Lindy, Debby and Laury Boone
CARTER FAMILY #2 .... Sara, Maybelle, Anita, June, Helen, Janette and Joe Carter
CHAMBERS BROTHERS, THE .... George Ernest, Willie Mack, Lester and Joe Chambers
CLANCY BROTHERS, THE #2 .... Pat, Bobby and Tom Clancy with cousin Bobbie O'Connell
COPPER FAMILY, THE .... Bob, Ron, John and Jill Cooper
COWSILLS, THE .... John, Bob, Bill, Dick, Paul, Sue and Mom (Barbara) Cowsill
DEBARGE .... James, Mark, Randy, Eldra and Bunny DeBarge
DeFRANCO FAMILY, THE .... Tony, Benny, Nino, Marisa and Merlina DeFranco
DILLARDS, THE .... Doug, Rodney, Homer Snr., Homer Jnr., Linda and Earling Dillard
FAMILY BROWN, THE .... Papa (Joe), Barry, Lawanda and Tracey Brown
FAMILY STONE, THE .... Sly (Sylvester), Rosie and Freddie Stone with cousin Larry Graham
FARQUAHR .... Barnswallow, Hummingbird, Condor and Flamingo Farquahr
FIVE STAIRSTEPS, THE .... Clarence, James, Aloha, Kenny and Dennis Burke
FUREYS, THE .... Finbar, Eddie, George and Paul Furey
GIRLS, THE .... Diane, Sylvia, Rosemary and Margaret Sandoval
GLADYS KNIGHT & THE PIPS .. Gladys and Merald 'Bubba' Knight, with cousins William Guest and Edward Patten
ISLEY BROTHERS, THE†††† .... Ronald, Rudolph, Kelly, Vernon, Ernest & Marvin Isley and cousin Chris Jasper
JACKSON 5/THE JACKSONS .... Jackie, Tito, Jermaine, Marlon, Michael and Randy Jackson
KIMBERLY SPRINGS .... Leah, Lizzy, Bo, Terry and Teddy Kimberly
KING SISTERS, THE .... Alyce, Donna, Louise and Yvonne Driggs
LENNON SISTERS, THE .... Diane, Peggy, Kathy and Janet Lennon
LEWIS FAMILY, THE .... Wallace, Talmage, Roy, Pollie, Miggie, Janis and Pop Lewis
LUCAS SISTERS, THE .... Diana, Neva, Rhonda and Myra Lucas
MADDOX BROTHERS & ROSE .... Cal, Henry, Fred, Don and Rosea Brogdon
MASSEY, LOUISE (& THE WESTERNERS) .... Louise, Curt, Allen and Dad Massey
MILLS BROTHERS, THE .... Herbert, Harry, Donald and John Jnr. (replaced by John Snr.) Mills
NEVILLE BROTHERS, THE .... Charles, Art, Aaron and Cyril Neville, plus (Aaron's son) Ivan Neville
OSMONDS, THE .... Alan, Wayne, Merrill, Jay, Donny, Marie and Jimmy Osmond
PICKARD FAMILY, THE .... Dad (Obey), Mom, Bubb (Obey Jnr.) Charlie, Ruth and Ann Pickard
POINTER SISTERS, THE .... Bonnie (Patricia), Anita, Ruth and June Pointer
ROBBS, THE .... Dee, Joe (George), Bruce and Craig Robb
SEGO BROTHERS & NAOMI .... James, Lamar, Naomi and the Rev. W. R. Sego
SHEPHERD SISTERS, THE .... Martha, Mary Lou, Gail and Judy Shepherd
SISTER SLEDGE .... Kathi, Debbie, Kim and Joni Sledge
STAPLE SINGERS, THE .... Mavis, Cleotha, Yvonne and Pop (Roebuck) Staples
STEWARTS OF BLAIRGOWRIE, THE .... Belle, Alex, Sheila and Cathie Stewart
STONEMAN FAMILY, THE #1††††† .... Pop (Ernest), Mom (Hattie) and assorted children
STONEMAN FAMILY, THE #2 .... Scotty, Jim, Van, Patsy, Donna and Roni Stoneman
SYLVERS, THE .... Leon, James, Olympia, Charmaine, Patricia, Angie, Ed, Ricky and Foster Sylvers
TAVARES .... Ralph, Arthur (Pooch), Feliciano (Butch), Perry Lee (Tiny) and Antone (Chubby) Tavares
WATERSONS, THE
.... Mike Lal and Norma Waterson with second cousin John Harrison (replaced by Norma's husband Martin Carthy)

THE SYLVERS — Leon, Edmund, Olympia, Pat, Foster, Ricky, James and Angie Sylver

WILBURN FAMILY, THE .... Lester Lloyd, Leslie Floyd, Vinita Geraldine and Thurman Theodore (Teddy) Wilburn
WILLIAMS BROTHERS, THE .... Andy, Bob, Dick and Don Williams

      * Refer to index for real or full name.
      † This duo later expanded into The Newbeats.
    †† The Dinning Sisters' brother was pop heart throb Mark Dinning.
  ††† The O'Donnell siblings have done most of their recording as Clannad and Bothy Band.
 †††† Vernon was killed in a car accident.
††††† 'Assorted children' is as close as possible a description of the early formation of the Stoneman Family from
       Virginia. Ernest and Hattie Stoneman had 23 children, most of whom played some form of music. The family
       began recording in 1924 and in the late sixties a group of the younger children (designated as #2) found
       acceptance at rock venues such as the Fillmores.
(h/w)=husband and wife team, although surnames differ.

Diane, Peggy, Kathy and Janet Lennon

NEVILLE BROTHERS — Charles, Art, Aaron and Cyril Neville

THE STAPLE SINGERS— Mavis, Pop (Roebuck), Yvonne and Cleotha Staples

SISTER SLEDGE —— Debbie, Kathie, Kim and Joni Sledge

THE LENNON SISTERS ON THE GROOVY SIDE

UP, UP AND AWAY
NEVER MY LOVE
SUNNY
GOIN' OUT OF MY HEAD
ODE TO BILLY JOE
COUNT ME IN
I WILL WAIT FOR YOU
TILL
GYPSY, WHAT CAN I DO
I LOVE
PRISONER OF LOVE

SURNAME BANDS

(Rock bands titles after the surname of the leading member/s)

ARBUCKLE .... Ronnie Arbuckle*
ARGENT .... Rod Argent
BAUTISTA .... Roland Bautista
BRUFORD .... Bill Bruford
CARILLO .... Frank Carillo
CHASE .... Bill Chase
CHRISTIE .... Jeff Christie
COUCHOIS .... Chris, Pat and Mike Couchois
CRANE .... Chuck Crane
DERRINGER .... Rick Derringer*
DIO .... Ronnie James Dio*
DOKKEN .... Don Dokken
DOUCETTE .... Jerry Doucette
ELLIS .... Steve Ellis
FINESILVER .... Mike Finesilver
FOX .... Noosha Fox
GILLAN .... Ian Gillan
GREENSLADE .... Dave Greenslade
GUIFFRIA .... Greg Guiffria
KEEL .... Ron Keel
KING .... Paul King
LABELLE .... Patti Labelle*
MILLINGTON .... Jean and June Millington
MONTROSE .... Ronnie Montrose
MYRIAD .... Carrl Myriad
NITZINGER .... John Nitzinger
PATTO .... Mike Patto*
RIGGS .... Jerry Riggs
RODWAY .... Steve Rodway
SABU .... Paul Sabu
SAMSON .... Paul Samson
SANTANA .... Carlos Santana
SCHOENHERZ .... Richard Schoenherz
VANDENBERG .... Adrian 'Adje' Vandenberg
VAN HALEN .... Edward and Alex Van Halen
VAN-ZANT .... Johnny Van-Zant
WET .... Kevin Wet
WOOL .... Edward and Claudia Wool
ZWOL .... Walter Zwol

VAN HALEN — Eddie and Alex Van Halen

Honourable Mentions:

ALAN BOWN, THE .... Alan Bown
ALICE COOPER .... Alice Cooper*
APPLEJACKS, THE (U.S.) .... Dave Appell
ARTWOODS, THE† .... Art(hur) Wood
BAKER GURVITZ ARMY, THE .... Ginger Baker* and Adrian Gurvitz
BATTEAUX .... David and Robin Batteau*
BLISS BAND, THE .... Paul Bliss
BOZ PEOPLE, THE .... Boz Burrell*
BRINSLEY SCHWARZ .... Brinsley Schwarz
BRONSKI BEAT .... Steve Bronski
COLWELL WINFIELD BLUES BAND, THE .... Bill Colwell and Mike Winfield
DALY WILSON BIG BAND, THE .... Warren Daly and Ed Wilson
DREW-VELS, THE .... Patti Drew
FLEETWOOD MAC .... Mick Fleetwood/John McVie
GAYLORDS, THE .... Ronnie Gaylord
GOLDIE & THE GINGERBREADS .... Goldie Zelkowitz and Ginger Panebianco
GRAHAM CENTRAL STATION .... Larry Graham
HILLMEN, THE .... Chris Hillman
JAYWALKERS, THE .... Peter Jay
LEWIS & CLARK EXPEDITION, THE .... Travis Lewis* and Boomer Clark*
MANFRED MANN .... Manfred Mann*
McKENDREE SPRING .... Fran McKendree
McKENNA MENDELSON MAINLINE .... Mike McKenna and Joe Mendelson
McKENZIE THEORY .... Robert McKenzie
PAGES .... Richard Page
PETER B's LOONERS .... Peter Bardens
ROSSINGTON COLLINS BAND .... Gary Rossington and Allen Collins
RITCHIE FAMILY, THE .... Ritchie Rome
ROEMANS, THE .... Tommy Roe
RUBINOOS, THE .... Jon Rubin
SANFORD/TOWNSEND BAND .... Ed Sanford and John Townsend
SONS OF CHAMPLIN ....∴. Bill Champlin
SRC .... Scott Richardson Case
STANKY BROWN .... James 'Stanky' Brown
SWANEE .... John Archibald Dixon Swan
TENPOLE TUDOR .... Edward Tudorpole
THUNDERCLAP NEWMAN .... Andy 'Thunderclap' Newman
TOMMY TUTONE .... Tommy 'Tutone' Heath
TRENIERS, THE .... Claude & Cliff Trenier
TYLA GANG, THE .... Sean Tyla
YOUNG HOLT UNLIMITED... Eldee Young and Isaac 'Red' Holt

* — Refer to index for real name.
† — Art is the brother of Rolling Stone Ronnie Wood.

BRUFORD — Bill Bruford

THE RUBINOOS — Jon Rubin

119

Actor GARY BUSEY plays
drums as Teddy Jack Eddy

JACKIE DeSHANNON has
worked under five
pseudonymns.

JOHN B. SEBASTIAN was a member of The Even Dozen
Jug Band as John Benson and played harmonica for the
Doors as Guiseppi Puglesi.

DONNIE BROOKS aka Johnny
Jordan and Johnny Faire

ALSO KNOWN AS...
(Working Aliases)

It is only in relatively recent times that musicians have been able to freely appear on the recordings of their peers without fear of censure and disciplinary action from their own record companies. During the jazz years and into the first rock era of the fifties, it was not uncommon for well known entities to have to guest on other recordings under a pseudonym.

These pseudonyms or working aliases have also been employed by established artists seeking to 'market test' a new musical style which they feel might confuse or alarm their followers; or, in the case of bits of studio nonsense, insult them. Some artists have successfully carried on dual recording careers by the use of a pseudonym, such as Ferlin Husky/Simon Crum and Sheb Wooley/Ben Colder.

A great many artists have also employed pseudonyms for reasons not entirely legitimate, and usually related to a desire to record for one company while still under contract to another. In the case of protracted contractural disputes, artists find themselves unable to legitimately record for extended periods and so resort to false names in order to continue working.

The reasons are as manifold as the pseudonyms themselves. Paul McCartney wrote, produced and played for other artists respectively as Bernard Webb, Apollo C. Vermouth and Paul Ramon so that his efforts would be judged on their merits and not on the basis of him being a Beatle.

He is not the only performer to have feared prejudice and preconceived notions, jazz and country artists have long felt pseudonyms necessary for breaking into the lucrative pop market.

For others the choice is out of their hands as manipulative label owners and managers try to cash in on booms or just milk a market dry. The Legrand recordings of Gary U.S. Bonds, for instance, were marketed under about eight variations of his false name (The U.S. Bonds, Gary Bonds, U.S. Bonds, Ulysses Samuel Bonds, The Bonds Brothers, etc.). When Cherilyn Sarkasian LaPier (Cher sang on a Beatle novelty single, *I Love You Ringo,* she had a copy thrust into her hands a few weeks later with the name Bonnie Jo Mason on the label.

A common feature of new wave recording in Britain and Australia over the past decade or less has been pseudonyms to fool the dole office. I mean, until the record actually 'makes it' and the loot starts rolling in, there's not much point in abandoning one's only weekly income, is there now?

The practice, for whatever reasons, has been commonplace for literally centuries and many of the great (and not so great) composers participated in the charade. Matyas Seiber used the name G.S. Mathis when writing music for the accordion, while Russian composer Boris Asafiev operated as a music critic under the name Igor Glebov.

Those featured in this section are in the main performers, with songwriter pseudonyms covered elsewhere. The activities related to these pseudonyms range from a simple guest session on somebody else's album (Eric Clapton as King Cool and George Harrison as L'Angelo Misterioso) to a complete album project (Tommy Boyce as Christopher Cloud).

The actual pseudonyms have no common ground whatsoever in derivation. Art Garfunkel, obviously uncomfortable with his clumsy monicker, recorded under the abbreviated version of Artie Garr but then had second thoughts and reverted. The same situation occured with Adrian Gurvitz, who was a member of The Gun as Adrian Curtis; with Kris Kristofferson who cut early singles as Kris Carson; and with folkie Judy Henske who made 'girlgroup' singles as Judy Hart.

When Stevie Wonder cut a jazz instrument album, he merely effected the mirror-reverse, Eivets Rednow. Rock guru Kim Fowley had the audacity to try and pass himself off as his own son, Kim Fowley Jnr., complete with an old school photo on the album cover. Micky Dolenz auditioned for the Monkees under his mother's maiden name Braddock, to avoid unfair association with his actor father. John Benson Sebastian merely dispensed with his surname when he was a member of the Even Dozen Jug Band in his pre-Spoonful days. And the venerable John D. Loudermilk showed remarkable acumen when he released the single *Asiatic Flu* as Ebe Sneezer & his Epidemics.

BARBARA ACKLIN .... Barbara Allen
LAUREN AGNELLI (NERVUS REX) .... Trixie A. Balm
TOMMY ALDRIDGE (BLACK OAK ARKANSAS) .... Dork Jackson
WILLIE ALEXANDER .... Willie Loco
DAEVID ALLEN (GONG) .... Bert Camembert/Dingo Virgin
WALLY ALLEN (PRETTY THINGS) .... Wally Waller
MYRA ANDERSON .... Myra Barnes/Vicki Anderson
CHRIS ANDREWS .... Chris Ravel (& The Ravers)
GINNY ARNELL .... (Jamie &) Jane
*GENE AUTRY .... John Hardy/Overton Hatfield/Tom Long/Bob Clayton/
Jimmie Smith/Gene Johnson/Sam Hill/Johnny Dodds
RON BAINBRIDGE (FORTUNES) .... Rod Allen
*LAVERN BAKER .... Bea Baker
*MICKEY 'GUITAR' BAKER (MICKEY & SYLVIA) .... Big Red McHouston
BOB BALDORI (WOOLIES) .... Boogie Woogie Bob
BOBBY BARE† .... Bill Parsons
BILLY BARTON .... Hillbilly Barton/Billy Boy Barton
MAGGIE BELL (STONE THE CROWS) .... Mags McGlint
PETER BELL (SULTANS) .... Johnny Lynn
RONALD BELL (KOOL & THE GANG) .... Khalis Bayyan
BERT BERNS .... Bert Russell/Russell Byrd
BILL BLACK .... Bill Robbins
BRUCE BLACKMAN (STARBUCK) .... Karl Marion
BOBBY BLOOM .... Captain Groovy
*DAVID BLUE .... David Bluestein
COLIN BLUNSTONE (ZOMBIES) .... Neil MacArthur
CURT BOETCHER .... Friar Tuck
NEIL BOGART .... Neal Scott/Wayne Roberts
*MARC BOLAN .... Mark Bowland/Big Carrot/Toby Tyler
*SONNY BONO .... Don Christy/Ronny Sommers
*DANIEL BOONE .... Peter Lee Stirling
MARK BOSTON (MALLARD) .... Rockette Morton
JIMMY BOWEN .... Wes Bryant
*DAVID BOWIE .... Davie Jones/Tom Jones (& Jonahs)
*TOMMY BOYCE .... Christopher Cloud
*BOY GEORGE .... Lieutenant Lush
DONNIE BROOKS .... Johnny Jordan/Johnny Faire
*ARTHUR BROWN .... Arthur Zarathustra
JAMES BROWN .... Walter Foster
VICTOR BROX(RETALIATION) .... Sam Crozier
DAVE BURGESS .... Dave Dupree
SOLOMON BURKE .... Lucas Lollipop
JAMES BURTON .... Jimmy Dobro
GARY BUSEY†† .... Teddy Jack Eddy
JO CALLIS (REZILLOS/HUMAN LEAGUE) .... Luke Warm
JOE CAMILLERI/JO JO ZEP .... Joey Vincent
GLENN CARDIER .... Sydney Hill
*VICKI CARR .... Carlita
WILF CARTER .... Montana Slim
RIC CARTEY .... Feelin' Joyous
*BUZZ CASON .... Garry Miles
ED CASSIDY (SPIRIT) .... Cass Strange
*JOEY CASTLE .... Cliff Rivers
GENE CHANDLER .... The Duke of Earl
*RONNIE CHARLES (ATLAS) .... Captain Australia (& The Honky Tonk)
CLIFTON CHENIER .... Cliston Chanier
*CHER .... Bonnie Jo Mason/Black Rose/Cher Allman/Cherilyn
TERRY CHIMES (CLASH) .... Tory Crimes
ROGER CHRISTIAN .... Hot Rod Rog
*LOU CHRISTIE .... Lou Christie Sacco
JIMMY CLANTON .... Jimmy Dale
*ERIC CLAPTON .... King Cool
CLAUDINE CLARK .... Joy Dawn
EDDIE COCHRAN .... Eddie Dano
*JOE COCKER .... Vance Arnold
*NAT KING COLE .... Shorty Nadine/Eddie Laguna
CRAIG COLLINGE (M. MANN EARTH BAND) .... Craig Collins
RAY COLUMBUS (& INVADERS) .... Ray Bell (& Bell Tones)
*CAROL CONNORS .... Annette Bard/Carol Collins
*SAM COOKE .... Dale Cooke

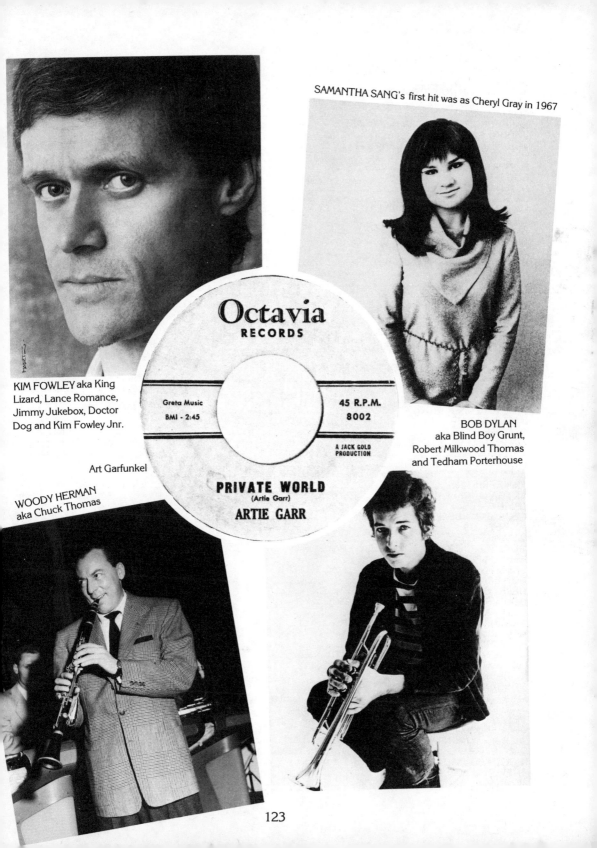

SAMANTHA SANG's first hit was as Cheryl Gray in 1967

KIM FOWLEY aka King Lizard, Lance Romance, Jimmy Jukebox, Doctor Dog and Kim Fowley Jnr.

Art Garfunkel

Octavia
RECORDS

Greta Music
BMI - 2:45

45 R.P.M.
8002

A JACK GOLD
PRODUCTION

PRIVATE WORLD
(Artie Garr)
ARTIE GARR

BOB DYLAN
aka Blind Boy Grunt, Robert Milkwood Thomas and Tedham Porterhouse

WOODY HERMAN
aka Chuck Thomas

STEWART COPELAND (POLICE)	Klark Kent
*ELVIS COSTELLO	The Imposter
JAMES COTTON	Joe Denim
JEFF COTTON (MAGIC BAND)	Antennae Jim Semens
DON COVAY	Pretty Boy
*BOB CREWE	Bobby Dimple
BARRY CROCKER ('BAZZA' McKENZIE)	Daddy Long Legs (& Spiders)
JOHNNY CYMBAL	Derek
JOHN R.T. DAVIES (TEMPERANCE 7)	Sheikh Haroun Wadi El Yadounir
MILES DAVIS	Cleo Henry
RONNIE DAWSON	Ronnie Dee
*BOBBY DAY	Bobby Flare
PETER DePOE (REDBONE)	Last Walking Bear
JACKIE DeSHANNON	Jackie Dee/Jackie Shannon/Sharon Lee/Sherry Lee Myers/Sharon Lee Dain
GREG LEROY DEWEY (MAD RIVER)	Dewey DaGrease
WILLIE DIXON	James Dixon
KLAUS DOLDINGER	Paul Nero
*MICKEY DOLENZ	Mike Swain/Mickey Braddock
LAMONT DOZIER	Lamont Anthony
DARYL DRAGON (THE CAPTAIN)	Rumbo
GEORGE DUKE	Dawille Gonga
AYNSLEY DUNBAR	Junior Dunn
LESLIE DUNCAN	Leslie Crowther
DAVID DUNDAS	Lord David Paul Nicholas Dundas, 2nd son of the 5th Earl of Zetland
*BOB DYLAN	Blind Boy Grunt/Robert Milkwood Thomas/Tedham Porterhouse
*RAMBLING JACK ELLIOT	Buck Elliot
JOHN ENTWISTLE (WHO)	John Browne
FENRUS EPP (KALEIDOSCOPE)	Connie Crill/Max Buda/Templeton Parcely
*ROKY ERICKSON	Emil Schwartze
ROY ESTRADA (MOTHERS OF INVENTION)	Orejon
*ESQUERITA	S.Q. Reeder/Esquerita Malochi/The Magnificent Malochi
*CHRIS FARLOWE	Little Joe Cook
RICKY FATAAR(FLAME/BEACH BOYS)	Stig O'Hara (Rutles)
DAVE FAULKNER (HOODOO GURUS)	Dave Flick
JOSE FELICIANO	Werbley Finster
GEORGE FORMBY	Harold Bright
KIM FOWLEY	King Phantom Lizard/Kim Fowley Jnr./Lance Romance/Jimmy Jutebox/Doctor Dog
INEZ FOXX	Inez Johnston
*BILLY FURY	Stormy Tempest
ALAN FREED	Moondog
ERNIE FREEMAN	Sir Chauncery/Bill Bumble
ART GARFUNKEL	Artie Garr/Tom Graph
DAVID GATES	Arthur James/Del Ashley
GEORGIA GIBBS	Freda Gibson
MICKEY GILLEY	Gary Michaels
*GARY GLITTER	Paul Raven/Rubber Bucket/Paul Monday
GODLEY & CREME	Frabjoy & Runcible Spoon
EARL GAINES	A. Friend
LESLEY GORE	(Billy &) Sue
*DON GRADY	Luke R. Yoo
GERRY GRANAHAN	Jerry Grant
*GOGI GRANT	Audrey Brown
LES GRAY (MUD)	Tulsa McLean
RUDY GRAYZELL	Rudy Grey/Rudy Gray
R.B. GREAVES	Sonny Childe
ELLIE GREENWICH	Ellie Gaye/Ellie Gee (&The Jets)
LUTHER GROSVENOR (SPOOKY TOOTH)	Ariel Bender (Mott The Hoople)
ADRIAN GURVITZ	Adrian Curtis (Gun)
BOBBY HACKETT	Pete Pesci
*BOBBY HART (BOYCE & HART)	Nick Landers
GEORGE HARRISON	Hari Georgeson/L'Angelo Misterioso/George O'Hara/George Harrysong/ P. Roducer/Jai Raj Harisein/George O'Hara Smith/George H./Son of Harry/Carl Harrison
MELANIE HARROLD†††	Joanna Carlin/Irma Cetas
*JIMI HENDRIX	Jimmy James
RICK HENN (SUNRAYS)	Dan & Jean
JUDY HENSKE	Judy Hart
*WOODY HERMAN	Chuck Thomas
STEVE HILLAGE	Simeon Sasparella
JOHNNY 'RABBIT' HODGES	Cue Porter

*BILLIE HOLIDAY‡	Lady Day
CHRISTINE HOLMES (FAMILY DOGG)	Kristine Sparkle
*ENGLEBERT HUMPERDINCK	Gerry Dorsey
FERLIN HUSKY	Simon Crum/Terry Preston
CHRISSIE HYNDE (PRETENDERS)	Christine Hindley (Moors Murderers)
ERIC IDLE (MONTY PYTHON)	Dirk McQuickly (Rutles)
NEIL INNES (BONZO DOG BAND)	Ron Nasty (Rutles)
MICK JAGGER & KEITH RICHARD	The Glimmer Twins
BOB JAXON	Bobby Jack
BILLY JOEL	Billy Joe (Hassles)/Bill Martin
DAVID JOHANSEN	Buster Poindexter (& Banshees of Blue)
CLIVE JOHN (MAN)	Clint Space
*ELTON JOHN	Rockaday Johnny
BRUCE JOHNSTON	Bob Sled (& The Tobbogans)
*BRIAN JONES (ROLLING STONE)	Elmo Lewis
GEORGE JONES	Thumper Jones
*PAUL JONES (MANFRED MANN)	P.P. (Permanently Pissed) Pond
*TOM JONES	Tommy Scott
GEORG KAJANUS (SAILOR)	Georg Hultgren
PETER KAUKONEN (JEFFERSON STARSHIP)	Peter Kangaroo
YUZO KAYAMA	Kosaku Dan
LENNY KAYE (PATTI SMITH BAND)	Link Cromwell
GIBSON KEMP (PADDY, KLAUS & GIBSON)	Stuart Gibson
ANDY KIM	Baron Longfellow
*EARL KING	Earl Connelly
*JONATHAN KING	Count Giovanni De Regina/Sean Hoff/Father Abraphart
MARSHAL KLEINBARD (TEDDY BEARS)	Marshal Howard Connors
AL KOOPER	Roosevelt Cook
BILL KREUTZMANN (GRATEFUL DEAD)	Bill Sommers
KRIS KRISTOFFERSON	Kris Carson
LENNY LaCOUR	Paul Perry
CLIVE LANGER (& BOXES)	Cliff Hanger
AMANDA LEAR	Peki d'Oslo/John Lear
ARTHUR LEE (LOVE)	Arthurly
JACKIE LEE	Jacky
*PEGGY LEE	Susan Melton/(Ten Cats and) A Mouse
JACKIE LEVEN (DOLL BY DOLL)	John St. Field
JERRY LEE LEWIS	The Hawk
DAVID LINDLEY	DeParis Letante
BOB LINKLETTER	Bob Preston
JACKIE LOMAX	Rick Redstreak
*PROFESSOR LONGHAIR	Roy Byrd/Little Loving Henry
JERRY LORDAN	Jerry Elvin
*DONNA LOREN	, Donna Dee/Barbie Ames/Donna Lee
JOHN D. LOUDERMILK	Johnny Dee/Ebe Sneezer (& Epidemics)
FRANKIE LYMON	Eddie Robbins
STEVE LYNDSEY (DEAF SCHOOL)	Mr. Average
EWAN MacCOLL	Jimmy Miller
*JOHNNY MAESTRO	Johnny Masters
DIDIER MALHERBE (GONG)	Bad Bloom Diode
*MANN & LOWE	Anthony September
BARRY MANN	Buddy Brooks
SHELLY MANNE	Manny Shell
MANTOVANI	Gandino
*MOON MARTIN	John Martine
*NICK MASSI (FOUR SEASONS)	Alex Alda
ERNIE MARESCA	Artie Chicago
JOHN MAUS/WALKER	John Stewart
*PAUL McCARTNEY	Percy Thrillington/Apollo C. Vermouth/Paul Ramon
DELBERT McCLINTON	Mac Clinton
RED McKENZIE	Bob Murray
ROD McKUEN	Dor
JOHN McLAUGHLIN	Mahavishnu John McLaughlin
TONY McPHEE (GROUNDHOGS)	John Lee/T.S. McPhee
TERRY MELCHER‡‡	Terry Day
FREDDIE MERCURY (QUEEN)	Larry Lurex
*TERRY LEE MIALL (ADAM & ANTS)	Terry Day
YVONNE MILLS (& SENSATIONS)	Yvonne Baker
MITCH MITCHELL (HENDRIX EXPERIENCE)	Henry Manchovitz

PIERRE MOERLEN (GONG)	Piere Cusluar/Pierre DeStrassbourg
*MATT MONRO	Fred Flange
HUGH MONTGOMERY-CAMPBELL (EGG)	Mont Campbell
KEITH MOON (WHO)	Kief Spoon
LIZA MORROW	Kit Carson
FRANCIS MOSE/MOZE (GONG/MAGMA)	Francis Bacon
TED MULRY (TMG)	Steve Ryder
MICHAEL MURPHY	Travis Lewis
JUNIOR MURVIN	Junior Soul
MARK NAFTALIN (BUTTERFIELD BLUES BAND)	Naffy Markham
*WAZMO NARIZ	Gunderson Peters
EARL NELSON (BOB & EARL)	Earl Cosby/Jay Dee/Jackie Lee
MIKE NESMITH	Michael Blessing
HANK NOBLE	Billy Guitar
JOHNNY O'KEEFE	Eddie Cash Jnr.
*OLIVER	Billy (& Sue)
JIMMIE O'NEILL (FINGERPRINTZ)	Jimmie Shelter
*TONY ORLANDO	Bertell Dache/Billy Shield
JERRY OSBORNE	Jerry Day/Dan Rathernot/Ratmore Slinky
TOMMY OVERSTREET	Tommy Dean from Abilene
JEAN OWEN (VERNONS GIRLS)	Samantha Jones
*BUCK OWENS	Corky Jones
*HOT LIPS PAGE	Papa Snow White
ALAN PARKER (CCS)	Andrew Balmain
CHARLIE PARKER	Charlie Chan
VAN DYKE PARKS	George Washington Brown
ANDY PARTRIDGE (XTC)	Mr. Partridge
ANDY PASK (LANDSCAPE)	Captain Whorlix
*LES PAUL	Rhubarb Red
GARY PAXTON	Lurch
JONNY PAYCHECK	Donny Young
LEON PAYNE	Rock Rogers
ART PEPPER	Art Salt
CLAUDE PEPPER	John Mack
GENE PITNEY	Billy Brian/Jamie (& Jane)

Tommy Boyce

Paul Weston and Jo Stafford

Tony Orlando

UA 290
Time: 2:48
ZTSP 66238

Aldon Music.
Inc. - BMI
Produced By
Don Costa

BERTELL DACHE
NOT JUST TOMORROW, BUT ALWAYS
(C. King-J. Goffin) Arranged
by Carol King

® UNITED ARTISTS RECORDS, INC. MADE IN U.S.A.

JOHN D. LOUDERMILK
aka Johnny Dee and Ebe Sneezer

MARY KAY PLACE	Loretta Haggers
BEN POLLACK	Ted Bancroft
*PRINCE	Jamie Starr
*P.J. PROBY	Jett Powers
SUZI QUATRO	Suzi Soul
ELLIOT RANDALL	Enrico Ronzoni
MICHAEL RASHKOW	Mike Lendell
*GENYA RAVAN	Goldie Zelkowitz
JOHNNIE RAY	A.Guy
CHRIS REA	Benny Santini
NOEL REDDING (HENDRIX EXPERIENCE)	Clit McTorius
*JERRY REED	Muvva Guitar Hubbard
KEITH RELF (YARDBIRDS)	Keith Dangerfield
CHARLIE RICH	Bobby Sheridan
*KEITH RICHARD (ROLLING STONES)	Valerie Masters
MINNIE RIPERTON	Andrea Davis
BOBBY RIO (& REVELLES)	Bobby Christo
*TOMMY ROCK	Tommy Knight/Tommy Jay
GIL RODIN	Clark Randell
KENNY ROGERS	Kenneth Rogers
SHORTY ROGERS	Roger Short
FRANCIS ROSSI (STATUS QUO)	Mike Rossi
JOHN ROWLES	Ja Ar
LEON RUSSELL	Hank Wilson
MITCH RYDER	Billy Lee
SAMANTHA SANG	Cheryl Gray
*SAM THE SHAM	Sam Samudio
JERRY SAMUELS	Napoleon XIV/Scott David
*SKY SAXON (SEEDS)	Marcus Tybolt/Sky Sunlight
JOHN B. SEBASTIAN	John Benson/Guiseppi Puglesi
PETE SEEGER	Pete Bowers
RONNIE SELF	Johnny Fallin
STEVE SEVERIN (BANSHEES)	Steve Havoc
DAVID SEVILLE	Alfi & Harry/Alvin, Simon & Theodore (Chipmunks)
GLENN SHORROCK (LITTLE RIVER BAND)	Andre L'Escargot

PAUL SIMON .... Jerry Landis/Paul Kane/True Taylor
EARL SINKS .... Sinx Mitchell
*WHISTLING JACK SMITH .... Coby Wells
GILLI SMYTH .... Shakti Yoni
LIMMIE SNELL (FAMILY COOKING) .... Lemmie B. Good
PHIL SPECTOR .... Phil Harvey
*RONNIE SPECTOR .... Veronica
JEREMY SPENCER (FLEETWOOD MAC) .... Earl Vance (& Valiants)
JO STAFFORD .... Cinderella G. Stump/Darlene Edwards
*ALVIN STARDUST .... Shane Fenton
FRANK STARR .... Andy Starr
*LUCILLE STARR .... Fern Regan
*RINGO STARR .... Ritchie Snare/English Ritchie
*RAY STEVENS .... Sweetie Jones
*RORY STORME .... Jet Storm
FRED STRAUKS (SKYHOOKS) .... Freddie Kaboodleschnitzer
RICHARD STRANGE .... Kid Strange
*STEVE STRANGE (VISAGE) .... Steve Brady (Moors Murderers)
THOMAS GILMORE STUART (RUBBER BAND) .... Christopher Toboggan
BIG JIM SULLIVAN .... Lord Sitar
STUART SUTCLIFFE (BEATLES) .... Stu de Stael
*AUSTEN TAYSHUS .... Isaac Cox
*JOE TEX .... Joseph X
DAVID THOMAS (PERE UBU) .... Crocus Behemoth
*JOHNNY THUNDERS (N.Y. DOLLS) .... Johnny Volume
DAVE TICE (COUNT BISHOPS) .... Mike Spenser (& Cannibals)
ART(HUR) TRIPP (MOTHERS/MALLARD) .... Ed Marimba
PETE TOWNSHEND (WHO) .... Bijou Drains
DAVE LEE TRAVIS & PAUL BURNETT .... Laurie Lingo (& Dipsticks)
TANYA TUCKER .... Misty
IKE TURNER .... Icky Remut
*CONWAY TWITTY .... Sonny Wilson
*RITCHIE VALENS .... Arvee Allens
*FRANKIE VALLI (FOUR SEASONS) .... Billy Dixon/Hal Miller/Frankie Valley/Frankie Vally
*VANDA & YOUNG .... Marcus Hook
DAVE VANIAN (DAMNED) .... Naz Nomad (& Nightmares)
*TEDDY VANN .... The Dixie Drifter
JOHN LEWIS WAGSTAFF .... Lee Kristofferson
*T-BONE WALKER .... Oak Cliff T-Bone
*DIONNE WARWICK .... Dionne Warwicke
*BABY WASHINGTON .... Justine Washington
ETHEL WATERS .... Mamie Jones/Martha Pryor
JOHNNY 'GUITAR' WATSON .... Young John Watson
ADRIENNE WEBBER .... Hazel Gummidge
CYNTHIA WEIL .... Miss Prim (& Classroom Kids)
PAUL WESTON‡‡‡ .... Jonathon Edwards
JANE WIEDLIN (GO GO'S) .... Jane Drano
*MARTY WILDE .... Zappo/Shannon
JOHN BUCK WILKIN .... Ronny Dayton/Bucky Wilkin
JOHNNY WINTER .... Texas Guitar Slim
STEVE WINWOOD .... Steve Angelo
MARC WIRTZ .... Marc Rogers/Philwit (& Pegasus)
JAH WOBBLE (PIL) .... Dan McArthur
STEVIE WONDER .... Eivets Rednow/El Toro Negro (The Black Bull)
SHEB WOOLLEY .... Ben Colder
STEVIE WRIGHT (EASYBEATS) .... Chris Langdon
ALEX YOUNG (GRAPEFRUIT) .... M. James
NEIL YOUNG .... Bernard Shakey
FRANK ZAPPA .... Bob Guy/Baby Ray/Captain Glasspack/Ron Roman
GARY ZEKELY (YELLOW BALLOON) .... Yodar Critch

* Refer to index for real name.

† This was an unintentional pseudonym . Bill Parsons actually existed and was signed to RCA around the same time as Bobby Bare. However when Bobby cut the 1958 hit single *The All American Boy*, Parsons' name was mistakenly appended to it.

†† Gary, star of *The Buddy Holly Story* film, used this pseudonym to play drums on albums by Leon Russell, Kinky Friedman and others.

††† Melanie issued one album on DJM as Joanna Carlin in 1977 and another on the same label in 1979 as Melanie Harrold.

‡ Although generally used as a nickname/billing name, Billie's 1943 release of *Trav'lin Light* was issued under the name of Lady Day.

‡‡ Terry is the son of Doris Day. He was the actual target of the Manson tribe, who murdered Sharon Tate in error.

‡‡‡ Paul Weston was the husband of Jo Stafford and the pair made goofy albums under the alias of Darlene & Jonathan Edwards.

Special Note:

In 1971 the Decca label in America released a bluesy guitar-dominated studio jam album by a mystery outfit called Green Bullfrog. The personnel listing was confined to brief pseudonymns — Boots, Pinta, The Boss and The Vicar on guitar, Sleepy on bass, Speedy on drums, Bevy and Sorry on keyboards, and Jordan on vocals.

In a 1978 interview with Guitar Player magazine, Deep Purple's Ritchie Blackmore was asked about Green Bullfrog and stated: "That was me, Albert Lee and Jim Sullivan. Ian Paice and Roger Glover were on it and whoever else was around at the time." As to which of those famous identities matched which pseudonym is still a mystery, though we can presume that Speedy is Ian Paice.

BOBBY BARE's biggest hit All American Boy, was credited to Bill Parsons.

GEORGE HARRISON has used ten pseudonymns as a producer and musician.

129

BUNNY WAILER — Neville O'Riley Livingston

BURNING SPEAR —
Winston Rodney

Manley Augustus Buchanan

TOOTS — Frederick Hibbert

SCREAMING
Target
BIG YOUTH

130

REGGAE/SKA/ CALYPSO IDENTITIES

BOB ANDY .... Keith Anderson
PABLO BLACK .... Paul Dixon
LORD BURGESS .... Irving L. Burgie
MIKEY DREAD .... Michael Campbell
SLY DUNBAR .... Noel Charles Dunbar
JACKIE EDWARDS .... Wilfred Edwards
RUPIE EDWARDS .... Robert Edwards
JUNIOR HANSON .... Marvin J. Hanson
DEADLY HEADLEY .... Felix Headley
LORD INVADER .... Rupert Grant
JANET KAY .... Janet Kay Bogle
BYRON LEE (& DRAGONAIRES) .... Ken Lazarus
JERRY MATHIAS (TOOTS & MAYTALS) .... Nathaniel Mathias
SUGAR MINOTT .... Lincoln Minott
PABLO MOSES .... Paul Henry
STEELIE NELSON .... Anthony Nelson
AUGUSTUS PABLO .... Horace Swaby
MICHAEL PROPHET .... Michael George Haynes
JACKIE ROBINSON (PIONEERS) .... Loren Robinson
MAX ROMEO .... Max Smith
SUGAR SIMONE .... Tito Simon
BUNNY SIMPSON (MIGHTY DIAMONDS) .... Fitzroy Simpson
DUCKIE SIMPSON (BLACK UHURU) .... Derrick Simpson
CHINNA SMITH .... Earl Smith
STICKY THOMPSON .... Uzziah Thompson
BUNNY WAILER .... Neville O'Riley Livingston
BLUBBER WAUL .... Franklyn Waul
TONY ZAP (GLADIATORS) .... Hughes Edmunds

Stage/Trade Names:

BIG YOUTH .... Manley Augustus Buchanan
BURNING SPEAR .... Winston Rodney
DILLINGER .... Lloyd Bullock
DR. ALIMANTADO .... James Winston Thompson
EEK-A-MOUSE .... Ripton Hilton
IJAHMAN .... Trevor Sutherland
I-ROY .... Roy Reid
JAH CRIPPLE .... Errol 'Tarzan' Nelson
JUDGE DREAD .... Alex Hughes
NINEY THE OBSERVER .... Winston Holness
PLUTO .... Leighton Shervington
PRINCE BUSTER .... Buster Campbell
SCIENTIST .... Overton Brown
SCRATCH THE UPSETTER+ .... Lee Perry
SIR COXONE THE DOWNBEAT .... Clement Dodd
SIR LANCELOT .... Lancelot Victor Pinard
TOOTS (& MAYTALS) .... Frederick Hibbert
U-ROY .... Ewart Beckford
YABBY-U .... Vivian Jackson
YELLOW MAN .... Winston Foster
+ — aka Pipecock Jackson, The Gong

Harold F. Hawkins

HAWKSHAW HAWKINS
Exclusive on RCA Victor Records

an RCA VICTOR
COUNTRY
and WESTERN
ATTRACTION

HANK LOCKLIN — Lawrence Hankins Locklin

DALE EVANS — Francis Octavia Smith/Fox/
Slye, with husband ROY ROGERS — Leonard Slye

COUNTRY & WESTERN PERFORMERS

JOHNNY ABRAHAM	Curtis Eugene Grothoff III
DERROLL ADAMS	Derroll Lewis Thompson
JERRY ALLEN	Jerry Atinsky
ROSALIE ALLEN	Julie Marlene Bedra
LIZ ANDERSON	Elizabeth Jane Haaby
BOB ATCHER	James Robert Owen Atcher
TEX ATCHISON	Shelby David Atchison
CHET ATKINS	Chester Burton Atkins
RAZZY BAILEY	Rasie Bailey
MOLLY BEE	Molly Beachboard
DOCK BOGGS	Moran L. Boggs
ELTON BRITT	James Britt Baker
SLIM BRYANT	Thomas Hoyt Bryant
GOOBER BUCHANAN (KENTUCKIANS)	James Gilbert Buchanan
BUDDY CANNON	Murray Franklin Cannon
THUMBS CARLLILE	Kenneth Ray Carllile
MARTHA LOU CARSON	Martha Ambergay
A. P. CARTER	Alvin Pleasant Delaney Carter
YODELING SLIM CLARK	Raymond LeRoy Clark
BIFF COLLIE	Hiram Abiff Collie
TOMMY COLLINS	Leonard Raymond Sipes
SHORTY COOK	Everett Roland Honderer
SPADE COOLEY	Donell C. Cooley
WILMA LEE COOPER	Wilma Lee Leary
COWBOY COPAS	Lloyd T. Copas
COUSIN HERB	Herbert Lester Henson
HOWARD CROCKET	Howard Hausey
TED DAFFAN	Theron Eugene Daffan
PAPPY DAILEY	Harold W. Dailey
VERNON DALHART	Marion Try Slaughter
BARBARA DANE	Barbara Spillman
DANNY DAVIS	George Nowlan
EDDIE DEAN	Edgar Dean Glosup
LORENE 'DEAREST' DEAN	Lorene St. Clare Glosup
MARV DENNIS	Marvin Blihovde
AL DEXTER	Albert Poindexter
JIMMIE DRIFTWOOD	James Morris
JIMMY EDWARDS	James Wiley Bullington
DALE EVANS†	Francis Octavia Smith/Fox/Slye/Rogers
SHUG FISHER	George Clinton Fisher
RED FOLEY††	Clyde Julian Foley
HOWDY FORRESTER (BLUEGRASS BOYS)	Howard Wilson Forrester
LEFTY FRIZZELL	William Orville Frizzell
GIB GUILBEAU	Floyd Guilbeau
BONNIE GUITAR	Bonnie Buckingham
HARDROCK GUNTER	Sidney Louie Gunther Jnr.
JACK GUTHRIE†††	Leon Guthrie
REDD HARPER	Maurice Coe Harper
KELLY HARRELL	Crockett Kelly Harrell
CHAPIN HARTFORD	Paula Hartford nee Foster
PETE BUTCH HAWES (ALMANAC SINGERS)	John Hawes
HAWKSHAW HAWKINS	Harold F. Hawkins
JASON HAWKINS	Jack Powell
AUTRY INMAN	Robert Inman
AUNT MOLLIE JACKSON	Mary Magdalene Garland
GRANDPA JONES	Louis Marshall Jones
MERLE KILGORE	Wyatt Merle Kilgore
PEE WEE KING	Frank King
RED LANE	Hollis DeLaughter
ERNIE LEE	Ernest Eli Cornelison
JONI LEE	Joni Lee Prater nee Twitty (Jenkins)
JIMMY LLOYD	James Lodgson

133

Rubye Blevins

CHET ATKINS — Chester Burton Atkins

KITTY WELLS — Muriel Deason   DEL WOOD — Adelaide Hazelwood

REDD STEWART .... Henry Redd Stewart
CLIFFIE STONE .... Clifford Gilpin Snyder
POP STONEMAN .... Ernest Van Hayden Stoneman
SCOTTY STONEMAN‡ .... Calvin Scott Stoneman
JOE SUN .... James Paulsen
TOM TALL .... Tommie Lee Guthrie
GID TANNER .... James Gideon Tanner
JIMMY TARLETON .... Johnny James Rimbert Tarleton
TUT TAYLOR .... Robert Taylor
AL TERRY (THE SOUTHERNERS) .... Allison Joseph Theriot
SONNY THROCKMORTON .... James Fron Throckmorton
JOHNNY TRITT .... John Pistritto
GABE TUCKER (KENTUCKY RAMBLERS) .... Gaylord Bob Tucker
T. TEXAS TYLER .... David Luke Myrick
HANK WALLIS (NASHVILLE SUPERPICKERS) .... Henry P. Strzelecki
HANK WANGFORD .... Sam Hutt
KITTY WELLS .... Muriel Deason
DOTTIE WEST .... Dorothy Marie West
SPEEDY WEST .... Wesley Webb West
DOC WILLIAMS .... Andrew John Smik Jnr.
LEONA WILLIAMS .... Leona Belle Helton
TEX WILLIAMS .... Solomon Williams
HAL WILLIS .... Leonard Francois Joseph Guy Gauthier
GUY WILLIS .... James Willis
BOB WILLS (TEXAS PLAYBOYS) .... James Robert Wills
KITTY WILSON (CIRCLE 3 RANCH GANG) .... Mary K. Wilson
SMILEY WILSON‡‡ .... Hamilton K. Wilson
MAC WISEMAN .... Malcolm B. Wiseman
MISS DEL WOOD .... Adelaide Hazelwood
SKEETS YANEY .... Clyde A. Yaney

† Smith was her maiden name, Fox was from her first husband, Slye from her next husband (Leonard Slye), who
became King of the Cowboys Roy Rogers. Evans is a stage name only.
†† Red is Pat Boone's father-in-law.
††† A cousin of Woody Guthrie who found moderate success in the country field.
‡ Fiddle champion Scotty is the most famous of Pop Stoneman's large brood.
‡‡ Smiley is the husband of Kitty Wilson.

WOLFMAN JACK — Robert Smith

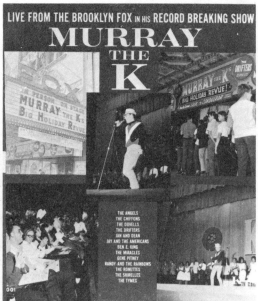

KENNY EVERETT — Maurice Cole

Murray Kaufman

DISC JOCKEYS

Britain

TONY BLACKBURN .... Kenneth Blackburn
RICK DANE .... Randall Gautier
SIMON DEE .... Carl Nicholas Henty-Dodd
ALAN DELL .... Alan Mandell
KENNY EVERETT .... Maurice Cole
PETE MURRAY .... Peter Murray James
ANNE NIGHTINGALE .... Avril Anne Nightingale
JOHN PEEL .... John Robert Parker Ravenscroft
TONY PRINCE .... Thomas Whitehead
MIKE RAVEN .... Churton Fairman
EMPEROR ROSKO .... Michael Pasternak
ED STEWART .... Edward Stewart Mainwaring

JOHN PEEL — John Robert Parker Ravenscroft

America

COUSIN BRUCIE .... Bruce Morrow
DEEJAY HOLLYWOOD .... Anthony Holloway
DR. DEMENTO .... Barret Hansen
GODFREY† .... Godfrey Kerr
HOUND DOG, THE .... George Lorenz
WINK MARTINDALE†† .... Winston Conrad Martindale
MURRAY THE K. .... Murray Kaufman
WOLFMAN JACK .... Robert Smith

† This legendary L.A. jock cut a number of singles in the sixties, including a cover of Kim Fowley's *The Trip*.

†† Wink had a #7 American hit in 1959 with *Deck of Cards*.

DR. DEMENTO — Barret Hansen

BILL GRAHAM — Wolfgang Wolodja Grajonka
Robert George Meek

COLONEL TOM PARKER — Andreas Cornelius Van Kuyk

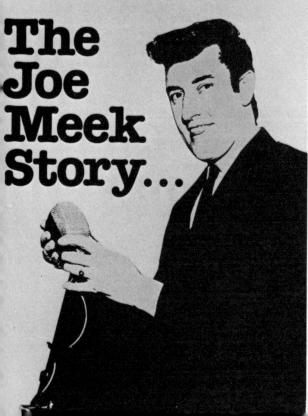

The Joe Meek Story...

THE SPRINGFIELDS (from left): MIKE HURST — Michael Pickworth
DUSTY SPRINGFIELD — Mary Isobel Catherine O'Brien
TOM SPRINGFIELD — Thomas O'Brien

MUSIC INDUSTRY FIGURES

RECORD PRODUCERS

STIG ANDERSON .... Stikkan Anderson
BASSMAN .... Paul Bass
BAZZA .... Barry Farmer
BLUEBIRD .... Dennis Bovell
TUTTI CAMARATA .... Salvatore 'Toots' Camarata
DENNY CORDELL .... Dennis Laverack
STEVE 'SHUTDOWN' DOUGLAS .... Steven Douglas Kreisman
FRANK FARIAN .... Franz Reuther
SNUFF GARRETT .... Thomas Garrett
BONES HOWE .... Dayton Howe
MIKE HURST .... Michael Pickworth
FELTON JARVIS .... Charles Felton Jarvis
ANDY JOHNS .... Jeremy Andrew Johns
SKY KEEGAN .... James Magner Keegan Jnr
MUTT LANGE .... Robert John Lange
MIKE LEANDER .... Michael George Farr
JAY LEWIS .... Jay Donnellan
JOE MEEK .... Robert George Meek
FRAZIER MOHAWK .... Barry Friedman
MICKIE MOST .... Michael Peter Hayes
LARRY PAGE .... Lenny Davis
CONNY PLANK .... Konrad Plank
VIC SMITH .... Victor Coppersmith-Heaven
NICK VENET .... Nikolas Kostantinos Venetoulis
ANDY WARHOL .... Andrew Warhola
RICKY WILDE .... Richard Smith
JOE WISSERT .... Joel Wissert
MARTIN ZERO .... Martin Hannett

MUSIC JOURNALISTS/AUTHORS
(Real Names)
MILES .... Barry Miles
PEREGRINE PICKLE .... George Putnam-Upton
JOHN TOBLER .... John Hugen-Tobler
(Pseudonyms)
GLENN A. BAKER .... Rudi Raven
LENNY KAYE .... Doc Rock
RICHARD MELTZER .... Mr. Vom
ARNOLD SHAW .... Ken Sloan†
GREG SHAW .... Nigel Strange††

FRINGE FIGURES
MAGIC ALEX (APPLE CORPS) .... Alexis Mardas
WAXIE MAXIE .... Max Needham

† Arnold, author of *Honkers & Shouters*, used this as a songwriting pseudonymn, one of his efforts being *A Man Called Peter*.
†† Bomp magazine editor Greg used this name to write the liner notes for the *Pebbles* garage rock album series.

MIKE NICHOLS — Michael Igor Peschowsky

William Szathmary (Bill Dana)

Donald James Yarmy

Mary Jean Tomlin

COMEDIANS ON RECORD

ABBOTT & COSTELLO .... William Abbott and Louis Francis Cristillo
DON ADAMS .... Donald James Yarmy
ALLEN & ROSSI .... Marty Allen and Steve Rossi
DAVE ALLEN .... David Tynan O'Mahoney
FRED ALLEN .... John F. Sullivan
WOODY ALLEN .... Allan Stewart Konigsberg
BELLE BARTHE .... Annabelle Salzman
ORSON BEAN .... Dallas F. Burrows
MILTON BERLE .... Milton Berlinger
JOEY BISHOP .... Joseph A Gottlieb
VICTOR BORGE .... Borge Rosenbaum
LENNY BRUCE .... Leonard Alfred Schneider
LORD BUCKLEY .... Richard M. Buckley
GEORGE BURNS .... Nathan Birnbaum
JUDY CANOVA .... Juliet Canova
JASPER CARROT .... Robert Davies
CHEECH & CHONG .... Richard Anthony Marin and Thomas Chong
CHICKENMAN .... Dick Orkin
FRED DAGG .... John Clarke
DAMASKAS .... Daniel Hollombe
BILL DANA/JOSE JIMINEZ .... William Szathmary
DEREK & CLIVE .... Peter Cook and Dudley Moore
DAME EDNA EVERAGE .... Barry Humphries
W.C. FIELDS .... William Claude Dunkenfield
WILD MAN FISCHER .... Larry Fischer
RED FOXX .... John Elroy Sandford
DAVID FRYE .... David Shapiro
GALLAGHER & SHEAN .... Edward Gallagher and Allan Shean
NORMAN GUNSTON .... Garry McDonald
BOB HOPE .... Leslie Townes Hope
HUDSON & LANDRY .... Robert Hudson and Ronald Landry
JONES & HARE .... Billy Jones and Ernest Hare
SPIKE JONES .... Lindley Armstrong Jones
ISH KABIBBLE .... Merwyn Bogue
TEDD LAWSON .... Theodore Howard Lehrman

JOAN RIVERS — Joan Molinsky

WOODY ALLEN — Allan Stewart Konigsberg

JERRY LEWIS	Joseph Levitch
MOMS MABLEY	Loretta Mary Aiken
MAD RUSSIAN, THE	Bert Gordon
PIGMEAT MARKHAM	Dewey Markham
GROUCHO MARX	Julius Henry Marx
MAX MILLER	Harold Sargent
SPIKE MILLIGAN	Terence Alan Milligan
MORAN & MACK (TWO BLACK CROWS)	George Searchy and Charles Emmett Sellers
ERIC MORCOMBE	Eric Bartholomew
BOB NEWHART	George Robert Newhart
MIKE NICHOLS	Michael Igor Peschowsky
JACK OAKIE	Lewis D. Offield
THORNDIKE PICKLEDISH	Robert O. Smith
JOAN RIVERS	Joan Molinsky
RODNEY RUDE	Rodney Keft
PETER SELLERS	Richard Henry Sellers
FRANKIE SIDEBOTTOM	Frank Sievey
SOUPY SALES	Milton Hines Supman
SMOTHERS BROTHERS, THE	Tom and Dick Smothers
AUSTEN TAYSHUS	Alexander Jacob Gutman
LILY TOMLIN	Mary Jean Tomlin
VAN & SCHENCK	Gus Van and Joseph Schenck
WAYNE & SHUSTER	Johnny Wayne and Frank Shuster
WEBER & FIELDS	Joe (Morris) Weber and Lew Fields (Moses Schanfield)

BOB HOPE —
Leslie Townes Hope

JASPER CARROT — Robert Davies

Borge Rosenbaum

Lindley Armstrong Jones

CHEECH & CHONG — Richard Anthony Marin and Thomas Chong

LOUIS BELLSON — Louis Balassoni

JAZZ MUSICIANS
Altered Full Names
or Surnames

GENE ADAMS	Raymond R. Saraceni	Piano
JOE ALBANY	Joseph Albani	Piano
DON ALBERT	Albert Dominique	Trumpet
DANNY ALVIN	Daniel Viniello	Drums
SIDNEY T. ARODIN	Sidney J. Arnondrin	Reeds
MARVIN ASH	Marvin Ashbaugh	Piano
GEORGE AULD	John Altwerger	Reeds
LOVIE AUSTIN	Cora Calhoun	Piano
LOUIS BELLSON	Louis Balassoni	Drums
LOU BENNETT	Louis Benoit	Organ
VIC BERTON	Victor Cohen	Percussion/Vibes
ARTHUR BLACK	Arthur Murray Blythe	Saxes
JERRY BLAKE	Jachinto Chabania	Reeds/Vocals
WILLIE BOBO	William Correa	Percussion
WILL BRADLEY	Wilbur Schwichtenberg	Trombone
GEORGE BRAITH	George Braithwaite	Reeds
GEORG BRUNIS	George Clarence Brunies	Trombone
BARBARA CARROLL	Barbara Carole Coppersmith	Piano
BOB CARTER	Robert Kahakalau	Bass
LEE CASTLE	Lee Castaido	Trumpet
TEDDY CHARLES	Edward Charles Cohen	Vibes
ARNETT CLEOPHUS COBB	Arnette Cobbs	Tenor Sax
CHRIS COLUMBUS	Joseph Christopher Columbus Morris	Drums
DICK CONTI	Richard Frank Cuchetti	Trumpet
BERT DALE	Nils-Bertil Dahlander	Drums/Piano
FRANK DE LA ROSA	Francisco Estaban Jnr.	Bass
WILLIE DENNIS	William De Berardinis	Trombone
WILL DENTON	William Joseph Nieberding	Trombone
PAUL DESMOND	Paul Breitenfeld	Alto Sax
PAUL DE SOUZA	Joao Jose Periera De Souza	Multi Inst.
JOAO DONATO	Joao Donato de Oliviera	Piano/Trombone
DON ELLIOTT	Donald Elliott Helfman	Vibes/Trumpet
ZIGGY ELMAN	Harry Finkelman	Trumpet
RICHARD ESTES	Richard Scott Dickey	Trumpet
GIL EVANS	Ian Ernest Gilmore Green	Piano
SLIM (RAY) EVANS	Otis Neirouter	Reeds
JOE FARRELL	Joseph Carl Firrantello	Reeds
IRVING HENRY FAZOLA	Irving Henry Prestopnik	Reeds
MARTY FLAX	Martin Flachsenhaar	Bar. Sax
LOU GARDNER	Louis Joseph Guardino	Violin
DUSKO GOYKOVICH	Dusan Gojkovic	Trumpet
TOMMY GRECO	Thomas Giangreco	Trumpet/Trombone
FERDE GROFE	Ferdinand Rudolph Von Grofe	Piano
SADIK HAKIN	Argonne Dense Thornton	Piano
JOHNNY HAMMOND	John Robert Smith	Piano
NOBUO HARA	Nobuo Tsu Kahara	Reeds
MORT HERBERT	Morton Herbert Pelovitz	Bass
ANDREW HILL	Andrew Hille	Piano
BART HOWARD	Howard Joseph Gustafson	Piano
GENE MAC HOWELL	Alfred Howell Bartles	Piano
PRESTON JACKSON	James Preston McDonald	Trombone
PETE JOLLY	Peter A. Ceragioli	Keyboards
CONNIE KAY (MJQ)	Conrad Henry Kirnon	Drums
BOB KEENE	Robert Kuhn	Clarinet
STUART KIRK	Charles Kincheleo	Piano
STEVE LACY	Steven Lackritz	Soprano Sax
EDDIE LANG	Salvatore Massaro	Guitar

145

RONNIE LANG	Ronald Langinger	Alto Sax
YUSEF LATEEF	William Evans	Flute
CHARLES LAVERE	Charles LaVere Johnson	Piano/Reeds
ARNIE LAWRENCE	Arnold Lawrence Finkelstein	Reeds
YANK LAWSON	John R. Lausen	Trumpet
BERNIE LEIGHTON	Bernard Lazeroff	Piano
GEORGE LEWIS	George Louis Francis Zeno	Reeds
MEL LEWIS	Melvin Sokoloff	Drums
EDDY LOUISS	Edouardo Louise	Organ/Trumpet
JOHNNY LUCE	John Lucciola	Sax
JIMMY LYTELL	James Sarrapede	Clarinet
ADAM MAKOWICZ	Adam Matyszkowicz	Piano
CHARLES MARLOW	Charles Margulis	Trumpet
CHINK MARTIN	Martin Abraham	Bass/Tuba/Guitar
PAT MARTINO	Patrick Azzara	Guitar
BROTHER JACK McDUFF	Eugene McDuffy	Keyboards
TODD McKAY	Mansell Brown McKalip	Reeds
BUDDY MERRIL	Leslie Merrill Behunin	Guitar
MEZ MEZZROW	Milton Mesirow	Reeds
BUTCH MILES	Charles J. Thornton Jnr.	Drums
EDDIE MILLER	Edward Lisbona	Piano
KID PUNCH MILLER	Ernest Burden	Trumpet
JOHNNY MINCE	John Henry Muenzenberger	Reeds
BUDDY MORROW	Muni 'Moe' Zudekoff	Trombone
SNUB MOSLEY	Lawrence Leo Mosely	Trombone
PHIL NAPOLEON	Fillippo Napoli	Trumpet
JAMIL SULIEMAN NASSER	George Leon Joyner	Bass
BIG EYE NELSON	Louis DeLisle	Clarinet
PAUL NERO	Kurt Polnarioff	Violin
DON NICHOLAS	Nicholas De Collibus	Violin
RED NORVO	Kenneth Norville	Percussion/Piano
MAMIE O'DELL	Marybelle Cruger DeLoriea	Piano
CHARLES M. OWENS	Charles M. Brown	Tenor Sax
TONY PASTOR	Antonio Pestritto	Tenor Sax
SANTO J. PECORA	Santo J. Pecoraro	Trombone
BUDDY PETIT	Buddy Crawford	Cornet
FLIP PHILLIPS	Joseph Edward Filipelli	Reeds
DEE DEE PIERCE	Joseph De Lacrois	Trumpet

Wilbur Schwichtenberg

Kenneth Norville

GEORGE AULD — John Altwerger

CHARLES VENTURA — Charles Venturo

TEDDY (THEODORE) POWELL	Alfred Paolella	Violin/Guitar
OLLIE POWERS	Oliver Powell	Drums
CHANO POZO	Luciano Pozo Y. Gonzales	Bongos
JOHN RAE	John Anthony Pompeo	Drums
LIONEE RAND	Lionel Randolph Clouser	Piano
KID RENA	Henry Rene	Trumpet
EMIL RICHARDS	Emilio Joseph Radocchia	Vibes
VIN RODDIE	Vincent Rodomista	Piano
RED RODNEY	Robert Chudnick	Trumpet
MILT ROGERS	Milton Adelstein	Piano
FELIX ROVIN	Fisher Asher Rabinovitch	Drums/Percussion
BENNY SAKS	Benjamin Sakamaki	Piano
JOE SAYE	Joseph Shulman	Piano
TONY SCOTT	Anthony Sciacca	Clarinet
SHORTY SHEROCK	Clarence Francis Cherock	Trumpet
HYMIE SHERTZER	Herman Schertzer	Alto Sax
BOBBY SHEW	Robert Joratz	Trumpet
SHAIB SHIHAB	Edmund Gregory	Reeds
EDDIE SHU	Edward Shulman	Reeds/Harmonica
WILLIE 'THE LION' SMITH	William Henry Joseph Bonoparte Bertholoff	Piano
TONY SPARGO (ODJB)	Antonio Sharbaro	Drums/Kazoo
LES STRAND	Leslie Roy Strandt	Organ/Piano
JOE SULLIVAN	Dennis Patrick Terence Joseph O'Sullivan	Piano
JOE TARTO	James Tortoriello	Bass/Tuba
LARRY THOMAS	Lawrence A. Miner	Percussion
NICK TRAVIS	Nicholas Anthony Travascio	Trumpet
TURK VAN LAKE	Vanig Hovespian	Guitar
CHARLIE VENTURA	Charles Venturo	Reeds
VINNIE WALLACE	Vincent Gambino	Tenor Sax
GEORGE WALLINGTON	Giorgio Figlia	Piano
CHUCK WAYNE	Charles Jagelka	Guitar
MARY LOU WILLIAMS	Mary Alfrieda Winn/Burleigh	Piano
RAY WILLOW	Raymond Lawrence Wierzbowski	Reeds
ANTHONY ZAND	Anthony Joseph Ferranzo	Piano

T. BONE WALKER — Aaron Thibeaux Walker

BULLMOOSE JACKSON —
Benjamin Clarence Jackson

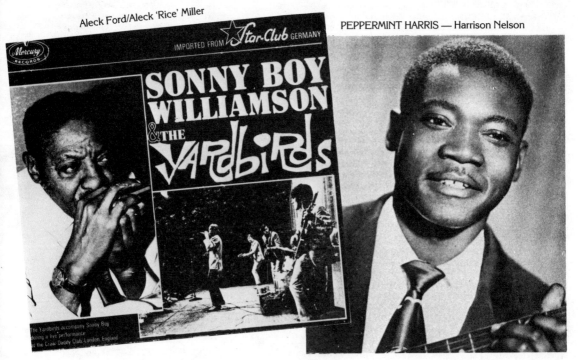

Aleck Ford/Aleck 'Rice' Miller

PEPPERMINT HARRIS — Harrison Nelson

148

BLUES PERFORMERS
Real Names

TEXAS ALEXANDER	Alger Alexander
MAE ALIX†	Liza May Alix
KOKOMO ARNOLD (GITFIDDLE JIM)	James Arnold
JOHN HENRY BARBEE	William George Tucker
JUKE BOY BARNER/BONNER	Weldon H. Philip Bonner
ED BARRON	Clyde Edric Barron Bernhardt
ALLEN BAUM (TARHEEL SLIM)	Alden Bunn
CAREY BELL	Carey Bell Harrington
LONG JOHN BINDER	Dennis Binder
SCRAPPER BLACKWELL	Francis Hillman Blackwell
LITTLE JOE BLUE	Joseph Valery Jnr.
EDDIE BO	Edward Bocage
BEA(TRICE) BOOZE	Muriel Nicholls
LONNIE BROOKS (GUITAR JUNIOR)	Lee Baker Jnr.
ADA BROWN	Ada Scott
GATEMOUTH BROWN	Clarence Brown
LILLIAN BROWN	Lillian Thomas
NAPPY BROWN	Napoleon Brown
RABBIT BROWN	Richard Brown
BUTCH CAGE	James Cage
GUNTER LEE CARR	Cecil Gant
JEANNE CARROLL	Albertha Jeanne Carroll
BO CARTER/CHATMAN	Armenter Chatmon
BOOZOO CHAVIS	Wilson Chavis
DOC CLAYTON	Peter Joe Cleighton
EDDY CLEARWATER (GUITAR EDDY)	Eddy Harrington
JAYBIRD COLEMAN	Burl Coleman
PEE WEE CRAYTON	Connie Curtis Crayton
BARBARA DANE	Barbara Jean Spillman
COW COW DAVENPORT	Charles Edward Davenport
MERCY DEE	Mercy Dee Walton
BLIND SNOOKS EAGLIN	Ford Eaglin
HONEYBOY EDWARDS	David Edwards
PETE FRANKLIN (GUITAR PETE)	Edward Lamonte Franklin
BLIND BOY FULLER	Fulton Allen
LITTLE BOY FULLER	Rich Trice
GRANDPAPPY GIBSON	Clifford Gibson
LEOLA B. GRANT	Leola B. Pettigrew
LIL GREEN	Lillian Johnson
BUDDY GUY	George Guy
VERA HALL	Vera Hall Ward
W. C. HANDY	William Christopher Handy
HI-TIDE HARRIS††	William Boyd/Gitry
PEPPERMINT HARRIS	Harrison Nelson
BUDDY BOY HAWKINS	Walter Hawkins
ROSALIE HILL	Rosa Lee Hemphill
MABLE HILLERY	Mable Henderson
SMOKEY HOGG	Andrew Hogg
LIGHTNIN' HOPKINS	Samuel Hopkins
PUG HORTON	Barbara Joanne Horton nee Kitcheman
SON HOUSE	Eddie James House Jnr.
PEG LEG HOWELL	Joshua Barnes Howell
J. B. HUTTO	Joseph Benjamin Hutto
BO-WEAVIL JACKSON	James Jackson

BULLMOOSE JACKSON	Benjamin Clarence Jackson
LEE JACKSON	Warren George Harding Lee
SAM JACKSON	Arthur Jackson
SKIP JAMES	Nehemiah James
HALF PINT JAXON	Frankie Jaxon
BO BO JENKINS	J. P. Jenkins
LUTHER JOHNSON	Lucius Brinson Johnson
STUMP JOHNSON	James Johnson
SYL JOHNSON	Sylvester Thompson
BIRMINGHAM JONES	Wright Birmingham
MAGGIE JONES	Fae Barnes
AL KING	Alvin K. Smith
JEAN KITTRELL	Ethel Jean Kittrell nee McCarty
JOHN LEE	John Lee Henley
TOMMY LEE	Thomas Lee Thompson
FURRY LEWIS	Walter Lewis
PETE 'GUITAR' LEWIS	Carl Lewis
SMILEY LEWIS	Overton Amos Lemons
PAPA LIGHTFOOT	Alexander Lightfoot
ABBEY LINCOLN	Anna Marie Woolridge
JOHNNY LITTLEJOHN	John Funchess
JOE HILL LOUIS	Lester Hill
SHORTSTUFF MACON	John Wesley Macon
SARAH MARTIN	Sara Dunn
VIOLA McCOY	Amanda Brown
BROWNIE McGHEE	Walter Brown McGhee
LIZZIE MILES	Elizabeth Mary Pajaud nee Landeraux
BIG MILLER	Clarence Horatio Miller
LITTLE BROTHER MONTGOMERY	Eurreal Wilford Montgomery
ROBERT NIGHTHAWK	Robert Lee McCollum
HAMMIE NIXON	Hammie Davis
TINY POWELL	Vance Powell
SNOOKY PRYOR	James Edward Pryor
YANK RACHELL	James Rachell
MA RAINEY	Gertrude Rainey nee Pridgett
MEMPHIS MA RAINEY	Lilian Glover
DOCTOR ROSS	Charles Isaiah Ross
SON SEALS	Frank Junior Seals
GEORGE 'HARMONICA' SMITH	Allen George Smith
PINETOP SMITH	Clarence Smith
THUNDER SMITH	Wilson Smith
WHISPERING SMITH	Moses Smith
SMOKEY SMOTHERS	Otis Smothers
KING SOLOMON	Ellis Solomon
BIG BOY SPIRES	Arthur Spires
BABE STOVALL	Jewell Stovall
EVA TAYLOR	Irene Gibbons
HOUND DOG TAYLOR	Theodore Roosevelt Taylor
KOKO TAYLOR	Cora Taylor nee Walton
LITTLE JOHNNY TAYLOR	John Lamar Young
DOC TERRY	Terry Adail
SONNY TERRY	Saunders Terrell
RAMBLIN' THOMAS	Willard Thomas
BIG MAMA THORNTON	Willie Mae Thornton
BIG SON TILLIS	Ellas Tillis
T. BONE WALKER	Aaron Thibeaux Walker
T. BONE WALKER JNR.	R. S. Rankin
SIPPIE WALLACE	Beaulah Wallace nee Thomas
BABY BOY WARREN	Robert Warren
D. C. WASHINGTON	D. C. Bendy
CROWN PRINCE WATERFORD	Charles Waterford

```
JUNIOR WELLS ................................................................................................................ Amos Blackmore
PEETIE WHEATSTRAW ...................................................................................................... William Bunch
ЬUKKA WHITE ................................................................................... Booker T. Washington White
GEORGIA WHITE ........................................................................................................... Georgia Lawson
HUDSON WHITTAKER (TAMPA RED) ........................................................ Hudson Woodbridge
DOC WILEY ......................................................................................................................... Arnold Wiley
HENRY 'RUBBER LEGS' WILLIAMS ........................................................... Henry Williamson
SUNNY WILLIAMS .............................................................................................................. Enoch Williams
JAMES WILLIAMSON (HOMESICK JAMES) ........................ John William Henderson
SONNY BOY WILLIAMSON #1††† ............................. Aleck Ford/Aleck 'Rice' Miller (b. 1899)
SONNY BOY WILLIAMSON #2 .......................................... John Lee Williamson (b. 1914)
HOP WILSON ................................................................................................................... Harding Wilson
MAMA YANCEY ............................................................................................................ Estella Yancey
PAT YANKEE ................................................................................... Patricia Millicent Weigum
```

† May Alix was also used as a pseudonymn by Alberta Hunter and Edna Hicks.
†† Harris was Huddie Ledbetter's singing voice in the movie *Leadbelly*.
††† Aleck was the illegitimate son of Millie Ford. He adopted stepfather Jim Miller's surname. Rice was a childhood pet name.

BLUES TRADE NAMES

With apologies to the amazing Sheldon Harris, anybody who attempts a serious quantification of any aspect of the blues is either a fool or a masochist. The entire subject is a researcher's nightmare, for a variety of reasons.

Although the form as we know it is around 75 years old, press coverage and enthusiast's documentation dates back only 30-35 years. Even those eras, regions and styles that have received attention still offer a maze of contradictions and confusions.

In the southern states of America where black performers created the raw, honest music that is commonly referred to as 'the blues', artists worked in virtual isolation, their contact with other performers and songs generally limited to their own state or portion thereof. As long as the name they chose was not being used by anyone else in their neck of the woods, they staked claim to it. Thus we have three Guitar Slims, two Sonny Boy Williamsons, two Harmonica Slims, three Piano Reds and two Washboard Sams; with no Musicians Union or Patents Office to adjudicate one way or another. Blues names were dispensed with like broken guitar picks. Some performers came up with a new handle for every new town, sometimes every new club. If a record on one tiny label failed under one name, it was off to the next city for another record, on another label, under another name. Not surprisingly, great quantities of recordings have still to be matched with the right performer, a work that may never be complete. A number of artists, such as Red Minter, Blind Willie McTell and Big Bill Broonzy, operated under at least ten different names. Sometimes name variations could be put down to basic illiteracy on the part of both singer and employer.

This humble attempt at coverage of blues names tends to concentrate on significant recording artists and makes no pretense of being complete. Further Blues Trade Names (generally those employed by known artists as an adjunct to their more common identities) are included in the next section.

```
ALABAMA SLIM ......................................................................................................................... Ralph Willis
BABY DOO ........................................................................................................................... Leonard Caston
BANJO JOE ................................................................................................................................ Gus Cannon
BARBEQUE BOB ....................................................................................................................... Robert Hicks
BARRELHOUSE BUCK ...................................................................................................... Buck McFarland
BIG AMOS ............................................................................................................................... Amos Patton
BIG LOUISIANA .................................................................................................................. Rodney Mason
BIG MACEO .................................................................................................... Maceo Merriweather
BIG MAYBELLE ........................................................................................... Mabel Louise Smith
BIG MOOSE ............................................................................................................................ John Walker
BIG SUNFLOWER ...................................................................................................................... Bob Hall
BIG WALTER #1 ................................................................................................................. Walter Horton
BIG WALTER #2 ................................................................................................................... Walter Price
BILLY BOY .......................................................................................................................... William Arnold
BLACK ACE .............................................................................................. Babe Kyre Lemon Turner
BLACK DIAMOND ....................................................................................................................... James Butler
BLIND BLAKE ............................................................................................................. Blake Alphonso Higgs
BLIND TOM ........................................................................................... Thomas Greene Bethune
BLUE SMITTY ..................................................................................................................... Clarence Smith
BOOGIE JAKE ..................................................................................................................... Matthew Jacobs
BOOGIE WOOGIE RED ................................................................................................... Vernon Harrison
BUMBLE BEE SLIM ................................................................................................................ Amos Easton
COOL PAPA ............................................................................................................... Haskell Robert Sadler
```

COUNTRY JIM	James Bledsoe
COUNTRY SLIM	Ernest Lewis
COUSIN LEROY	Leroy Rozier
DIRTY RED	Nelson Wilborn
DOCTOR HEPCAT	Lavada Durst
FOREST CITY JOE	Joseph Pugh
GATOR TAIL	Willis Jackson
GOOD ROCKIN' SAM	Sam Beasley
GUITAR NUBBITT	Alvin Hankerson
GUITAR SHORTY	John Henry Fortesque
GUITAR SLIM #1	Eddie Jones
GUITAR SLIM #2	Norman Green
GUITAR SLIM #3	Alec Seward
HARMONICA FRANK	Frank Floyd
HARMONICA KING, THE	George Smith
HARMONICA SLIM #1	James Moore
HARMONICA SLIM #2	Travis L. Blaylock
HARP BLOWIN' SAM	Sam Fowler
HOMER THE GREAT	Connie Curtis Crayton
HOMESICK JAMES	John A. Williamson
HOWLIN' WOLF	Chester Arthur Burnett
JELLY BELLY	Louis Hayes
KING IVORY LEE	Lee Semiens
LAZY BILL	William Lucas
LAZY LESTER	Leslie Johnson
LIGHTNIN' SLIM	Otis V. Hicks
LITTLE AL	Al Gunter
LITTLE DAVID	David Wylie
LITTLE SON/SONNY	Aaron Willis
LITTLE WALTER #1	Marion Walter Jacobs
LITTLE WALTER #2	'Babyface' Leroy Foster
LONESOME LEE	Jimmy Lee Robinson
LONESOME SUNDOWN	Cornelius Green
LONG JOHN	John Hunter
LONG TALL LESTER	Lester Foster
LU BLUE/BLUE LU	Louisa Barker
MAGIC SAM	Sam Maghett
MAGIC SLIM	Morris Holt
MEMPHIS MINNIE #1	Lizzie Douglas
MEMPHIS MINNIE #2	Mamie Smith
MEMPHIS SLIM #1	Peter Chatman
MEMPHIS SLIM #2	Charles Davenport
MEMPHIS WILLIE B.	William Borum
MERCY BABY	Jimmy Mullins
MISS PEACHES	Elsie Griner Jnr.
PIANO RED #1 (aka DR. FEELGOOD)	William Lee Perryman
PIANO RED #2	Vernon Harrison
PIANO RED #3	Vance Patterson
POLKA DOT SLIM	Vincent Monroe
POOR BOB	Bob Woodfork
POPPY HOP	Wilson Harding
ROCKIN' SIDNEY	Sidney Semien
SHAKEY JAKE	James D. Harris
SLIM HARPO	James Moore
SLY FOX, THE	Eugene Fox
SON BRIMMER	Will Shade
SONNY BOY	Arthur Smith
SPECKLED RED/DETROIT RED	Rufus G. Perryman
SPIDER SAM	Harry Van Walls
SWEET EMMA	Emma Barrett
TAMPA RED	Hudson Whittaker
TOO TIGHT HENRY #1	Henry Townshend
TOO TIGHT HENRY #2	Henry Lee Castle
TREE TOP SLIM	William Ealey
T.V. SLIM	Oscar Wills
UKULELE KID	Charlie Burse
WASHBOARD SAM #1	Robert Brown
WASHBOARD SAM #2	Albert Johnson
WASHBOARD WILLIE	William Paden Hensley

BIG MAYBELLE — Mabel Louise Smith

BLUES ALIASES

LOTTIE BEAMAN .... Jennie Brooks/Lottie Brown/Clara Cary/Lottie Everson/
Lottie Kimbrough (MN)/Lena Kimbrough/Mae Morgan

*SCRAPPER BLACKWELL .... Frankie Black

BIRLEANNA BLANKS .... Berlina/Berlevia/Birlianna/Biriliannia/Berlina

LUCILLE BOGAN .... Bessie Jackson

'BIG' BILL BROONZY .... Big Bill/Blues Boy Bill/Big Bill Broomsley/Chicago Bill/
Slim Hunter/Big Bill Johnson/Little Son/
Little Sam/Natchez/Sammy Sampson

BESSIE BROWN #1 .... Sadie Green/Caroline Lee

*LILLIAN BROWN .... Fannie Baker/Elbrown/Mildred Fernandez/Maude Jones/Lillyn Brown

ROBERT BROWN .... Washboard Sam/Ham Gravy/Shufflin' Sam/Smoky Babe

EDDIE BURNS .... Slim Pickens/Big Ed/Swing Brother

SAMUEL COLLINS .... Bunny Carter/Jim Foster/Salty Dog Sam/Big Boy Woods/Cryin' Sam

IDA COX .... Velma Bradley/Kate Lewis/Julia Powers/Jane Smith/Ida Prather (MN)

ARTHUR CRUDUP .... Percy Lee Crudup/Art Crudux/Arthur Crump/
Elmer James/Big Boy Crudup

THEODORE DARBY .... Blind Squire Turner

TOM DORSEY .... Barrelhouse Tommy/Georgia Tom/Memphis Jim/Memphis Mose/
George Ramsey/Railroad Bill/Smokehouse Charley/Texas Tommy

LIZZIE DOUGLAS .... Memphis Minnie/Minnie McCoy/Texas Tessie/Gospel Minnie

WILLIAM THOMAS DUPREE .... Champion Jack Dupree/Big Tom Collins/Blind Boy Johnson/
Meathead Johnson/Jordan Lightning Jnr./Brother Blues

JOHN J. ERBY .... George Seymour/Guy Smith/J. Guy Suddoth/Jack Erby

EDDIE HARRIS .... Carolina Slim/Country Paul/Georgia Pine/Jammin' Jim/Lazy Slim Jim

LUCILLE HEGAMIN .... Fanny Baker

ROSA HENDERSON .... Flora Dale/Rosa Green/Mae Harris/Mamie Harris/Sara Johnson/
Sally Ritz/Josephine Thomas/Gladys White/
Bessie Williams/Rosa DeChamps (MN)

CHARLEY HICKS .... Cat Juice Charley/Laughin' Charley/Charley(ie) Lincoln

JOHN LEE HOOKER .... Birmingham Sam/John Lee Booker/Boogie Man/John Lee Cooker/
Delta John/Johnny Lee/Texas Slim/Johnny Williams

WALTER HORTON .... Shakey Horton/Big Walter/Tangle Eye/Shakey Walter/Mumbles/Walter

ALBERTA HUNTER .... Josephine Beatty/Helen Roberts/May Alix

*BULLMOOSE JACKSON .... Sam Taylor/Panama Francis/Moose Jackson

ELMORE JAMES .... Elmo James/Joe Willie

'BLIND' LEMON JEFFERSON .... Deacon L.J. Bates/Elder J.C. Brown

GUS JENKINS .... The Young Wolf/Little Temple/Gus Jinkins

*LUTHER JOHNSON .... Georgia Boy/Luther King/Little Luther/Snake Johnson

*STUMP JOHNSON .... Little Man/Snitcher Roberts/Shorty George

PLEASANT JOSEPH .... Cousin Joe/Brother Joshua/Cousin Joseph/
Cousin Joe Pleasant/Smiling Joe/Pleasant Joe

ALBERT LAUNDREW .... Sunnyland Slim/Delta Joe/Doctor Clayton's Buddy

*LEADBELLY .... Walter Boyd

*PAPA LIGHTFOOT .... Little Papa Walter/Papa George/George Lightfoot

*JOE HILL LOUIS .... Chicago Sunny Boy/Johnny Lewis/Little Joe

*SARAH MARTIN .... Margaret Johnson/Sally Roberts/Sara Withers (MN)

JOE McCOY .... Big Joe/Georgia Pine Boy/Halleluja Joe/Hamfoot Ham/Kansas Joe/
Mississippi Mudder/Mud Dauber Joe/Bill Wilber

*VIOLA McCOY .... Violet McCoy/Daisy Cliff/Fannie Johnson/Gladys Johnson/
Clara White/Susan Williams/Bessie Williams

*BROWNIE McGHEE .... Brother McGhee/Big Tom Collins/Blind Boy Fuller #2/Henry Johnson/
Spider Sam/Tennessee Gabriel/Blind Boy Williams

'BLIND' WILLIE McTELL .... Barrelhouse Sammy/Blind Doogie/Blind Sammy/Blind Willie/
Georgia Bill/Red Hot Willie Glaze/Hot Shot Willie/
Pig 'n' Whistle Red/Red Hot Willie

ELMON MICKLE .... Driftin' Slim/Driftin' Smith/Harmonica Harry/Model T. Slim

JOSIE MILES .... Evangelist Mary Flowers/Pearl Harris/Augusta Jones

*LIZZIE MILES .... Mandy Smith

IVERSON 'RED' MINTER .... Iverson Bey/Cryin' Red/Playboy Fuller/Guitar Red/
Walkin' Slim/Richard Lee Fuller/Rocky Fuller/
Elmore James Jnr./Rockin' Red/Louisiana Red

MONETTE MOORE .... Ethel Mayes/Nettie Potter/Susie Smith/Grace White

*ROBERT NIGHTHAWK .... Robert Lee McCoy/Pettie's Boy/Ramblin' Bob

JIMMIE ODEN .... Old Man/Big Bloke/Poor Boy/St. Louis Jimmy

CHARLEY PATTON .... Charley Peters/The Masked Marvel

ARTHUR PHELPS	Blind Blake #2/Blind Arthur/Gorgeous Weed/Billy James/Blind George Martin
GERTRUDE 'MA' RAINEY	Mama Can Can/Madame Rainey/Lila Patterson/Anne Smith/Black Nightingale
ALEC SEWARD	Guitar Slim/Slim Seward/Georgia Slim/Blues Boy/Blues King
MICK SIMMONS	Mac Sims/Little Mack/St. Louis Mac/Mac Simmons
EARL SINKS	Earl Henry/Sinx Mitchell/Snake Richards/Earl Richards
CLARA SMITH	Violet Green
GEORGE 'HARMONICA' SMITH	George Allen/Harmonica King/Little Walter Jnr.
VICTORIA SPIVEY	Jane Lucas
ROOSEVELT SYKES	The Honeydripper/Easy Papa Johnson/Willie Kelly/Dobby Bragg/The Blues Man
*EVA TAYLOR	Catherine Henderson/Irene Williams
*SONNY TERRY	Sanders Terry/Sonny T./Sonny
LOU WATTS	Tommy Lewis/Tommy Louis/Kid Thomas
WILL WELDON	Casey Bill/Kansas City Bill/Levee Joe
VIOLA WELLS	Viola Underhill/Miss Rhapsody
JOSH WHITE	Pinewood Tom/The Singing Christian/Tippy Barton
JOE LEON WILLIAMS	Jody Williams/Sugar Boy Williams/Little Papa Joe
SONNY BOY WILLIAMSON #1	Little Boy Blue/Sib

* Refer to index for real name.   (MN) Maiden Name

'HIS MINNIE #1 — Lizzie Douglas

EVA TAYLOR — Irene Gibbons, aka
Catherine Henderson, Irene Williams

JOHN LEE HOOKER used eight pseudonymns.

CHAMPION JACK DUPREE — William Thomas Dupree, used six pseudonymns.

DANNY THOMAS — Amos Jacobs

Betty Carter-Social Call

BETTY

Lillie Mae Jones

Oswald George Nelson and Peggy Lou Hilliard nee Snyder

IMPERIAL LP-9049
HI-FIDELITY

OZZIE and HARRIET

STEREO-SPECTRUM

DENNIS DAY SINGS

Christmas is for the Family

WITH ORCHESTRA AND BOYS CHOIR

DESIGN

Eugene McNulty

156

BIG BAND/TORCH/ JAZZ/BROADWAY/ GOSPEL SINGERS

ROBERT ALDA .... Alphonso D'Abruzzo
LAURIE ALLEN .... Jean Ann Delgrosso
LEE ROY ANTHONY .... Lee Roy Abernathy
BOBBY ARVON .... Robert Anthony Arvonio
JAN AUGUST .... Janet Augustoff
GENE AUSTIN .... Eugene Lucas
ALICE BABS .... Alice Nilson
MILDRED BAILEY .... Mildred Rinker
BONNIE BAKER .... Evelyn Nelson
MICKEY BASS .... Lee Oddis Bass III
YOLANDE BAVAN .... Yolande Mari Wolffe
NORA BAYES .... Dora Goldberg
JOHN BRADFORD .... John Milton Levinson
BENNY BELL .... Paul Wynn
SUE BENNETT .... Susan Benjamin
JANET BLAIR .... Martha Janet Lafferty
CONNEE BOSWELL† .... Constance Foore'Boswell
JOHN BRADFORD .... John Milton Levinson
PHIL BRITO .... Philip Colombrito
HENRY BURR .... Harry McClasky
VIC CAESAR .... Victor Louis Cesario
LEW CAREY .... Lewis D. Conetta
NANCY CARROLL .... Ann Veronica Lahiff
JAMES CARSON .... James William Roberts
BETTY CARTER .... Lillie Mae Jones
JUNE CHRISTY .... Shirley Luster
STEVE CLAYTON .... Patrick Louis Tedesco
BUDDY CLARK .... Samuel Goldberg
JOE COOK .... Joseph Lopez
KEN CURTIS .... Curtis Gates
VIKKI DALE .... Rose Leonore Victoria Biondo
CASS DALEY .... Catherine Dailey
DON DARCY/D'ARCY .... John Arcesi
RUSTY DAVIS .... James Russell Cheeseman
DOLLY DAWN (& HER DAWN PATROL) .... Theresa Maria Stabile
HAZEL DAWN .... Hazel Latout
DENNIS DAY .... Eugene McNulty
ALFRED DRAKE .... Alfred Capurro
DUKE DUMAS (STAMPS QUARTET) .... James Madison Dumas
BOB EBERLY .... Robert Eberle
BILL FARRELL .... William Fiorelli
TEX FENSTER .... Harry Fenster
KITTY FURNISS .... Cathy Cowan
OTTHO GAINES .... Leo Gaines
SID GARRY/GARY .... Sidney Garfunkel
ALMA GLUCK .... Reba Fiersohn
MAXIE GREEN .... Susan M. Greenberg
CONNIE HAINES (aka YVONNE MARIE) .... Yvonne Marie Jamais

JOHN HODGKINSON	John Meadowcraft
LIBBY HOLMAN	Elspeth Holtzman
BOB HOWARD	Howard Joyner
CAROLYN HOWARD	Caroline Horowitz
BETTY HUTTON	Betty June Thornburg
MARION HUTTON	Marion Thornburg
ROBERTO INGLEZ	Robert English
PINOCCHIO JAMES	Cornelius James
BEVERLY JANIS	Beverly Myers Shapiro
ELSIE JANIS	Elsie Bierbauer
SALENA JONES	Joan Shaw
EDDIE KAIN	Edward Howard Kimmel
ALVIN KALEOLANI	Alvin Kalanikauikealaneo
HELEN KANE	Helen Schroder
BILL KAY	William Myron Kaufman
BENNY KAYE	Benjamin Katz
GERRY KAYE	Geraldine Dolores Klug
PETER KAYE	Peter Kunatz
LINDA KEENE	Florence McCrory
BONNIE B. KING	Julia Helen Berndt
DENNIS KING	Dennis Pratt
ROBERT KOLE	Robert Kolodin
KARIN KROG	Karin Krog Bergh
NATALIE LAMB	Natalie Elston
SCRAPPY LAMBERT	Harold Lambert
FRANCES LANGFORD	Frances Newbern
SNOOKY LANSON	Roy Lanson
JIMMY LAWTON	James Dwaine Degraw
YAKIMA LEE	Lee L. Graham
EDDIE LEONARD	Lemuel Gordon Toney
WINNIE LIGHTNER	Winifred Hansen
ARTHUR LONDON	Art Lund
LILLIAN LORRAINE	Ealallean De Jaques
JON LUCIEN	Jon Lucien Harrigan
PEGGY MANN	Margaret Germano
LEO MANNES	Zeke Manners
MIRANDO MARAIS	Rosa Lily Odette Marais nee Baruch de la Pardo
BENNY MARTINI	Benjamin Anthony Azzara
ILONA MASSEY	Ilona Hajmassey
DAVID MASTERS	David Mark Burger
GARY McCLINTIC	Lambert Gerhardt McClintic
FRED MEADOWS	Ben Gordon
MARILYN MILLER	Mary Ellen Reynolds
MARIAN MONTGOMERY	Marian M. Holloway nee Runnels
DENNIS MORGAN	Stanley Morner
HELEN MORGAN	Helen Riggins
MAE MURRAY	Marie Koenig
HARRIET NELSON††	Peggy Lou Hilliard nee Snyder
RONNIE NELSON	Ronald Edward Niedhammer
ANITA O'DAY	Anita Colton
DODIE O'NEILL	Dolores O'Neill
JANIS PAIGE	Donna Marie Tjaden
TONY PASTOR	Antonio Pestritto
OTTILIE PATTERSON	Anna Ottilie Patterson
PENNY PRICE	Mayme Watts
SUE RANEY	Raelene Claire Claussin
CARL RAVELL	Carl Ravazza
JIMMY RAY	James Genovese
ANN RICHARDS	Margaret Ann Borden
HARRY RICHMAN	Harold Reichman
JIM ROBERTS	James Robert Caudle
DON RODNEY	Donald Ragonese
LILLIAN RUSSELL	Helen Louise Leonard

JULIA SANDERSON .... Julia Sackett
JOSEPH SANTLEY .... Joseph Mansfield
SERENA SHAW .... Lita De Saxe nee Davison
ETHEL SHUTTA .... Ethel Schutte
LEO SIEZAK .... Leo Schonberg
SINGIN' SAM .... Harry Frankel
SUNNY SKYLAR .... Selig Sidney Shaftel
JENNI SMITH .... Jo Ann Callison
KATE SMITH .... Kathryn Elizabeth Smith
BUTCH STONE .... Henry Stone
EDDIE STONE .... Edward Marblestone
BEVERLY STYLES .... Juanita Robins Carpenter
MAXINE SULLIVAN .... Marietta Williams
SISTER ROSETTA THARPE .... Rosetta Nubin
DANNY THOMAS ††† .... Amos Jacobs
PINKY TOMLIN .... Truman Tomlin
DES TOOLEY .... Amy Tooley nee Ruwald
RANDY VAN HORNE .... Harry Van Horne
LUPE VELEZ .... Guadaloupe Velez de Villa Lobos
NANCY WALKER .... Anna Myrtle Swoyer
DICK WALTERS .... Richard Showalter
RUSTY WARREN .... Ilene Goodman
FRANCIS WAYNE/CLAIRE .... Chiarina Francesca Berticci
TED WHITE .... Ted Weitz
JOAN WHITNEY .... Zoe Parenteau Whitney nee Kramer
JOHN WILDER .... John Balfour Ireson
CHICKIE WILLIAMS .... Jessie Wanda Williams nee Crupe
FRANCES WILLIAMS .... Frances Jellinek
BARRY WOOD .... Louis Rapp
FRAN ZIFFER .... Francis Burgid

† Ms Boswell changed her billing from Connie to Connee after dabbling in numerology.
†† Harriet married bandleader Ozzie Nelson and the pair became the parents of Rick and Dave Nelson.
††† Band singer, comedian and television star Danny Thomas adopted his name from the Christian names of his two brothers — Daniel and Thomas.

Harold Lambert

Dora Goldberg

Scrappy Bill
LAMBERT & HILLPOT
WITH BEN BERNIES ORCH.

159

NORA BAYES

BOB CROSBY — George Robert Crosby

GERALDO — Gerald Bright

James Monte Maloney

DAME NELLIE MELBA —
Helen Porter Mitchell

160

BAND/ORCHESTRA LEADERS

RAY ANTHONY .... Ray Antonini
MITCHELL AYRES .... Mitchell Agress
BEN BERNIE .... Benjamin Anzelwitz
LOU BREESE .... Louis Calabreese
SONNY BURKE .... John Francis Burke
FRANKIE CARLE .... Francis Nunzio Carlone
BOB CROSBY .... George Robert Crosby
DON DONSON .... Salvatore Scarpa
RAVEN GRAY EAGLE .... Andrea Nicola Florio
WALTER EDDY .... Walter Edelstein
DON ELLIOTT .... Donald Elliott Helfman
SKINNAY ENNIS .... Robert Ennis
LARRY FOTINE/'CONSTANTINE' .... Lawrence Constantine Fotinakis
GIL FULLER .... Walter Gilbert Fuller
AARON GANZ .... Aaron Ruben Gonzalez
GERALDO .... Gerald Bright
TOM GERUN .... Thomas Gerunovitch
TERRY GIBBS .... Julius Gubenko
JOHNNY GILES .... Giles Edward Mellenbruch
JERRY GRAY .... Jerry Graziano
GLEN GRAY (CASA LOMA ORCH.) .... Glen Gray Knoblaugh
NORMAN GREENE .... Norman Greenberg
MACHITO GRILLO .... Frank R. Grillo
SPIKE HAMILTON .... George Hamilton
CHICO HAMILTON .... Foreststorm Hamilton
BUSTER HARDING .... Lavere Harding
HAP HAZARD/JUSTIN CASE .... Paul Dean Hammett
SKITCH HENDERSON .... Lyle Henderson
SMACK HENDERSON .... James Fletcher Henderson
WILL HENRY .... William Henry Davies
CARL HOFF .... Carl Hoffmayr
LEROY HOLMES .... Alvin Holmes
SPIKE HUGHES .... Patrick C. Hughes
INA RAY HUTTON† .... Odessa Cowan
RED INGLE .... Ernest Jansen Ingle
JOHNNY JOHNSON .... Malcolm Johnson
JIMMY JOY .... James Monte Maloney
BERT KAEMPFERT .... Berthold Kaempfert
BERNIE KANE .... Frank Joseph Aquino
KAY KYSER .... James Kern Kyser
PAPA JACK LAINE .... George Vitelle Laine
SOL LAKE .... Soloman Lachoff
FRANK LA MARR .... Frank Joseph La Motta
ELLIOTT LAWRENCE .... Elliott Lawrence Broza
TED LEWIS .... Theodore Laopold Friedman
DOODLES LIEBER .... Marcus Edward Lieberstein
STEPHEN LORD/S. J. LOY .... Stephen Loyacano
ABE LYMAN .... Abraham Simon
CHICO MARX .... Leonard Marx
HOOTIE McSHANN .... Jay McShann
DEKE MOFFITT .... De Loyce Moffitt
OZZIE NELSON .... Oswald George Nelson
CHICO O'FARRILL .... Arturo O'Farrill
KING OLIVER .... Joseph Oliver
WILL OSBORNE .... William Oliphant
PAUL APGE .... Paul D. Brown
JOHNNY PINEAPPLE .... David Kaonhi
TITO PUENTE .... Ernest Puente Jnr.
SCOTT RAYMOND .... Harry Warnow
ALVINO REY .... Al McBurney
KING RICHARD('S FUEGEL KNIGHTS) .... Dick Behrke

DOC SEVERINSEN .... Carl H. Severinsen
ALLAN SMALL .... Alexander Scheibman
BLUE STEELE .... Gene Staples
CAPTAIN STUBBY (& BUCCANEERS) .... Thomas C. Fouts
DON SWAN .... Wilbur Clyde Schwandt
JOHNNY UKELELE .... John Kaaihue
AL VEGA .... Aram Vagramian
JERRY WALD .... Jervis Wald
TED WEEMS .... Wilfred Theodore Weymes
KAI WERNER†† .... Werner Last

† This sister of singer June Hutton and daughter of pianist Marvel Ray Hutton led an all-girl band.
†† Brother of James Last.

OPERA SINGERS

Being orientated toward popular music forms, this book presents only a modest opera listing, concentrating mostly upon well known identities.

As a contrast to pop/rock performers of European heritage who have traditionally tried to lose all trace of their origins by way of a name change and crash courses in American vernacular, many 'serious' singers have shown a tendency toward abandoning quite sturdy Anglo-Saxon names in favour of more exotic identities which, presumably, would not be out of place at La Scala.

EMMA ALBANI .... Marie Louise Cecile Emylie de Lajeunesse
NORBERT ARDELLI .... Norbert Adler
CESARE BAROMEO .... Chase Baromeo
RUDOLF BING† .... Rudolf Landau
EMMA CALVE .... Rosa Calvert
CASTLEMARY .... Comte Armand de Castan
MARIO CHAMLEE .... Archer Chalmondeley
HARRIET HENDERS .... Harriet Henderson
ALBERT LANCE .... Lance Ingram
ERNEST LERI† .... Ernest Joseph Maria Levi
DAME NELLIE MELBA†† .... Helen Porter Mitchell
ROBERT MERRILL .... Moishe Miller
EMMA NEVADA .... Emma Wixom
LILLIAN NORDICA .... Lillian Norton
ADELINA PATTI .... Adela Juana Maria Patti
JAN PEERCE .... Jacob Pearlman
ROSA PONSELLE .... Rosa Ponzillo
NORMAN SCOTT .... Norman Schultz
MARCELLA SEMBRICH .... Praxede Marcelline Kochanska
BEVERLY SILLS .... Belle Silverman
RISE STEVENS .... Rise Steenberg
RICHARD TUCKER .... Reuben Tickle
LEONARD WARREN .... Leonard Varenoff

† Opera managers/directors.   †† Assumed in tribute to her Australian birthplace, Melbourne.

POP SONGWRITING TEAMS

All record collectors are familiar with the recurring names which appear in the tiny brackets below the song title on a record label. So many of the truly great pop/rock hits bear the same credits — Leiber/Stoller, Goffin/King, Greenwich/Barry, Mann/Weil, etc. Rarely are these ace teams presented to us as anything more than two simple surnames. Accordingly their complete names are presented hereunder.

ADLER & ROSS .... Richard Adler and Jerry Ross
ANDERS & PONCIA .... Pete Anders* and Vinnie Poncia
ASHFORD & SIMPSON .... Nicholas Ashford and Valerie Simpson
BACHARACH & DAVID .... Burt Bacharach and Hal David
BATCHELOR & ROBERTS .... Ruth Batchelor and Bob Roberts
BICKERTON & WADDINGTON .... Wayne Bickerton and Tony Waddington
BONNER & GORDON .... Garry Bonner and Alan Lee Gordon
BOYCE & HART .... Tommy Boyce* and Bobby Hart*
BRECHT & WEILL .... Berthold Brecht and Kurt Weill

BRICUSSE & NEWLEY	Leslie Bricusse and Anthony Newley
F. & B. BRYANT	Felice and Boudleaux Bryant
BUIE & COBB	Buddy Buie* and James Cobb
BURKE & VAN HEUSEN	Johnny Burke and Jimmy Van Heusen*
CAMPBELL & CONNELLY	James Campbell and Reginald Connelly
CAHN & STYNE	Sammy Cahn and Julius Kerwin Styne
CARTER & LEWIS†	John Carter* and Ken Lewis*
CHINN & CHAPMAN (CHINNICHAP)	Nicky Chinn and Mike Chapman
CASON & GAYDEN	Buzz Cason* and Mac Gayden
COOK & GREENAWAY	Roger Cook and Roger Greenaway
CREWE & GAUDIO	Bob Crewe* and Bob Gaudio
DARYLL & RICHARDS	Ted Daryll* and Greg Richards
DE SYLVA, BROWN & HENDERSON	Buddy DeSylva*, Lew Brown and Ray Henderson
EVANS & LIVINGSTON	Ray Evans and Jay Livingston
FELDMAN, GOLDSTEIN & GOTTEHRER††	Robert Feldman, Gerald Goldstein and Richard Gottehrer
GAMBLE & HUFF	Kenny Gamble and Leon Huff
GARFIELD & BOTKIN JNR.	Gil Garfield and Perry Botkin Jnr.
GELD & UDELL	Gary Geld and Peter David Udell
GENTRY & CORDELL	Bo Gentry* and Ritchie Cordell*
GIANT, BAUM & KAYE	Bill Giant, Bernie Baum and Florence Kaye
GIMBEL & FOX	Norman Gimbel and Charles Fox
GOFFIN & KING	Gerry Goffin and Carole King*
GREENE & STONE	Charles Greene and Brian Stone
GREENWICH & BARRY	Ellie Greenwich and Jeff Barry
HAMMOND & HAZLEWOOD	Albert Hammond and Mike Hazlewood
HAYES & PORTER	Isaac Hayes and David Porter
HEMRIC & STYNER	Guy Hemric and Jerry Styner
HOLLAND, DOZIER & HOLLAND	Eddie Holland, Lamont Dozier and Brian Holland
HOWARD & BLAIKLEY	Ken Howard and Alan Blaikley
HUGO & LUIGI	Hugo Peretti and Luigi Creatore
KASENETZ & KATZ	Jerry Kasenetz and Jeff Katz
KORNFELD & DUBOFF	Artie Kornfeld and Steve Duboff
KALMAR & RUBY	Bert Kalmar and Harry Ruby*
LAMBERT & POTTER	Dennis Lambert and Brian Potter
LEIBER & STOLLER	Jerry (Jerome) Leiber and Mike Stoller
LEKA & PINZ	Paul Leka and Shelley Pinz
LERNER & LOWE	Alan Jay Lerner and Frederick Lowe
LINZER & RANDELL	Sandy Linzer and Denny Randell
MADARA & WHITE	John Madara and David White
MANN & LOWE	Kal Mann and Bernie Lowe
MANN & WEIL	Barry Mann and Cynthia Weil
MARCUS & BENJAMIN	Sol Marcus and Benny Benjamin
MARGO, MEDRESS, MARGO & SIEGEL	Mitchell Margo, Henry Medress, Philip Margo and Jay Siegel
MARTIN & COULTER	Bill Martin and Phil Coulter
MURRAY & CALLANDER	Mitch Murray* and Peter Callander
OLDHAM & PENN	Spooner Oldham* and Dan Penn*
POMUS & SHUMAN	Jerome 'Doc' Pomus and Mort Shuman
RAGNI, RADO & MacDERMOT	Gerome Ragni, James Rado* and Galt MacDermot
RALEIGH & BARKAN	Ben Raleigh and Mark Barkan
RAMBEAU & REHAK	Eddie Rambeau* and Bud Rehak
REED & MASON	Les Reed and Barry Mason
RESNICK & YOUNG	Artie Resnick and Kenny Young
RICE & WEBER	Tim Rice and Andrew Lloyd-Weber
RODGERS AND HAMMERSTEIN	Richard Rodgers and Oscar Hammerstein III
RODGERS & HART	Richard Rodgers and Lorenzo Hart
RUSSELL & MEDLEY	Bert Russell (Berns) and Phil Medley
R. & R. SHERMAN	Bob and Dick Sherman
SAWYER & BURTON	Pam Sawyer and Lori Burton
SCHROEDER & GOLD	Aaron Schroeder and Wally Gold
SEDAKA & GREENFIELD	Neil Sedaka and Howard Greenfield
SHEELEY & DeSHANNON	Sharon Sheeley and Jackie DeShannon*
SLAY & CREWE	Frank Conley Slay Jnr. and Bob Crewe*
SLOAN & BARRI	P. F. Sloan* and Steve Barri*
TEPPER & BENNETT	Sid Tepper and Roy C. Bennett
TRENT & HATCH	Jackie Trent and Tony Hatch
TUCKER & MANTZ	Annette Tucker and Nancie Mantz
USHER & CHRISTIAN	Gary Usher and Roger Christian
VANDA & YOUNG	Harry Vanda* and George Young
WARREN & DUBIN	Harry Warren and Al Dubin

* Refer to index for real name.   † This duo recorded as Carter Lewis and The Southerners.
†† As The Strangeloves, this trio masqueraded as Niles, Miles and Giles Strange.

CHUCK BERRY wrote *Let It Rock* as Edward Anderson.

THE WEAVERS — (l-r) Pete Seeger, Lee Hays, Ronnie Gilbert and Fred Hellerman, wrote collectively as Paul Campbell. Hellerman wrote as Fred Brooks.

PAUL McCARTNEY wrote *Woman* as Bernard Webb.

PETULA CLARK wrote album tracks as Al Grar

164

SONGWRITING PSEUDONYMS OF ESTABLISHED WRITERS AND PERFORMERS

CLINT BALLARD JNR. .... B. L. Porter
*BEN BERNIE .... Ben Green
BERT BERNS .... Bert Russell
*CHUCK BERRY .... Edward Anderson
OTIS BLACKWELL .... John Davenport
JOHNNY BURKE .... K. C. Rogan
*CAMPBELL & CONNELLY .... Irving King
ALAN CLARK, TONY HICKS & GRAHAM NASH (HOLLIES) .... L. Ransford
PETULA CLARK .... Al Grant
H. ROBINSON CLEAVER .... Roy King
SAM COOKE, HERB ALPERT & LOU ADLER .... Barbara Campbell
KEN DARBY .... Vera Matson
HOWARD DEITZ .... Dick Howard
AHMET ERTEGUN .... A. Nugetre
*BENT FABRIC .... Frank Bjorn
*NOEL GAY .... Stanley Hill
*IRA GERSHWIN .... Arthur Francis
CARL GROSSMAN (TIN TIN)† .... Carl Keats
TONY HATCH .... Mark Anthony
FRED HELLERMAN (WEAVERS) .... Fred Brooks
FLETCHER 'SMACK' HENDERSON .... George Brooks
JOHN HILL HEWITT .... Eugene Raymond
DIANE HILDERBRAND .... Diane S. Skye
*HUGO & LUIGI .... Mark Marwell
MICK JAGGER & *KEITH RICHARD .... Nanker-Phelge
*ELTON JOHN & BERNIE TAUPIN .... Ann Orson & Carte Blanche
BILL JUSTIS .... Bill Everette
*LEADBELLY .... Joel Newman
*LEIBER & STOLLER .... Elmo Glick/Joel & Chuck Kaye
BUNNY LEWIS .... Lee Lange
*MANTOVANI .... Tulio Trapani
PAUL MAURIAT .... Del Roma
*PAUL McCARTNEY .... Bernard Webb/A. Smith
JOHNNY MERCER .... Joe Moore

LEIBER & STOLLER wrote as Elmo Glick, and Joel & Chuck Kaye

IRVING MILLS .... Joe Primrose
*SYD NATHAN .... Lois Martin
NORMAN NEWELL .... David West
JACK O'HAGAN .... John Quinlan
JIMMY PHILLIPS & MARCEL STELLMAN .... Leo Johns/John Turner
*DOC POMUS .... Jerome Felder
FRANK POURCELL .... J. W. Stole
*PRINCE .... Alexander Nevermind
JERRY RAGAVOY .... Norman Meade
*BUCK RAM .... Ande Rand/Lynn Paul
CARSON ROBINSON .... Maggie Andrews
MIKE RUDD (SPECTRUM) .... My Crudd
RONNIE SCOTT .... Jack Gellar
SHARON SHEELEY .... Shari Sheeley
JESSE STONE .... Charles Calhoun
ALLAN TOUSSAINT .... Naomi Neville
*SCOTTY TURNBULL (SHARKS) .... Allison Dewar
*VANDA & YOUNG .... Nick A. Teen & Al K. Hall/'Russell'
WEAVERS, THE .... Paul Campbell
*MARTY WILDE .... Frere Manston
MURRAY WILSON†† .... Reggie Dunbar
SEPTIMUS WINNER .... Alice Hawthorne
*JOHNNY WORTH††† .... Les Van Dyke

   * Refer to index for complete or real name.
   † Grossman, who wrote *Down The Dustpipe* for Status Quo, has the distinction of being the only person to ever write
     a song specifically *for* the Bee Gees. That song was *Lonely Winter*, which he wrote as Carl Keats when he was a
     member of Australian group Steve & The Board (led by *Physical* writer Steve Kipner)
  †† A moderately successful fifties pop songwriter Murray is best known as the father of Beach Boys Brian, Dennis and
     Carl Wilson.
††† Worth took his writing pseudonymn from his London telephone exchange.

BENT FABRIC (Bent Fabricus Bjerre)
wrote *Alley Cat* as Frank Bjorn.

MANTOVANI co-wrote *Cara Mia* as Tulio Trapani.

166

POPULAR COMPOSERS/ SONGWRITERS
Real Names

BOBBY ADANO .... Milo Angelo Adamo
BILLY ADOR .... William Albimoor
VAN ALEXANDER .... Al Feldman
KENNETH J. ALFORD .... Frederick J. Ricketts
HARRY ARCHER .... Harold Auracher
JOE ARIZONA .... Arthur Kongbrake
HAROLD ARLEN .... Hyman Arluk
BOBBY ARTHUR .... Art Shaftel
L.E. AUTE .... Luis Eduardo Aute Gutierrez
PAT BALLARD .... Francis Drake Ballard
LIONEL BART .... Lionel Begleiter
BAYETTE .... Todd Cochran
JOHNNY BLACK .... John Huber
BUMPS BLACKWELL .... Robert A. Blackwell
D. DANNY BOONE .... Daniel B. Faulkerson
LEW BROWN .... Louis Brownstein
DAN BRYANT .... Daniel W.O. Brien
LORD BURGIE .... Burgess Attaway
IVAN CARYLL .... Felix Tilken
CASSIO .... Giosy & Maria Capuano
DICK CHARLES .... Richard Charles Kreig
ARTHUR CLIFTON .... Philip Anthony Corri
BUD COLEMAN .... Ervan F. Coleman
CY COLEMAN .... Seymour Kaufman
MARTY COLEMAN .... Martin Cohen
CON CONRAD .... Conrad K. Dober
AARON COPLAND .... Aaron Kaplan
RITCHIE CORDELL .... Richard Rosenblatt
HAROLD CORNELIUS .... Harold Fields
PAUL CRESTON .... Guiseppe Guttoveggio
JIMMY CURTIS .... James Stulberger
MANN/MANNY CURTIS .... Emmanuel Kurtz
TED DARYLL .... Theodore Henry Meister
JIMMY DeKNIGHT .... James Myers
BUDDY DeSYLVA .... George Gard De Sylva
SAXIE DOWELL .... Horace Kirby Dowell
EDDIE DOWLING .... Joseph Nelson Goucher
PAUL DRESSER .... Paul Dreiser
VERNON DUKE .... Vladimir Dukelsk
GEORGE EDDY .... George Paxton
STEPHEN FAY .... David Stephens
JERRY FIELDING .... Joshua Feldman
CHET FORREST .... George Forest Chichester
ARTHUR FREED .... Arthur Grossman
FREDDY FRIDAY .... Murray Sporn
NOEL GAY .... Richard Moxon Armitage
BO GENTRY .... Robert Ackoff
IRA GERSHWIN .... Ira Gershovitz
JAY GORNEY .... Daniel Jason Gorney
YIP HARBURG .... Edgar Yipsel Harburg
GEORGE HANDY .... George Joseph Handleman
OTTO HARBACH .... Otto Haverbach

JIMMY HARRIS	James Holvay
DAVID HILL	David Alexander Hess
ROLLIN' HOWARD	Ebenezer G.B. Holder
DAN HOWELL	David Kapp
DICK JAMES†	Richard Leon Vapnick
MARK JAMES	Francis Rodney Zambon
DOMINIC JOHN	Joe Roncoroni
JESSE LEE KINCAID	Nick Gerlach
BUDDY KILLEN	William D. Killen
ROBERT A. KING	Robert Keiser
GARY KNIGHT/WESTON	Harold P. Tempkin
HERB LEIGHTON	Herbert Leventhal
PAT LEWIS	Eli Oberstein
JERRY LIVINGSTON	Jerry Levinson
TONY MacAULEY	Anthony Instone
CECIL MACK	Richard C. McPherson
DAVID MARKS	David Markantonatos
JOHNNY MacRAE	Frederick Aylor MacRae
HOLT MARVELL	Eric Maschwitz
LORD MELODY	Fitzroy Aledander
MURRAY MENCHER	Ted Murray
HANK MILLS	Samuel Garrett
ISSACHAR MIRON	Issachar Michrovsky
MOGOL	Guillo Rapetti
NEIL MORET	Charles N. Daniels
MITCH MURRAY	L. Michael Stitcher
HORATIO NICHOLL	Lawrence Wright
IVOR NOVELLO	David Ivor Davies
ROLF NORMAN	Rolf Norman Elsmo
DAN PENN	Wallace Daniel Pennington
CURLY PUTNAM	Claude Putnam Jnr.
MILDRED PHILLIPS	Mildred Pressman
JAMES RADO	James Radomski
BUCK RAM	Samuel Ram

L. Michael Stitcher

IVOR NOVELLO — David Ivor Davies   TONY MacAULEY — Anthony Instone

EDDIE RAMBAU	Edward Fluri
DON RAYE	Donald MacRae Wilhoite Jnr.
SCOTT RAYMOND	Harry Warnow
ANDY RAZAFF	Andreamentania Paul Razafinkeriefo
BUD REHAK	Andrew Rachek
JOHNNY RICHARDS	John Cascales
HARRY RUBY	Harold Rubenstein
PAUL SANDERS	Paul Santoro
RONNIE SAVOY	Eugene Hamilton
JOHN SIRAS	Ira Schuster
TOM SPRINGFIELD	Thomas O'Brien
PATTY STAIR	Martha Greene
RANDY STARR	Warren Nadel
LONA STEPHENS	Lona Spector
LESLIE STUART	Thomas A. Barrett
MARION SUNSHINE	Mary Tunstall Ijames
HOWARD TALBOT	Ricahrd Munkittrick
DOROTHY TERRIS/D.A. ESTROM	Theodora Morse
BUCK TRAIL	Ronald B. Killette
VAN TREVOR	Robert Francis Boulanger
JACK TROMBEY	Jules Staffaro
JAMES VAN HEUSEN	Edward Chester Babcock
ALBERT & HARRY VON TILZER	Albert & Harry Gumm
FRANK WAXMAN	Franz Wachsmann
ROBERT WELLS	Robert Wells Levinson
RED WEST††	Robert West
PAUL WESTON	Paul Westein
SLIM WILLET	Winston Moore
HUGH WILLIAMS	Will Grosz
P.G. WODEHOUSE	Pelham Grenville Wodehouse
KEN WOOD	Walter R. Moody
JOHNNY WORTH	Yani Skordalides

† Best known as a famous British music publisher (the Beatles being his most prominent clients), Dick was also a dance band singer and occasional writer, best known for singing the title song of the *Robin Hood* TV series. The DJM record label (Dick James Music) carried Elton John's recordings until 1976.
†† Red West was an army buddy of Elvis Presley who became the head of his 'Memphis Mafia', undertook bit parts in many of his movies and wrote a number of songs for him, including *If Every Day Was Like Christmas* and *You'll Be Gone*.

CLASSICAL COMPOSERS
– Real Names

Generally, those dedicated gents labouring in lofts and sweating in cellars over their beloved symphonies and suites had little interest in adopting nifty names to elevate their public profile. However, as in every other avenue of musical endeavour, the classics had its share of masquerades, often on the part of European writers trying to sell their work in the New World.

STEPHEN ADAMS .... Michael Maybrick
ALEXANDER AGRICOLA .... Alexander Ackerman
HENRICO ALBICASTRO .... Heinrich Weyssenburg
CHARLES ALKAN .... Charles Henri Valentin Morhange
JEAN BARTAUD .... Jean Barraud
ARCIMELO .... Arcangelo Corelli
PAUL ARMA .... Imre Weisshaus
LEWIS BENNETT .... Louis Benoit
FRANCIS CHAGRIN .... Alexander Paucker
VAN CLIBURN .... Harvey Lavan Cliburn
GIOVANNI COPERARIO .... John Cooper
ALEXANDRE D'ARAGON .... Pierre LeFrancq
JOHN LODGE ELLERTON .... John Lodge
FEDELE .... Daniel Gottlieb Treu
LUKAS FOSS .... Lukas Fuchs
SIGNEY FOREST .... Louise E. Stairs
ROBERT FRANZ .... Robert Franz Knauth
EDWARD GERMAN .... Edward German Jones
J. F. F. E. HALEVY .... Jacques Francois Fromental Elie Levy
F. X. HAMMER .... Franz Xavier Marteau
ALAN HOVHANESS .... Alan Chakmakjian
JACOB le POLONAIS/le REYS .... Jacob Polak
KELER-BELA .... Adalbert Von Keler
ISIDORE de LARA .... Isidore Cohen
LOUIS LOTHAR .... Paul Dupin
MELANTE ...., G. P. Telemann
MOONDOG .... Louis Thomas Hardin
MOSONYI .... Michael Brandt
JACQUES OFFENBACH† .... Jacques Eberst
OLOCIN OZZANIUGNAS .... Nicolo Sanguinazzo
PIERGUIGI PALESTRINA .... Giovanni Pierluigi
GIOVANNI PUNTO/JOHANN WENZEL STICH .... Jan Vaclav Stich
FREDERIC REGNAL .... Frederic d'Erlanger
ERNEST RAYER .... Louis Etienne Ernst Rey
ROLAND-MANUEL .... Roland Alexis Manuel Levy
JOHN ROTH .... Philip Pfeil/Phile
DANE RUDHYAR .... Daniel Chenneviere
HENRI SAUGET .... Jean-Pierre Poupard
CORONA SCHROTER .... Elisabeth Schmelling
CAMILLE de SENEZ .... Count Gabriel Wayditch von Verhovac
SHARM .... John Marsh
ETERIO STRINFALICO .... Alessandro Marcello
FRANZ VON SUPPE .... Francesco Ermengildo Ezechiele Suppe-Demelli
JOSEPH TAL .... Joseph Gruenthal
HOWARD TALBOT .... Richard Lansdale Munkittrick
CARLO GIUSEPPE TOESCHI .... Carlo Giuseppe Toesca della Castellamonte
URTICA .... Vaclav Jan Kopriva
JOSEF VENATORINI .... Josef Myslivecek
LODOVICI VIADANA .... Lodovici Grossi
BRUNO WALTER†† .... Bruno Schlesinger
PETER WARLOCK .... Philip Heseltine
HERMANN ZENTA .... Augusta May Anne Holmes

† Offenbach was borrowed from the name of Eberst's German birthplace.
†† Orchestra conductor.

CLASSICAL COMPOSERS – The Top 40

Somewhere over the past century or so, classical composers managed to lose their first names. Now we know them only as Beethoven, Mozart, Bach, Ravel, etc. However, be assured that these legendary gentlemen were not born defficient in the name department, as this selective list will adequately prove.

BACH	Johann Sebastian Bach
BARTOK	Bela Bartok
BEETHOVEN	Ludwig Van Beethoven
BERLIOZ	Hector Berlioz
BIZET	George Bizet
BRAHMS	Johannes Brahms
CHOPIN	Frederick Chopin
DEBUSSY	Claude Debussy
DVORAK	Antonin Dvorak
ELGAR	Edward Elgar
GRIEG	Edvard Hagerup Grieg
HANDEL	George Frederick Handel
HAYDN	Joseph Haydn
HOLST	Gustav Von Holst
LIZST	Frank Lizst
MAHLER	Gustav Mahler
MENDELSSOHN	Jacob Ludwig Felix Mendelssohn-Bartholdy
MOZART	Wolfgang Amadeus Mozart
MUSSORGSKY	Modest Mussorgsky
PAGANINI	Niccolo Paganini
PROKOFIEV	Serge Prokofiev
PUCCINI	Giacomo Puccini
PURCELL	Henry Purcell
RACHMANINOV	Sergei Rachmaninov
RAVEL	Maurice Ravel
RIMSKY-KORSAKOV	Nikolai Rimsky-Korsakov
ROSSINI	Gioacchino Rossini
SCHOENBERG	Arnold Schoenberg
SCHUBERT	Farnz Schubert
SCHUMANN	Robert Schumann
SCHUTZ	Heinrich Schutz
SIBELIUS	Jean Sibelius
STOCKHAUSEN	Karlheinz Stockhausen
STRAUSS	Johann Strauss
STRAVINSKY	Ivor Stravinsky
TCHAIKOVSKY	Piotr Ilyich Tchaikovsky
VARESE	Edgard Varese
VERDI	Guiseppe Verdi
VIVALDI	Antonio Vivaldi
WAGNER	Richard Wagner

Gioacchino ROSSINI

Piotr Ilyich TCHAIKOVSKY

FRED ASTAIRE —
Frederick Austerlitz

MAMIE VAN DOREN —
Joan Lucille Oland

JUDY GARLAND —
Frances Ethel Gumm

MARILYN MONROE —
Norma Jean Baker/Mortensen

DANNY KAYE — David Daniel Kaminsky

SINGING STARS OF THE SILVER SCREEN

Even the most unlikely cinema stars, such as Jimmy Cagney, Jack Nicholson, Jayne Mansfield and Clint Eastwood, have been called upon to sing at some point in their careers. This list covers those who have dabbled in singing a little more seriously (though not as seriously as Doris Day and Debbie Reynolds, who can be found in the pop listings). Most of them managed to find their way onto disc at some point and a few sang with dance bands or on Broadway.

JUNE ALLYSON	Ella Geisman
JULIE ANDREWS	Julia Elizabeth Welles
DESI ARNAZ	Desiderio Alberto Arnaz y de Acha
FRED ASTAIRE	Frederick Austerlitz
DORA BRYAN†	Dora Broadbent
RED BUTTONS	Aaron Chwatt
DIAHANN CARROLL	Carol Diahann Johnson
RICHARD CHAMBERLAIN††	George Richard Chamberlain
SANDRA DEE	Alexandria Zuck
MARLENE DIETRICH	Maria Magdalena Von Losch
DIANA DORS	Diana Fluck
DEANNA DURBIN	Edna Mae Durbin
ALICE FAYE	Alice Jeanne Leppert
JUDY GARLAND	Frances Ethel Gumm
MITZI GAYNOR	Francesca Mitzi Marlene de Charney von Gerber
BETTY GRABLE†††	Elizabeth Ruth Grable
KATHRYN GRAYSON	Zelma Kathryn Hendrick
JUDY HOLLIDAY	Judith Tuvim
TAB HUNTER	Art Gelien or Arthur Andrew Kelm
GLORIA JEAN	Gloria Jean Schoonover
DANNY KAYE	David Daniel Kaminsky
HOWARD KEEL	Harold Clifford Keel
BERT LAHR	Irving Lahrheim
DOROTHY LAMOUR	Mary Leta Dorothy Kaumeyer
PRISCILLA LANE	Priscilla Mullican
JOAN LESLIE	Joan Agnes Theresa Sadie Brodel
CARMEN MIRANDA	Maria do Carmo Miranda da Cunha
MARILYN MONROE‡	Norma Jean Baker/Mortenson
YVES MONTANDT‡‡	Ivo Livi
ZERO MOSTEL	Samuel Joel Mostel
RAMON NOVARRO	Ramon Samaneigos
JANE POWELL	Suzanne Bruce
GINGER ROGERS	Virginia Katherine McMath
SHIRLEY ROSS	Bernice Gaunt
SABRINA‡‡‡	Norma Sykes
DINAH SHORE	Frances Rose Shore
ANN SOTHERN	Harriette Lake
SISSY SPACEK	Mary Elizabeth Spacek
MAMIE VAN DOREN	Joan Lucille Olander
VERA-ELLEN	Vera-Ellen Westmyr Rohe

† This cheeky Cockney actress kicked off the Beatle tribute record bandwagon with the 1963 single *All I Want For Christmas Is A Beatle*.

†† In 1962-63, when he was TV heart-throb *Dr Kildare*, Chamberlain notched up four American chart hits.

††† When Betty married bandleader Harry James she sang as Ruth Hagg, a combination of both their middle names. She was also called Frances Dean by MGM for a short time.

‡ Marilyn was born illegitimately to Edward Mortenson and Gladys Baker.

‡‡ Yves was a disciple of Edith Piaf, who helped make him a major singing star in France before he went to Hollywood in 1960.

‡‡‡ Britain's blonde bombshell of B-grade flicks recorded for Philips in the early sixties, cutting such essential ditties as *A Man Not A Mouse*.

PAT BENATAR — Patricia Andrejewski

MAIDEN NAMES

(of female performers who operate under married names)

PAT BENATAR .... Patricia Andrejewski
CARLA BLEY .... Carla Borg
DALE BOZZIO (MISSING PERSONS) .... Dale Consalvi
BONNIE BRAMLETT .... Bonnie Lynn
RUTH BROWN .... Ruth Weston
FELICE BRYANT .... Felice Scaduto
(MOTHER) MAYBELLE CARTER .... Maybelle Addington
SARA CARTER (CARTER FAMILY) .... Sara Dougherty
SARA DYLAN† .... Sara Lowndes nee Nozinsky
MIMI FARINA .... Mimi Baez
SUSAN JACKS (POPPY FAMILY) .... Susan Pesklevits
WANDA JACKSON .... Wanda Goodman
BIANCA JAGGER† .... Bianca Perez Moreno de Marias
LYNN MANN (JOHNNY MANN SINGERS) .... Lynn Marie Dolin
RITA MARLEY .... Rita Anderson
LINDA McCARTNEY (WINGS) †† .... Linda Louise Eastman (Epstein)
CHRISTINE McVIE (FLEETWOOD MAC) .... Christine Perfect
MARIA MULDAUR .... Maria Grazia Rosa Domenica d'Amato
ESTHER OFARIM .... Esther Zaled
DORY PREVIN .... Dory Langdon
JEANNIE C. RILEY .... Jeannie Carolyn Stephenson
SANDRA RHODES .... Sandra Chalmers
MARY RUSSELL ††† .... Mary McCreary
RONNIE SPECTOR .... Ronnie (Veronica) Bennett
APRIL STEVENS .... April LoTempio
LINDA THOMPSON .... Linda Peters
JULIE TIPPETS .... Julie Driscoll
RUTH UNDERWOOD .... Ruth Romanoff

† Strictly not performers, but nonetheless interesting.
†† Contrary to popular belief, Linda is not an heir of the Eastman-Kodak empire. Her father is actually a heavyweight New York Lawyer.
††† The wife of Leon Russell, who has enjoyed most success under her maiden name.

DALE BOZZIO (MISSING PERSONS) — Dale Consalvi

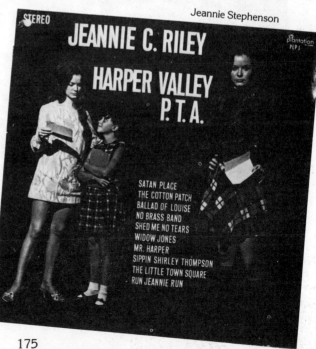

Jeannie Stephenson

175

William Evans

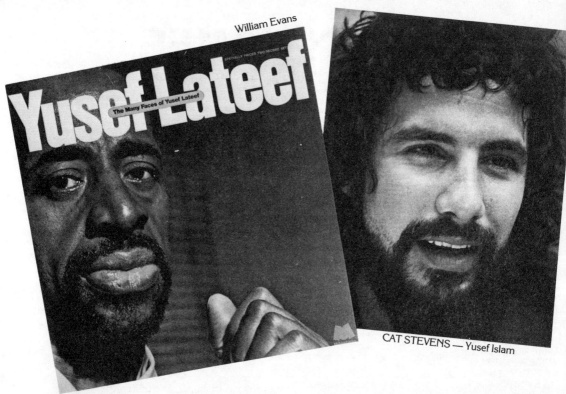

CAT STEVENS — Yusef Islam

WALTER/WENDY CARLOS

ADOPTED MUSLIM NAMES

The rise of 'Black Power' in America during the Sixties saw a move toward the embrace of the Islamic faith by a great many prominent negro figures, including many jazz musicians. This conversion involved the adoption of Muslim names, which were used in both a primary and secondary manner by professional musicians. Of course, not all Islamic converts were black, as the inclusion of Cat Stevens indicates.

A. T. ATKINSON	Ahmad Khatab Salim
BEA BENJAMIN	Sathima Ibrahim
ART BLAKEY	Abdullah Ibn Bahaina
*DOLLAR BRAND	Abdullah Ibrahim
*LA LA BROOKS (CRYSTALS)	Sakimah Muhammed
DOUG CARN	Abdul Rahim Ibrahim
WARREN CHEESEBORO	Khan Jamal
KENNY CLARKE	Liaquat Ali Salaam
BILL DAVIS	Abdul Samad
CASSIUS MARCELLUS CLAY JNR.†	Muhammed Ali
WILLIAM EVANS	Yusef Lateef
FRITZ JONES	Ahmad Jamal
LORNA LOGIC††	Syama-Manjari-Devi Daso
EMMANUEL KAYSI MacFOY	Abeodun Oju
LEO MORRIS	Idris Muhammad
RUDY POWELL	Musheed Karweem
*CAT STEVENS	Yusef Islam
*JOE TEX	Yusef Hazziez
ARGONNE THORNTON	Sadik Hakim
McCOY TYNER	Sulaimon Saud
CHARLES WEAVER	Abdullah Shakur
ORLANDO WRIGHT	Musa Kaleen
LARRY YOUNG	Khalid Yasin

  * Refer to index for real name.
  † Although primarily a boxer, Clay actually made a number of 'rant' records.
†† Lorna's is believed to be a Krishna name.

SEX CHANGE NAMES

Music entities who have altered their genders mid-career; thus generating material under both names.

WALTER CARLOS	to	WENDY CARLOS
WAYNE COUNTY	to	JAYNE COUNTY
WALLY STOTT†	to	ANGELA MORLEY

† Wally was a British record producer/arranger/conductor of the sixties who worked with, among others, The Walker Brothers. Angela is now a busy London arranger.

Note: Amanda Lear does not qualify for inclusion as her claim to have previously been John Lear has been proven false.

MUSIC BRAND NAMES

ARIA GUITARS	Shiro Aria
BURNS GUITARS	James Burns
DOLBY NOISE REDUCTION	Dr. Ray Dolby
FENDER GUITARS	Leo Fender
GIBSON GUITARS	Orville Gibson
GRETSCH GUITARS/DRUMS	Fred Gretsch
HAMER GUITARS	Paul Hamer
HAMMOND ORGANS	Laurens Hammond
HOFNER GUITARS	Karl Hofner
LUDWIG DRUMS	William F. Ludwig Snr.
MANSON GUITARS	Hugh & Andy Manson
MARTIN GUITARS	Christian Frederick Martin
MOOG SYNTHESIZERS	Dr. Robert Moog
OBERHEIM COMPUTER KEYBOARDS	Tom Oberheim
PEAVEY AMPLIFIERS/GUITARS	Hartley Peavey
RHODES ELECTRIC PIANOS	Harold Rhodes
RICKENBACKER GUITARS	Adolph Rickenbacker
ROGERS DRUMS	Joseph Rogers
STEINBERGER BASS GUITARS	Ned Steinberger
STRADIVARIUS VIOLINS	Antonio Stradivari
ZILDJIAN CYMBALS	Bob Zildjian

RINGO STARR — Richard Starkey, Ludwig Drums' most famous customer.

JETHRO TULL — invented the seed drill

Peter Woolnough and Chris Bell

NO SUCH ANIMAL

These groups are named after individuals who either do not exist or are not members of the band.

EDWARD BEAR†
BILLY BEETHOVEN
MATT BIANCO
SKIP BIFFERTY
BUSTER BROWN††
HENRY COW
LAMONT CRANSTON†††
PABLO CRUISE
TERRY DACTYL

BAXTER FUNT
JODY GRIND
JO JO GUNNE‡
SEBASTIAN HARDIE
BARCLAY JAMES HARVEST
MOLLY HATCHET
PYTHON LEE JACKSON‡‡
JUDAS JUMP
H.P. LOVECRAFT

JUDAS PRIEST‡‡‡
HARLEY QUINNE
MASON PROFFIT
MONTY PYTHON
JETHRO TULL‡‡‡‡
JASPER WRATH

  † The original name of Winnie The Pooh.
  †† This early seventies Australian hard rock band, which yielded up members of AC/DC and Rose Tattoo, took its
    name from the legendary 50's rocker of *Fannie Mae* fame.
  ††† The 'true identity' of The Shadow.
  ‡ An offshoot of Spirit, this group took its name from a Chuck Berry song title.
  ‡‡ Commonly assumed to be a pseudonymn of Rod Stewart, this name actually belonged to an Australian band
    which once used Stewart as a session vocalist in London.
  ‡‡‡ The name of a character in a Bob Dylan song.
‡‡‡‡ The medieval inventor of the seed drill.

BOGUS BROTHERS

Despite the group name employed, these outfits were/are not comprised of related members.

THE ALLEN BROTHERS†
THE ALLISONS
BARNES & BARNES*
THE BLUES BROTHERS
THE BOSS BROTHERS
THE BROTHERS FOUR
THE BUCHANAN BROTHERS††
THE CHEVALIER BROTHERS
THE COCTEAU TWINS
DAVE & ANSELL COLLINS*
THE COWARD BROTHERS
THE COYOTE SISTERS
THE DALTON BROTHERS†††
THE DAVIS SISTERS
THE DOOBIE BROTHERS
THE ELVIS BROTHERS
THE FLOATERS
THE KAYE SISTERS

THE LE ROI BROTHERS
THE MARSHALL BROTHERS
THE McKENZIE BROTHERS
THE MOST BROTHERS
THE NOYES BROTHERS
THE PELACO BROTHERS
JAMES & BOBBY PURIFY*
THE RIGHTEOUS BROTHERS
THE RAMONES
THE STATLER BROTHERS
THE THOMPSON TWINS
THE TWINKLE BROTHERS
THE TWINS
THE VIRGIL BROTHERS
THE WALKER BROTHERS
WAS (NOT WAS)
THE ZARSOFF BROTHERS

* Refer to index for real name.
†   This is the Australia Duo which yielded up Peter Allen and not the c/w duo which recorded for Columbia in the twenties.
†† The Buchanan Brothers were an early version of Cashman Pistilli & West
††† The Dalton Brothers were an early version of The Walker Brothers.

100 INTERESTING MIDDLE NAMES
(of performers using their real names)

Name	Middle Name	Name	Middle Name
ROY ACUFF	Claxton	BOB MARLEY	Nesta
PETER ALBIN (BIG BRO. & HOLDING CO.)	Scott	HUGH MASAKELA	Ramapolo
JERRY ALISON (CRICKETS)†	Ivan	NICK MASON (PINK FLOYD)	Berkeley
JOAN BAEZ	Chawdos	ROD McKEUN	Marvin
BOBBY 'BLUE' BLAND	Calvin	JEAN MILLINGTON (FANNY)	Yolanda
DAVE BRUBECK	Warren	BILL MONROE	Smith
TIM(OTHY) BUCKLEY	Charles	JIM MORRISON (DOORS)	Douglas
ERIC BURDON	Victor	JON(ATHAN) MOSS (CULTURE CLUB)	Aubrey
JOE BUTLER (LOVIN' SPOONFUL)	Campbell	JOHNNY NASH	Lester
GLEN CAMPBELL	Travis	ART(HUR) NEVILLE (METERS)	Lanon
LARRY CARLTON	Eugene	PHIL OCHS	David
ERIC CARMEN	Howard	ROY ORBISON	Kelton
BILL CHAMPLIN (SONS OF CHAMPLIN)	Bradford	DONNIE OSMOND	Clark
HARRY CHAPIN	Forster	JAY OSMOND (OSMONDS)	Wesley
JACK CLEMENT	Henderson	JIMMY PAGE (LED ZEPPELIN)	Patrick
JUDY COLLINS	Marjorie	DOLLY PARTON	Rebecca
MIKEY CRAIG (CULTURE CLUB)	Emile	DENIS PAYTON (DAVE CLARK 5)	West
ALANNAH CURRIE (THOMPSON TWINS)	Joy	DAN PEEK (AMERICA)	Milton
ROGER DALTREY	Harold	CARL PERKINS	Lee
MILES DAVIS	Dewey	OSCAR PETERSON	Emmanuel
DOUG DILLARD	Flint	MIKE PINERA (IRON BUTTERFLY)	Carlos
WALTER EGAN	Lindsay	DAVID POMERANZ	Hyman
JOSE FELICIANO	Monserrate	ELVIS PRESLEY†††	Aron
DAN FOGELBERG	Grayling	RAY PRICE	Noble
JOHN FOGERTY (CREEDENCE)	Cameron	JOHNNIE RAY	Alvin
'TENNESSEE' ERNIE FORD	Jennings	JIMMIE RODGERS #2	Frederick
MARVIN GAYE	Pentz	LINDA RONSTADT	Maria
ROBIN GIBB	Hugh	BOBBY SHERMAN	Cabot
JIM GORDON (DEREK & DOMINOES)	Beck	PAUL SIMON	Frederic
EDDY GRANT	Montague	FRANK SINATRA	Albert
BILL HALEY	John Clifton	STEPHEN SONDHEIM	Joshua
GREG HAM (MEN AT WORK)	Norman	PHIL SPECTOR	Harvey
OSCAR HAMMERSTEIN II	Greeley Glendenning	NORMA TANEGA	Cecilia
HERBIE HANCOCK	Jeffrey	MEL(VIN) TORME	Howard
RICHIE HAVENS	Pierce	PETER TOWNSHEND (WHO)	Dennis Blandford
ROY HAY (CULTURE CLUB)	Ernest	MARY TRAVERS (PETER, PAUL & MARY)	Allin
LENA HORNE	Calhoun	SARAH VAUGHAN	Lois
CHRISSIE HYNDE (PRETENDERS)	Ellen	LOUDON WAINWRIGHT III	Snowden
BURL IVES	Icle Ivanhoe	TOM WAITS	Alan
JERMAINE JACKSON	La Jaune	GORDON WALLER (PETER & GORDON)	Trueman Riviere
MICHAEL JACKSON	Joe	CHARLIE WATTS (ROLLING STONES)	Robert
MICK JAGGER	Philip	BRIAN WILSON (BEACH BOYS)	Douglas
HARRY JAMES	Haag	JACKIE WILSON	Leroy
JANIS JOPLIN	Lyn	JESSE WINCHESTER††††	James
SIMON KIRKE (BAD COMPANY)	Frederick	JOHNNY WINTER	Dawson
JOHN LENNON††	Winston	PHILIP WRIGHT (HUMAN LEAGUE)	Adrian
JOHN LEYTON	Dudley	STEVIE WRIGHT (EASYBEATS)	Carlton
BOB LIND	Neale	ANGUS YOUNG (AC/DC)	McKinnon
KENNY LOGGINS	Clarke	GEORGE YOUNG (FLASH & THE PAN)	Redburn
STEPHEN LUSCOMBE (BLANCMANGE)	Alfred	FRANK ZAPPA	Vincent

Note: Although the familiar forms of artist names have been listed, it should be noted that many of the first names are obvious contractions, i.e.: Bill is William, Tom is Thomas, Jim is James, Ernie is Ernest. Frank is Francis, Donnie is Donald, Bob is Robert, etc.

† Jerry actually released a single (*Real Wild Child*) under the name Ivan.
†† John changed his middle name by deed poll from Winston to Ono on April 22, 1969.
††† This is not a type error, Vernon & Gladys Presley omitted the customary second 'a' from Elvis' middle name. However, his gravestone bears the name Aaron.
†††† Jesse James Winchester sounds almost too absurd to be true, but if this singer-songwriter does have a real name, he has hidden it remarkably well.

John CAMERON Fogerty

Lena CALHOUN Horne

Glen TRAVIS Campbell

Eddy MONTAGUE Grant

JERRY LEE LEWIS — The Killer

NICKNAMES/ BILLING NAMES

These 'unofficial' names generally do not appear on record labels but are commonly associated with the artists by fans and critics. As there are as many of these names as there are artists, the listing is highly selective, concentrating on major entities and interesting names.

JOHNNY ADAMS	The Tan Canary
LEE ALLEN	Mr. Lee
REX ALLEN	The Arizona Cowboy
DUANE ALLMAN*	Skydog
LOUIS ARMSTRONG*	Satchmo (from 'Satchel Mouth')
EDDY ARNOLD*	The Tennessee Plowboy
PEARL BAILEY	Pearly Mae
CHARLIE BARNET	Mad Mab
ASTON BARRETT (WAILERS)	Family Man
SHIRLEY BASSEY	Burly Chassis
RODNEY BINGENHEIMER	The Mayor Of Sunset Strip
BOBBY 'BLUE' BLAND	The Soul Man
MARC BOLAN*	The Electric Warrior
JOHN BONHAM (LED ZEPPELIN)	Bonzo
DAVID BOWIE*	The Thin White Duke/Ziggy Stardust
ELKIE BROOKS*	Elk
JAMES BROWN	Soul Brother No. 1/Mr. Dynamite/The Hardest Working Man in Show Business
RUTH BROWN	Miss Rhythmn
JERRY BUTLER	The Ice Man
CAB CALLOWAY*	The Hi De Ho Man
GLEN CAMPBELL	The Rhinestone Cowboy
JO ANN CAMPBELL	The Blonde Bombshell
FREDDY CANNON*	Boom Boom
EARL CARROLL (CADILLACS)	Speedo/Mr. Earl
WILF CARTER	The Yodelling Cowboy
JOHNNY CASH*	The Man In Black
RAY CHARLES*	The Genius
ROGER CHRISTIAN	Hot Rod Rog/The Poet Of The Strip
ERIC CLAPTON*	Slowhand/God
DOUG CLIFFORD (CREEDENCE)	Cosmo
JUDY COLLINS	Judy Blue Eyes
BILLY CONNOLLY	The Big Yin
BING CROSBY*	The Old Groaner
DICK DALE*	King Of The Surf Guitar
BRIAN DAVIDSON (THE NICE)	Blinky
EDDIE DAVIS	Lockjaw
JOHN DAWSON (NEW RIDERS OF THE PURPLE SAGE)	Marmaduke
BO DIDDLEY*	The Black Gladiator/Big Bad Bo
LEE DORSEY	Kid Chocolate/Mr. T.N.T.
TOMMY DORSEY	That Sentimental Gentleman of Swing
DARYL DRAGON	Captain Keyboards
JULIE DRISCOLL	Jools
SLY DUNBAR*	Drumbar
BOB DYLAN*	The Great White Wonder/The Zim
BILLY ECKSTINE*	The Sepia Sinatra/The Great Mr. B.
JOHN ENTWHISTLE (WHO)	The Ox
EXUMA	The Obeah Man
TOMMY FACENDA	Bubba
ABDUL FAKIR (FOUR TOPS)	Duke
ELLA FITZGERALD	The First Lady of Jazz
ARETHA FRANKLIN	The Queen Of Soul
DONNIE FRITTS	The Elegant Alabama Leaning Man
JESSE FULLER	The Lone Cat
JERRY GARCIA (GRATEFUL DEAD)*	Captain Trips
JUDY GARLAND*	Miss Showbusiness
GEORGIA GIBBS*	Her Nibs
RUBEN GONZALEZ	Mr. Salsa
BENNY GOODMAN	The King Of Swing

NICK GRAVENITES (BUTTERFIELD BLUES BAND) .... Nick The Greek
DALE GRIFFIN (MOTT THE HOOPLE) .... Buffin
CLAUDE GRAY .... The Tall Texan
TOM T. HALL .... The Storyteller
W. C. HANDY* .... The Father Of The Blues
RONNIE HAWKINS .... The Hawk
ISAAC HAYES .... Black Moses
HEINTJE .... Wonder Boy
CLARENCE HENRY .... Frogman
BERTHA HILL .... Chippie
EARL HINES .... Fatha
AL HIRT .... The Monster
BOB HITE (CANNED HEAT) .... The Bear
BILLIE HOLIDAY* .... Lady Day
JULIO IGLESIAS .... The Spanish Sinatra
MAHALIA JACKSON .... The Gospel Queen
ETTA JAMES* .... Miss Peaches
BILLY JOEL .... The Piano Man
DR. JOHN* .... The Night Tripper
ELTON HERCULES JOHN* .... Captain Fantastic
AL JOLSON* .... The World's Greatest Entertainer
GEORGE JONES & TAMMY WYNETTE* .... Mr. & Mrs. Country Music
QUINCY JONES .... Q
JANIS JOPLIN .... Pearl
LOUIS JORDAN .... King Of The Jukeboxes
B. B. KING* .... Blues Boy
EARL KING* .... Trick Bag
EVELYN KING .... Champagne
PAUL KOSSOFF (FREE) .... Koss
KAY KYSER* .... Dean Of The Kollege Of Music Knowledge
RONNIE LANE (FACES) .... Plonk
BRENDA LEE* .... Little Miss Dynamite
LENNON & McCARTNEY* .... The Nurk Twins
JOHN LENNON .... Dr. Winston O'Boogie
JERRY LEE LEWIS .... The Killer
JOE LIGGINS† .... The Honeydripper
NICK LOWE .... The Jesus Of Cool
LYDIA LUNCH* .... The Priestess of Primordial Angst/Diva of the Disgusted
UNCLE DAVE MACON .... The Dixie Dewdrop
JOHN MAYALL .... The Father of British Blues
MECO .... The Wizard
JOHN COUGAR MELLENCAMP .... The Little Bastard
BETTE MIDLER .... The Divine Miss M.
STEVE MILLER .... The Space Cowboy/The Gangster of Love
THELONIOUS MONK* .... The High Priest of the Be Bop/The Mad Monk
CLYDE MOODY .... The Hillbilly Waltz King
CHAD MORGAN .... The Sheikh of Scrubby Creek
GEORGE MORTON .... Shadow
TONY MOTTOLA .... Mr. Big
ROSE MURPHY .... The Chee Chee Girl
MURRY THE K* .... The Fifth Beatle
MIKE NESMITH* .... Papa Nes
DAVID NEWMAN .... Fathead
JACK NITZSCHE .... Specs
RED NORVO & MILDRED BAILEY* .... Mr. & Mrs. Swing
JOHNNY O'KEEFE .... The Wild One/The Boomerang Boy
ROY ORBISON .... The Big 'O'
JOHNNY OTIS* .... The Godfather of Rhythmn and Blues
PATTI PAGE* .... The Singing Rage
CHARLIE PARKER .... Bird
LARRY PARNES .... Mr. Parnes, Shillings and Pence
MINNIE PEARL* .... The Queen of Country Comedy
EDITH PIAF* .... The Little Sparrow
BOBBY PICKETT .... Boris
GENE PITNEY .... The Rockville Rocket
PEREZ PRADO .... King Of The Mambo
ELVIS PRESLEY .... The King/The Hillbilly Cat/The Memphis Flash/El
LLOYD PRICE .... Mr. Personality
SUZI QUATRO .... Lady Leather

The Singing Rage

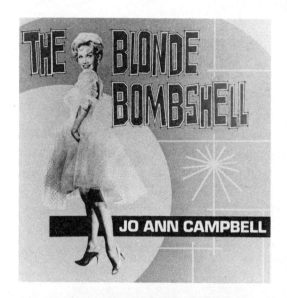

JAMES BROWN — Soul Brother No. 1/Mr Dynamite/
The Hardest Working Man in Show Business

LEE RITENOUR — Captain Fingers/Rit

ROY ORBISON — The Big 'O'

MA RAINEY* .... Mother of the Blues
JOHNNIE RAY .... The Prince of Wails/The Nabob of Sob/The Cry Guy
LOU REED* .... The Godfather of Punk
GOEBEL REEVES .... The Texas Drifter
TERRY REID .... Superlungs
CHARLIE RICH .... The Silver Fox
LEE RITENOUR .... Captain Fingers/Rit
MARTY ROBBINS .... Mr. Teardrop
BILLY 'BOJANGLES' ROBINSON .... Mr. Bojangles
JIMMIE RODGERS #1 .... The Singing Brakeman/The Father of Country Music
ROY ROGERS* .... The King of the Cowboys
IVY RORSCHACH (CRAMPS) .... Poison Ivy
TODD RUNDGREN .... Runt
JIMMY RUSHING .... Mr. Five by Five
ROBBIE SHAKESPEARE .... Basspeare
FRANK SINATRA .... Ol' Blue Eyes/The Voice
BESSIE SMITH .... Empress Of The Blues
FRED SMITH (MC5) .... Sonic
HANK SNOW* .... The Singing Ranger
PHIL SPECTOR .... The Tycoon Of Teen
ELTON ISLAND SPIVEY .... The Za Zu Girl
BRUCE SPRINGSTEEN .... The Boss
JOHN STEWART .... The Lonesome Picker
YMA SUMAC* .... The Voice of the Xtaby
DAME JOAN SUTHERLAND .... La Stupenda
BERNIE TAUPIN .... The Brown Dirt Cowboy
LARRY TAYLOR (CANNED HEAT) .... The Mole
CARLA THOMAS .... Queen of the Memphis Sound
MEL TORME .... The Velvet Fog
JACKIE TRENT & TONY HATCH .... Mr & Mrs Music
ERNEST TUBB .... The Texas Troubadour
SOPHIE TUCKER* .... The Last Of The Red Hot Mamas
BIG JOE TURNER .... The Boss Of The Blues
JIM VALLEY (RAIDERS) .... Harpo
STEVE VAN ZANDT (E. STREET BAND) .... Miami Steve
SARAH VAUGHAN .... Sassy/The Divine One
PHIL VOLK (RAIDERS) .... Fang
RUSTY WARREN * .... The Knockers-Up Girl
DINAH WASHINGTON*†† .... Queen Of The Blues
MUDDY WATERS* .... The Living Legend
NOBLE WATTS .... The Thin Man
PAUL WELLER (STYLE COUNCIL) .... The Cappuccino Kid
JUNIOR WELLS* .... The Little Giant of the Blues
IREENE WICKER .... The Singing Lady
HANK WILLIAMS* .... The Hillbilly Shakespeare
HANK WILLIAMS JNR.* .... Bocephus
CHUCK WILLIS* .... Sheikh Of The Blues
BOB WILLS* .... The King Of Western Swing
AL WILSON (CANNED HEAT) .... Blind Owl
JACKIE WILSON .... Mr. Excitement/Sonny
JIMMY WITHERSPOON .... Spoon
JOHN PAUL YOUNG .... Squeak/Mungy
LESTER YOUNG .... Pres
(JOHN) ZACHARLE .... The Cool Ghoul
* Refer to index for real name.
  † This billing was also claimed by Roosevelt Sykes.
†† A hotly contested billing.

The wedding of **MIAMI STEVE VAN ZANDT** (aka Little Steven), with **BRUCE SPRINGTSTEEN** (aka The Boss), left, as Best Man.

ELLA FITZGERALD — The First Lady of Jazz

JIMMY RUSHING — Mr. Five By Five

CHARLIE PARKER — Bird

DAME JOAN SUTHERLAND — La Stupenda

Victor

75c. in U.S.A.   Tenor with orchestra

My Waikiki Ukulele Girl
(Hawaiian Fox Trot Song)
(Jesse G. M. Glick–Chris. Smith)

Irving Kaufman

18202-A

VICTOR TALKING MACHINE CO. Camden, N.J.

SAM LANIN

VERNON DALHART

THE KINGS OF PSEUDONYMS

VERNON DALHART

Country & Western performer Vernon Dalhart was christened Marion Try Slaughter and took his stage name from the Texas towns of Vernon and Dalhart. However that wasn't the only alias he assumed. Born in 1883, he began recording on Edison cylinders around 1917. His 1924 disc of *The Wreck Of The Old '97* sold an estimated six million for RCA, and untraceable numbers for some 50 other labels which released the same recording under various false names. At the time of his death in 1948 it was estimated that Vernon Dalhart was responsible for more than 5,000 different record releases, under more than 150 pseudonyms, for collective sales exceeding 75 million. Following is a listing of most of his known false label credits.

INDIVIDUAL PSEUDONYMS:

PAUL ADAMS,
JAMES ADHERN,
JOH ALBIN,
MACK ALLEN,
WOLFE BALLARD,
JAMES BELMONT,
HARRY BLAKE,
HARRY BRITT,
BILLY BURTON,
JEFF CALHOUN,
JESS CALHOUN,
JIMMY CANNON,
JIMMY CANTRELL,
WALTER CLARK,
JACK CLEMMONS,
ED CLIFFORD,
JIMMY CONNOR,
AL CRAMER,
AL CRAVER,
JAMES CUMMINGS,
FRANK DALBERT,
FRANK DALHART,
VERNON DALL,
CHARLES DALTON,
VERNON DELL,
HUGH DONOVAN,
JOSEPH ELLIOT,
FRANK EVANS,
CLIFFORD FORD,
JEFF FULLER,
JEP FULLER,
ALBERT GORDON,
LESLIE GRAY,
DAVID HARRIS,
HARRY HARRIS,
FRANCIS HAROLD,
LOU HAYS,
FERN HOLMES,
HOWARD HULL,
FRANK HUTCHINSON,
WALTER HYDE,
JOE KINCAID,
FRED KING,
LOUIS LANE,
HUGH LATIMER,
HUGH LATTIMORE,
TOBE LITTLE,
THE LONE STAR RANGER,
BOB MASSEY,
GUY MASSEY,
BOB McAFEE,
CARLOS B. McAFEE,
WARREN MITCHELL,
GEORGE MORBID,
DICK MORSE,
CHARLES NELSON,
GWYRICK O'HARA,
SAM PETERS,

HARRY RAYMOND,
LES REIS,
JOSEPH SMITH,
JOSEPHUS SMITH,
CLIFF STEWART,
EDWARD STONE,
HOWARD STONE,
BILLY STUART,
WILL TERRY,
THE TEXAS TENOR,
BOB THOMAS,
AL TURNER,
ALLEN TURNER,
SID TURNER,
BILLY VERNON,
HERBERT VERNON,
VALREL VETERAN,
TOM WATSON,
CHARLIE WEST,
BOB WHITE,
BOBBY WHITE,
ROBERT WHITE,
WALTER WHITLOCK,
GEORGE WOODS,
MISTER X.

GROUP PSEUDONYMS:

ALLEN AND PARKER,
THE ARCHIE RUFF SINGERS,
THE ARKANSAS TRAVELLERS,
THE ARKANSAS TRIO,
BALLARD AND SUMUELS,
THE BARBARY COAST FOUR,
THE BIRMINGHAM BUGLES,
THE BROADWAY QUARTET,
CALHJOUN AND ANDREWS,
THE CALIFORNIA RAMBLERS,
THE CRAMER BROTHERS,
DALHART'S BIG CYPRESS BOYS,
DALHART'S TEXAS PANHANDLERS,
THE DOMINO QUARTET,
EVANS AND CLARK,
FRED OZARKS JUG BLOWERS,
THE HARMONY FOUR,
THE JEWEL TRIO,
THE JONES BROTHERS,
THE KANAWHA SINGERS,
LADD'S BLACK ACES,
MITCHELL AND WHITE,
THE NATIONAL MUSIC LOVERS QUARTET,
THE OLD SOUTHERN SACRED SINGERS,
THE ORIOLE TRIO,
PETERS AND JONES,
THE REGAL RASCALS,
SALT AND PEPPER,
THE SMOKEY MOUNTAIN SACRED SINGERS,
THE VIRGINIANS,
THE WINDY CITY DUO,
THE WINDY CITY JAZZERS.

SAM LANIN

This American bandleader recorded for just eleven years, from 1920 to 1931. But during this relatively short period his productivity was almost beyond belief. Biogrophers have established that he cut around 2,000 tracks, which were released on some 8,000 discs on well over 100 labels, under about 250 individual and group psuedonyms. By the mid-twenties it was common prodedure for a new Lanin recording (which usually presented itself every week) to be issued in a dozen different forms.

A perfect example would be *Get Out And Get Under The Moon*, recorded on May 29-30 1928. The known releases of this single recording are by: Miami Royal Palm Orchestra (Cameo), Ray Green & His Orch. (Angelus), Henry Halstead & HIs Congress Orch. (Electron), Bob Burton's Rosemont Orch. (Golden Tongue), Victor Morris' Orch. (Gracelon), Don Crawford's Syncopators (Melotone), The Western Wanderers (Paramount), Ed Black & His Band (Regent), The Plaza Dance Band (Starr), The Sterling Dance Orch. (Sterling), Art Carroll & His Band (Worth) and Sam Lanin & HIs Orch. (Perfect).

As well, any one of the various names might be used for release of the track on a number of other labels. For instance, the Miami Royal Palm Orchestra version of the song appeared not only on Cameo but on the Lincoln, Romeo and Dominion labels.

As a professional recording band leader, it is unlikely that Lanin was aware of even a fraction of the names his work was issued under; or that he was paid any royalties on the sales. He just churned out track for a set free and the major labels employing him (Columbia, Okeh, American Record Company, Plaza etc) used the recordings in any way they wished. Often, record companies in foreign markets, such as Australia, were sent masters and given free reign to invent their own spurious identities. Such procedure was very much commonplace at the time, with Sam Lanin being a major originator of the 'raw material'.

The same procedure which allowed Lanin's efforts to be appended with hundreds of false names, also resulted in more than 100 record releases credited to Sam Lanin's Orchestra/Lanin's Arcadians/Sam Lanin's Famous Players & Singers and other variations, bearing material that was *not* recorded by Lanin. It seems that most foreign territories presumed that the Lanin credit was as bogus as all the others and just used it indiscriminately to grace the studio efforts of other professional recording orchestras, such as those led by Ben Selvin, Fred Rich, Fletcher Henderson, Ted Wallace, Lou Gold and Harry Reser.

To complicate the issue even further, it should be understood that many of the names on the following list were not exclusive to Sam Lanin but were also used for the release of material by other professional recording orchestras. For instance, records by Tom Rock & His Orchestra carried the studio efforts of not only Lanin but also Fred Rich & His Orchestra, Harry Reser's Orchestra and Ted Wallace & His Orchestra. Some of the other pseudonyms which Lanin shared with his peers were Frank Auburn, Lloyd Keating, Ray Seeley, Sam Nash, Rudy Marlowe and Chester Leighton.

Space does not permit a complete listing of the man's pseudonyms, if indeed one were possible. Leaving aside group names (without leader preface) such as Broadway Broadcasters, Texas Ten, Red Headed Melody Makers, The Floridians etc, the following listing presents the greater majority of the actual personality identities assumed by the incredible Mr Lanin.

AL ALBERTS	LOU/BUDDY GOLDEN	RAY PERKINS
PAUL ALLEN	EDDIE GORDON	WILL PERRY
JACK ARCHER	JIMMY/RAY/BOB GREEN	JIMMIE POLLACK
FRANK AUBURN	EDEN HALL	JOHN PORTER
LES BACKER	HENRY HALSTEAD	ART POWELL
JENE BAILEY	LEWIS HANLEY	DICK PRICE
FRANK/HAL BAKER	BOB HARDING	HOTSPUR PYKE
WILL BENTON	BILY HAYES	HAL RADFORD
ED/TED BLACK	CARL HENRY	EARL/VIC RANDOLPH
BUDDY BLUE	JERRY HILL	LARRY RICH
BOB BURTON	BERT HILTON	VINCENT RICHARDS
ART CARROLL	GLEN INGRAHAM	JOE RICHARDSON
ERNEST CARLE	BILLY JAMES	JUSTIN RING
VAN CARLSON	JIMMY JOHNSON	DAN RITCHIE
FRED CHESS	WILL JOHNSTONE	CLIFF ROBERTS
PAUL CLICQUOT	LLOYD KEATING	TOM ROCK
ROY COLLINS	FRANK KEYES	ROY ROLLS
FRED COOPER	LAURIE KINLOCK	ARTHUR/GEORGE ROSE
LOU CONNOR	HART LAWSON	ARTHUR ROSS
LYNN COWAN	CHESTER LEIGHTON	JARDIN/WILLY ROYAL
DAN/DON/MATTY CRAWFORD	FRED LENNOX	JOSEPH SAMUELS
JOE CURRAN	ED LOYD	RAY/RED SEELEY
FRANK DAILEY	AL LYNN	CLARENCE/RALPH SHERMAN
BILLY DE REX	RUDY MARLOW	CAL SMITH
AL DOLLAR	TED MARSHALL	BOB STEPHENS
FRANK DOYLE	ALBERT MASON	SID TERRY
DAVID/WALLY EDWARDS	ROY/GENE MORGAN	HOWARD THOMAS
JOE EMANUEL	JOE/AL/VICTOR MORRIS	JOHN/TED VINCENT
JACK FORDHAM	EDDIE/RAY MILLER	GEO. WALLACE
HENRY FRISCO	SAM NASH	GEORGE WELLS
HENRI GENDRON	CHIC NELSON	JERRY/TED/HAROLD/HAL WHITE
NATHAN GLANTZ	ERNIE NOBLE	HAROLD/HAL WHYTE
LOU GLENRICH		

BEN SELVIN

Best known for his 1920 recording of *Dardanella,* on RCA Victor, the first 'pop' dance disc to sell a million (eventually 6.5 million), bandleader/violinist/recording manager Ben Selvin is reputed to have made more records than any other person; the figure being generally cited as 9,000, covering the years 1919 to 1934. Like Sam Lanin, his work was issued under more than a hundred pseudonyms, many of which he shared with his peers. Following is some of those which do not appear on the Lanin list.

MICKIE ALPERT	JERRY MASON	PERLEY STEVENS
BUDDY CAMPBELL	EARL MARLOW	EDDIE THOMAS
JERRY FENWYCK	ENRIQUE MADRIGUERA	BARRY TIMBLE
RUDY GRAHAM	ED PARKER	JOHNNY WALKER
ROY HENDERSON	RAY SINCLAIR	JACK WHITNEY
PHIL HUGHES		

IRVING KAUFMAN

Born in Syracuse, New York in 1890, tenor Irving Kaufman began peforming in vaudeville with his brother Jack in 1898. A bouyant star of stage and radio, he commenced recording in the 1920's. Blessed with perfect pitch and the ability to sing in the studio without arrangements, Kaufman and his Al Jolson-type voice found great favour with record company owners of the era. He recorded many thousands of sides under scores of pseudonyms and was still recording in 1960, at age 70. No definitive list of Kaufman's pseudonyms exists but this is a fair sampling. Interestingly, his brother Jack was almost as prolific!

JACK/JIM/JOHN ANDREWS	BILLY DAY	ROMEO KID
SAM ASH	CHARLES DISCKSON	J. SAUNDERS
DONALD BAKER	JIMMY FLYNN	ARTHUR/ROBERT SEELIG
TED BANCROFT	EDDY FORD	HARRY/WILLIAM/JOE SMITH
HENRY/GEORGE BEAVER	JOHN FRAWLEY	LOU SYDNEY
ARTHUR BROWN	HARRY GOODWIN	NOEL TAYLOR
AL BRUCE	FRANK HARRIS	IVAN TERRIBILINKSY
DICK BURNETT	ARTHUR HOLT	HENRY TOPPING
SAMMY BURTON	HENRY/REX IRVING	LANCE TRESHAM
BUZZING BOB	GEORGE KAY	JERRY UNDERHILL
BOB CARROLL	JOHN KELLY	VINCENT VAN TUYL
JOHN CHANNELL	PETE KILLEEN	MITCHELL VOGUE/VOGEL
FRANK CHRISTY	IRVING KNOWLES	GEORGE WALTERS
BILLY/IRVING CLARK	PIERRE LA FOND	L. WARWICK
CONFIDENTIAL CHARLIE	TOM NEVILLE	BRIAN WATT
IRVING COOMBS	HAROLD NOBLE	TONY WEST
LESTER CORTES	HAPPY JIM PARSONS	JACK/BUCK/WILSON
GEORGE CRANE	DONALD PIERCE	RAY WINN/WYNN
CHARLES DALE	IRVING POST	ROBERT WOOD
BILLY DALE	BILLY RAYMOND	MARVIN YOUNG
CHARLES DICKSON	ROMEO KID	

NOTE: Other American and British dance band era singers who employed a multiplicity of pseudonyms included Arthur Fields, Maurice Elwin, Henry Burr, Annette Hanshaw, Evelyn Preer, Jack Plant, Fred Douglas, Cavan O'Connor, Charles Penrose, Harold 'Scrappy' Lambert, John Thorne, Sam Browne, Ernest Pike and Seger Ellis.

BEN SELVIN and HIS VOCALION ORCHESTRA

CHARLES ARTHUR RAWLINGS

This Late Victorian writer of ballads and salon pieces enjoys the distinction of being the classical composer with the most pseudonyms. This listing is believed to be complete.

HAYDON AUGARDE
JEAN AUGARDE
JEANNE BARTELET
OTTO BONHEUR
EMILE BONTE
FAULKNER BRANDON
LOUIS BRANDON
HENRI CLERMONT
AUGUSTE CONS
EUGENE DELACASSA
LEO DELCASSE
EILEEN DORE
JEAN DOUSTE
DENIS DUPRE
LEON DU TERRAIL

SEYMOUR ELLIS
ROBERT GRAHAM
JOHN GRESHAM
MAXIME HELLER
EMERSON JAMES
HARRINGTON LEIGH
FRANÇOIS LEMARA
GILBERT LOEWE
ANGELO MARTINO
ALPHONSE MENIER
NITA
PAUL PERRIER
MAXIME PONTIN
WELLINGTON RAWLINGS
VERNON REY

CARL RITZ
CARL RUBINS
EMILE SACHS
HANS SACHS
RALPH SEYMOUR
HERMAN STRAUS
MAURICE TELMA
GORDON TEMPLE
PAUL TERRIER
THOMAS THOME
CLAUDE DE VERE
OSCAR VERNE
BERYL VINCENT
CHRISTINE WILLIAMS
SYDNEY WEST

PETER DAWSON

Australian baritone singer Peter Dawson (1882-1961) began recording on Edison Bell cylinders in 1904 as Leonard Dawson and approximately a quarter of his output through until 1958 was issued under pseudonyms, some of which are yet to be detected and documented. According to biographer Peter Burgiss, "Dawson can lay claim to being the most well known and respected recording artist of all time in the British Empire, her Colonies and Dominions." Burgiss estimates that Dawson sold up to 25 million records and cut well over 2,000 titles during a career that took him from cylinders to LP records. This is the most complete Dawson pseudonym list to date.

FRANK DANBY
WILL DANBY
FRED DAVIES
LEONARD DAWSON
VICTOR GRAHAM

HECTOR GRANT
CHARLES HANDY
MR. MILES
JAMES OSBORNE
DAVID PETERS

WILL STRONG
ARTHUR WALPOLE
GEORGE WELSH
PETER WENTWORTH
ROBERT WOODVILLE

ELVIS PRESLEY'S FILM NAMES

NOTE: In **That's The Way It Is**, **Elvis On Tour** and **This Is Elvis**, he portrayed himself.

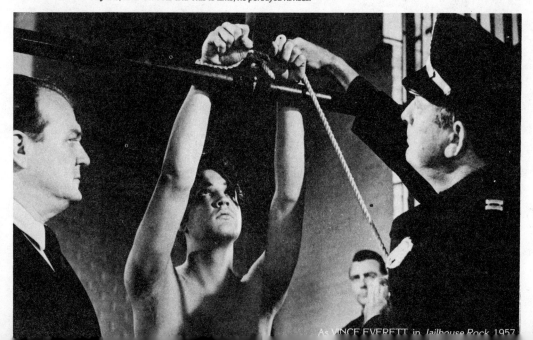

As VINCE EVERETT in *Jailhouse Rock* 1957

RAHSAAN ROLAND KIRK — Ronald T. Kirk

CAT ANDERSON — William Alonzo Anderson

CHUBBY JACKSON — Greig Stewart Jackson

CANNONBALL ADDERLY — Julian Adderly

JAZZ MUSICIANS —
Altered First Names

PEPPER ADAMS	Park Adams	Bar. Sax
CANNONBALL ADDERLY	Julian Adderly	Alto Sax
BUZZ ADLAM	Basil G. Adlam	Saxes
HOOLEY AHOLA	Sylvester Ahola	Cornet
MOUSEY ALEXANDERE	Elmer Alexander	Drums
JAP ALLEN	Jasper Allen	Bass/Tuba
RED ALLEN	Henry Allen	Trumpet
TRIGGER ALPERT	Herman Alpert	Bass
ANDY ANDERS	John Frank Anders	Reeds
BUDDY ANDERSON	Bernard Hartwell Anderson	Trumpet
CAT ANDERSON	William Alonzo Anderson	Trumpet
BENNY BAILEY	Ernest Harold Bailey	Trumpet
BUSTER BAILEY	William C. Bailey	Reeds
SHORTY BAKER	Harold Baker	Trumpet
TWO TON BAKER	Richard E. Baker	Piano
BUTCH BALLARD	George Edward Ballard	Drums
POLO BARNES	Paul D. Barnes	Reeds
DUD BASCOMB	Wilbur Odell Bascomb	Trumpet
GATO BARBIERI	Leonardo Barbieri	Tenor Sax
RIP BASSETT	Arthur Bassett	Banjo/Guitar
PUDDINGHEAD BATTLE	Edgar W. Battle	Reeds/K'brds
BIX BEIDERBECKE	Leon Bix Beiderbecke	Cornet/Piano
TEX BENEKE	Gordon Beneke	Tenor Sax
BUNNY BERIGAN	Rowland Bernard Berigan	Trumpet
SONNY BERMAN	Saul Berman	Trumpet
CHU BERRY	Leon Berry	Tenor Sax
BARNEY BIGARD	Albany Bigard	Clarinet
RAY BIONDI	Remo Biondi	Multi-Instrum.
BISH BISHOP	Wallace Henry Bishop	Drums
EUBIE BLAKE	Jamers Hubert Blake	Piano
MICKEY BLOOM	Milton Bloom	Trumpet
BUDDY BOLDEN	Charles Joseph Bolden	Cornet
SHARKEY BONANO	Joseph Bonano	Trumpet
BOZO BOSE	Sterling Belmont Bose	Trumpet
BUGS BOWER	Maurice Bower	Trumpet
TINY BRADSHAW	Myron Bradshaw	Drums/Piano
STUMPY BRADY	Floyd Maurice Brady	Trombone
RUBY BRAFF	Reuben Braff	Trumpet
DOLLAR BRAND	Adolph Johannes Brand	Piano
PETE BROWN	James Ostend Brown	Reeds/Violin
PUD BROWN	Albert Brown	Reeds
SANDY BROWN	Alexander Brown	Clarinet
SONNY BROWN	William Brown	Multi-Instrum.
YULE BROWN	Louis Brown	Piano
TOBY BROWNE	Scoville Browne	Reeds
RUSTY BRYANT	Royal G. Bryant	Saxes
MOUSE BURROUGHS	Alvin Burroughs	Drums
JACK BUTLER	Jacques Butler	Trumpet
JAKI BYARD	John A. Byard Jnr	Piano
DON BYAS	Carlos Wesley Byas	Tenor Sax
JOE BYRD	Gene Byrd	Guitar
HAPPY CALDWELL	Albert W. Caldwell	Reeds
RED CALLENDER	George Callender	Bass/Tuba
CONTE CANDOLI	Secondo Candoli	Trumpet
PETE CANDOLI	Walter Joseph Candoli	Trumpet
MUTT CAREY (aka PAPA MUTT)	Thomas Carey	Trumpet
WINGIE CARPENTER	Theodore Carpenter	Trumpet
PECK CARR	Mancy Carr	Banjo/Guitar
BENNY CARTER	Bennett Lester Carter	Reeds
OSCAR CASTRO-NEVES	Carlos Oscar de Castro Neves	Guitar/K'brds
BUDDY CATLETT	George James Catlett	Bass

195

PAPA CELESTIN	Oscar Celestin	Cornet
DOC CHEATHAM	Adolphus Cheatham	Trumpet
BUDDY CHILDERS	Marion Childers	Trumpet
BUDDY CHRISTIAN	Howard Seton Christian	Drums
SUNNY CLAPP	Charles Clapp	Trombone
JUNE CLARK	Algeria Junius Clark	Trumpet
SONNY CLARK	Conrad Yeatis Clark	Piano
KLOOK CLARKE	Kenneth Spearman Clarke	Drums
PETER CLARKE	Frank Clarke	Reeds
SONNY CLAY	William Rogers Campbell Clay	Drums/Misc.
BUCK CLAYTON	Wilbur Clayton	Trumpet
JIMMY COBB	Wilbur James Cobb	Drums
SONNY COHN	George Thomas Cohn	Trumpet
POLO COKER	Charles Mitchell Coker	Piano
BUDDY COLE	Edward Lamar Cole	Keyboards
BUDDY COLLETTE	William Marcel Collette	Reeds
SHAD COLLINS	Lester Rallington Collins	Trumpet
EDDIE CONDON	Albert Edwin Condon	Guitar/Banjo
JUNIOR COOK	Herman Cook	Tenor Sax
DOC COOKE	Charles L. Cooke	Piano
BUSTER COOPER	George Cooper	Trombone
CORKY CORCORAN	Gene Patrick Corcoran	Tenor Sax
CORKY CORNELIUS	Edward Cornelius	Trumpet
KAT COWENS	Herbert Cowens	Drums
BOB CRANSHAW	Melbourne Cranshaw	Bass
HANK CRAWFORD	Benny Ross Crawford Jnr.	Sax/Piano
SONNY CRISS	William Criss	Alto Sax
CUTTY CUTSHALL	Robert Dewees Cutshall	Trombone
PUTNEY DANDRIDGE	Louis Dandridge	Piano
BUD DANT	Charles Gustav Dant	Cornet
HAM DAVIS	Leonard Davis	Trombone
RUSTY DEDRICK	Lyle Dedrick	Trumpet
BUDDY DE FRANCO	Boniface Ferdinand Leonardo DeFranco	Clarinet
JUD DENAUT	George Matthews Denaut	Bass
BABY DODDS	Warren Dodds	Drums
MUTTONLEG DONNELLY	Theodore Donnelly	Trombone
KENNY DORHAM	McKinley Dorham	Trumpet
HANK DUNCAN	Henry James Duncan	Piano
NATTY DOMINIQUE	Anatie Dominique	Trumpet
BUZZY DROOTIN	Benjamin Drootin	Drums
SONNY DUNHAM	Elmer Lewis Dunham	Reeds
SWEETS EDISON	Harry Edison	Trumpet
BASS EDWARDS	Henry Edwards	Bass/Tuba
ROY 'LITTLE JAZZ' ELDRIDGE	David Roy Eldridge	Trumpet
ZIGGY ELMAN	Harry Elman	Trumpet
PEE WEE ERWIN	George Erwin	Trumpet
BUTCH EVANS	William Robert Evans III	Reeds
STREAMLINE EWING	John Ewing	Trombone
BUDDY FEATHERSTONHAUGH	Rupert Edward Lee Featherstonhaugh	Tenor Sax
KANSAS FIELDS	Carl Donnell Fields	Drums
POPS FOSTER	George Murphy Foster	Bass/Tuba
PANAMA FRANCIS	David A. Francis	Drums/Perc.
BUD FREEMAN	Lawrence Freeman	Reeds
VON FREEMAN	Earl Lavon Freeman	Tenor Sax
JOKI FREUND	Walter Jakob Freund	Reeds
IZZY FRIEDMAN	Irving Friedman	Reeds
KING GARCIA	Louis K. Garcia	Trumpet
JACK GARDNER (aka JUMBO JACK)	Francis Henry Gardner	Piano
MONTUDI GARLAND	Edward B. Garland	Bass
MEX GONSALVES	Paul Gonsalves	Tenor Sax
BIG BOY GOUDIE	Frank Goudie	Reeds
SONNY GREER	William Alexander Greer	Drums
CHRIS GRIFFIN	Gordon Griffin	Trumpet
TINY GRIMES	Lloyd Grimes	Guitar
RAM HALL	Minor Hall	Drums
SKIP HALL	Archibald Hall	Keyboards
BUGS HAMILTON	John Hamilton	Trumpet
CHICO HAMILTON	Foreststorn Hamilton	Drums

CAPTAIN HANDY	John Handy	Reeds
BUSTER HARDING	Lavere Harding	Piano
TOBY HARDWICKE	Otto Hardwicke	Saxes
BEAVER HARRIS	William Godvin Harris	Drums
BILL HARRIS	William Palmer Harris	Trombone
STAN HASSELGARD	Ake Hasselgarde	Clarinet
CLANCY HAYES	Clarence Leonard Hayes	Banjo
TUBBY HAYES	Edward Brian Hayes	Sax
MONK HAZEL	Arthur Hazel	Drums/Cornet
J.C. HEARD	James Charles Heard	Drums
TOOTIE HEATH	Albert Heath	Drums
SCAD HEMPHILL	Shelton Hemphill	Trumpet
HAYWOOD HENRY	Frank Henry	Reeds
SKEETS HERFURT	Arthur Herfurt	Reeds
EDDIE HIGGINS	Hayden Higgins	Piano
BASS HILL	Ernest Hill	Bass/Tuba
PEANUTS HOLLAND	Herbert Lee Holland	Trumpet
MULE HOLLEY	Major Quincy Hollley Jnr.	Bass/Tuba
RED HOLLOWAY	James L. Holloway	Reeds
STIX HOOPER	Nesbert Hooper	Drums
JOE HOWARD	Francis L. Howard	Trombone
KID HOWARD	Avery Howard	Trumpet
PEANUTS HUCKO	Michael Andrew Hucko	Reeds
BOBBI HUMPHREY	Barbara Ann Humphrey	Flute/Sax
FAT MAN HUMPHRIES	Frank Humphries	Reeds
PEE WEE HUNT	Walter Hunt	Trombone
IKE ISAACS	Charles E. Isaacs	Bass/Cello
BULLMOOSE JACKSON	Benjamin Clarence Jackson	Sax/Violin
BUTTER JACKSON	Quentin Leonard Jackson	Trombone/Bass
CHUBBY JACKSON	Greig Stewart Jackson	Bass
GATOR JACKSON	Willis Jackson	Saxes
BUD JACOBSON	Orville Kenneth Jacobson	Reeds/Piano
ILLINOIS JACQUET	Jean Baptiste Jacquet	Tenor Sax
SPIKE JANSON	Hugh Michael Janson	Piano
PAT JENKINS	Sidney Jenkins	Trumpet
POSEY JENKINS	Frederick Jenkins	Trumpet
JACK JENNEY	Truman Elliott Jenney	Trombone
BUDD JOHNSON	Albert J. Johnson	Reeds
BUDDY JOHNSON	Woodrow Wilson Johnson	Piano
BUNK JOHNSON	William Geary Johnson	Reeds/Piano
COUNTESS JOHNSON	Margaret Johnson	Piano
DINK JOHNSON	Oliver Johnson	Multi-Instrum.
J.J. JOHNSON	James Louis Johnson	Trombone
KEG JOHNSON	Frederic H. Johnson	Trombone/Guitar
LONNIE JOHNSON	Alonzo Johnson	Guitar
MONEY JOHNSON	Harold Johnson	Trumpet/Fluegel
SWAN JOHNSON	Howard William Johnson	Reeds/Piano
JONAH JONES	Robert Elliott Jones	Trumpet
PREACHER JONES	Wardell Jones	Trumpet
DUKE JORDAN	Irving Stanley (or Sydney) Jordan	Piano
SLICK JONES	Wilmore Jones	Drums
KID JORDAN	Edward Jordan	Reeds
TAFT JORDAN	James Taft Jordan	Trumpet
TINY KAHN	Norman Kahn	Drums
PECK KELLEY	John Dickson Kelley	Piano
HAL KEMP	James Harold Kemp	Reeds
RAHSAAN ROLAND KIRK	Ronald t. Kirk	Reeds
ED KIRKEBY	Wallace Theodore Kirkeby	Banjo/Piano
PAPA JACK LAINE	George Vitelle Laine	Drums/Sax
NAPPY LAMARE	Hilton Napoleon Lamare	Guitar
THUNDERBIRD LANCASTER	William Byard Lancaster	Reeds
BIG JIM LAWSON	Harry Lawson	Trumpet
SONNY LEE	Thomas Ball Lee	Trombone
MIN LEIBROOK	Wilfred F. Leibrook	Sax/Bass/Tuba
MIKE LEONARD	Harlan Quentin Leonard	Saxes
HOT LIPS LEVINE	Harry Levine	Trumpet
LUX LEWIS	Meade Anderson Lewis	Piano
BIG TINY LITTLE	Dudley Little	Piano

FUD LIVINGSTONE	Joseph Anthony Livingstone	Reeds
TRICKY LOFTON	Lawrence Ellis Lofton	Trombone
SLATS LONG	Don Long	Clarinet
BABY LOVETT	Samuel Lovett	Drums
CHUMMY MACGREGOR	J. Chalmers Macgregor	Piano
KID SHOTS MADISON	Louis Madison	Trumpet
JUNIOR MANCE	Julian Clifford Mance Jnr.	Piano
FESS MANETTA	Manuel Manetta	Multi-Instrum.
GAP MANGIONE	Gaspare Mangione	Keyboards
WINGY MANONE	Joseph Manone	Trumpet
SAXIE MANSFIELD	Maynard Mansfield	Tenor Sax
DODO MARMAROSA	Michael Marmarosa	Piano
KAISER MARSHALL	Joseph Marshall	Drums
SKIP MARTIN	Lloyd Martin	Reeds
SABU MARTINEZ	Luis Martinez	Percussion
KID MARTYN	Barry Martyn	Drums
FIDGY McGRATH	David Fulton McGrath	Piano
ROSY McHARGUE	James Eugene McHargue	Reeds
BIG MIKE McHENDRICK	Reuben Michael McHendrick	Banjo/Guitar
LITTLE MIKE MCKENDRICK	Gilbert Michael McKendrick	Banjo/Guitar
RED McKENZIE	William McKenzie	Kazoo
JACKIE McLEAN	John Lenwood McLean	Reeds
LUCKY MILLINDER	Lucius Millinder	Leader
GEEZIL MINERVE	Harold Minerve	Reeds
PIGGY MINOR	Orville Minor	Trumpet
SLAMFOOT MINOR	Dan Minor	Trombone
WHITELY MITCHELL	Gordon B. Mitchell	Bass
TOOTS MONDELLO	Nuncio Mondello	Reeds
LITTLE BROTHER MONTGOMERY	Eurreal Wilford Montgomery	Piano
TETE MONTOLIU	Vincente Montoliu	Piano
BIG CHIEF MOORE	Russell Moore	Trombone
BREW MOORE	Milton Aubrey Moore	Tenor Sax
SLIM MOORE	Alton Moore	Trombone
FLUTES MORTON	Norvel E. Morton	Reeds
LANNY MORGAN	Harold Lansford Morgan	Alto Sax
SONNY MORGAN	Howard Morgan	Percussion
BENNY MOTEN	Clarence Lemont Moten	Bass
MOON MULLENS	Edward Mullens	Trumpet
SPUD MURPHY	Lyle Murphy	Reeds
SUNNAY MURRAY	James Arthur Murray	Drums
BOOTS MUSSULLI	Henry W. Mussulli	Saxes
BUMPS MYERS	Hubert Maxwell Myers	Saxes
SERIOUS MYERS	Wilson Ernest Myers	Bass/Guitar
RAY NANCE	Willis Nance	Trumpet/Violin
TRICKY SAM NANTON	Joseph Nanton	Trombone
TEDDY NAPOLEON	George Napoleon	Piano
FATS NAVARRO	Theodore Navarro	Trumpet
BIG EYE NELSON	Louis Nelson	Clarinet
YELLOW NUNEZ	Alcide Nunez	Clarinet
SY OLIVER	Melvin James Oliver	Trumpet
ISLAND OSTLUND	Petur David Ostlund	Drums
GEORGE OTSUKA	Keiji Otsuka	Drums
TINY PARHAM	Hartzell Strathdene Parham	Piano/Organ
TRUCK PARHAM	Charles Valdez Parnham	Bass
KNOCKY PARKER	John William Parker	Piano
SLOW DRAG PAVAGEAU	Alcide Pavageau	Bass
DUKE PEARSON	Columbus Calvin Pearson Jnr	Piano
FATS PICHON	Walter Pichon	Piano
DEDE PIERCE	Joseph DeLacrois Pierce	Trumpet
NEELY PLUMB	Benjamin Plumb	Reeds
JAKE PORTER	Vernon Porter	Cornet
YANK PORTER	Allen Porter	Drums
DOC POSTON	Joseph E. Posten	Reeds
BUD POWELL	Earl Powell	Piano
RUDY POWELL	Everard Stephen Powell	Reeds
SPECS POWELL	Gordon Powell	Drums
KEG PURNELL	William Purnell	Drums
MOE PURTILL	Maurice Purtill	Drums

SNOOZER QUINN	Edwin McIntosh Quinn	Guitar/Banjo
JUNIOR RAGLIN	Alvin Redrick Raglin	Bass
RAM RAMIREZ	Roger Ramirez	Piano/Organ
MOUSE RANDOLPH	Irving Randolph	Trumpet
BILLY RAUCH	Russell Rauch	Trombone
SKIP REDWINE	Wilbur Redwine	Piano
DIZZY REECE	Alphonso Son Reece	Trumpet
RED REEVES	Reuben Reeves	Trumpet
RED RICHARDS	Charles Richards	Piano
BOOMIE RICHMAN	Abraham Samuel Richman	Reeds
TONY RIZZI	Trefoni Rizzi	Guitar
LUCKY ROBERTS	Charles Luckyeth Roberts	Piano
ZUE ROBERTSON	C. Alvin Robertson	Trombone
BIG JIM ROBINSON	Nathan Robinson	Trombone
BANJO ROBINSON	Ikey L. Robinson	Banjo/Guitar
ROD RODRIGUEZ	Nicholas Goodwin Rodriguez	Piano
SHORTY ROGERS	Milton M. Rogers	Trumpet
SONNY ROLLINS	Theodore Walter Rollins	Tenor Sax
CURLY RUSSELL	Dillon Russell	Bass
PEE WEE RUSSELL	Charles Ellsworth Russell	Reeds
BABE RUSSIN	Irving Russin	Reeds
RUDY RUTHERFORD	Elman Rutherford	Reeds
FATS SADI	Lallemand Sadi	Vibes/Bongos
PHAROAH SANDERS	Farrell Sanders	Sax
RED SAUNDERS	Theodore Saunders	Drums/Perc.
BUD SCOTT	Arthur Scott	Guitar/Banjo
HONEY BEAR SEDRIC	Eugene P. Sedrick	Reeds
BUD SHANK	Clifford Everett Shank Jnr.	Reeds
BUSTER SHAVER	Floyd Herbert Shaver	Piano
LIGE SHAW	Elijah W. Shaw	Drums/Perc.
SHEP SHEPHERD	Berisford Shepherd	Drums
LONNIE SIMMONS	Samuel Simmons	Reeds/Keyboards
PAZUZA SIMON	Stafford Simon	Reeds
ZOOT SIMS	John Haley Sims	Tenor Sax
ZUTTY SINGLETON	Arthur James Singleton	Drums
BUSTER SMITH	Henry Smith	Reeds/Guitar
JABBO SMITH	Cladys Smith	Trumpet
POPS SMITH	Russell T. Smith	Trumpet
STUFF SMITH	Hezekiah Leroy Gordon Smith	Violin
TAB SMITH	Talmadge Smith	Saxes
TATTI SMITH	Carl Smith	Trumpet
MUGGSY SPANIER	Francis Joseph Spanier	Cornet
TUT SOPER	Oro M. Soper	Piano
O'NEILL SPENCER	William Spencer	Drums
PEE WEE SPITELARA	Joseph T. Spitelara	Reeds
STEVE STEVENSON	Tommy Stevenson	Trumpet
SONNY STITT	Edward Stitt	Alto Sax
BUDDY SVARDA	William Ernest Svarda	Trombone
KING SWAYZEE	Edwin Swayzee	Trumpet
BUDDY TATE	George Holmes Tate	Reeds
JACK TEAGARDEN	Weldon Leo Teagarden	Trombone
TOOTS THIELMANS	Jean Thielmans	Harmonica
FOOTS THOMAS	Walter Purl Thomas	Reeds
CAL TJADER	Callen Radcliffe Tjader Jnr	Vibes
TRAPS TRAPPIER	Arthur Benjamin Trappier	Drums
BON BON TUNNELL	George N. Tunnell	Piano
McCOY TYNER	Alfred McCoy Tyner	Piano
SYD VALENTINE	Raymond Valentine	Trumpet
JOE VENUTI	Guiseppe Venuti	Violin
PINKY VIDACOVICH	Irving Vidacovich	Reeds
CLEANHEAD VINSON	Edward Vinson	Alto Sax
NUNN WARE	Winfred Nettleton Ware	Trombone
BAMA WARWICK	William Carl Warwick	Trumpet
COUNTRY WASHBOURNE	Joseph Washbourne	Bass/Tuba
BUCK WASHINGTON	Ford Lee Washington	Piano/Trumpet
DIAMOND WASHINGTON	Leon Washington	Reeds
JACK WASHINGTON	Ronald Washington	Saxes
MACK WASHINGTON	William Washington	Drums
HANK WAYLAND	Frederick Gregson Weyland	

CHICK WEBB	William Webb	Drums
SPEED WEBB	Lawrence Arthur Webb	Drums
DOC WEST	Harold West	Drums
PEANUTS WHALUM	Hugh David Whalum Jnr	Sax/Piano
FATHER WHITE	Harry Alexander White	Reeds
FRUIT WHITE	Morris White	Guitar
SONNY WHITE	Ellerton Oswald White	Piano
BEARCAT WILLIAMS	John Overton Williams	Reeds
COOTIE WILLIAMS	Charles Melvin Williams	Trumpet
FESS WILLIAMS	Stanley R. Williams	Reeds
FIDDLER WILLIAMS	Claude Williams	Guitar/Violin
HAPPY WILLIAMS	David Williams	Bass
SANDY WILLIAMS	B. Alexander Williams	Trombone
BUSTER WILSON	Albert W. Wilson	Piano
JUICE WILSON	Robert Edward Wilson	Violin
SHADOW WILSON	Rossiere Wilson	Drums
BOOTIE WOOD	Mitchell W. Wood	Trumpet
PREZ YOUNG	Lester Willis Young	Reeds
SNOOKIE YOUNG	Eugene Edward Young	Trumpet
TRUMMY YOUNG	James Osborne Young	Trombone
ZEKE ZARCHY	Rubin Zarchy	Trumpet

THE JAZZ SCENE

BUD FREEMAN QUINTET featuring RUBY BRAFF

Lawrence Freeman and Reuben Braff

BUDDY DE FRANCO — Boniface Ferdinand Leonardo De Franco

RED ALLEN — Henry Allen

BUCK CLAYTON — Wilbur C

75 HIT SONGS WRITTEN UNDER PSEUDONYMS

ABERGAVENNY by Marty Wilde
Frere Manston (Marty Wilde) and Jack Gellar (Ronnie Scott)

A BLOSSOM FELL by Nat King Cole
Harold Cornelius (Harold Fields), Dominic John (Joseph Roncoroni) and Howard Barnes

AINT MISBEHAVIN' by Fats Waller
Andy Razaf† (Andreamentania Paul Razafinkeriefo) and Fats Waller (Thomas Wright Waller)

BABY YOU COME ROLLIN' CROSS MY MIND by Peppermint Trolley Company
Jesse Lee Kincaid (Nick Gerlach)

BECAUSE by Perry Como
Edward Teschemaker (Edward Lockton) and Guy d'Hardelot (Helen Rhodes)

BOOGIE WOOGIE BUGLE BOY by Andrews Sisters/Bette Midler
Don Raye (Donald MacRae Wilhoite Jnr) and Hughie Prince

BORN TO BE WILD by Steppenwolf
Mars Bonfire (Dennis Edmonton)

BREAKWAY by The Beach Boys
Reggie Dunbar (Murray Wilson) and Brian Wilson

CALIFORNIA PARADISE by The Runaways
Kari Krome (Kari Lee Mitchell), Joan Jett (Joan Larkin) and Sandy West (Sandra Resavento)

CARA MIA by Jay & The Americans
Lee Lange (Bunny Lewis) and Tulio Trapani (Mantovani)

CHILD OF CLAY by Jimmie Rodgers #2
Jimmy Curtiss (James Stulberger)

DON'T GO BREAKING MY HEART by Elton John & Kiki Dee
Ann Orson (Elton John) and Carte Blanch (Bernie Taupin)

DON'T YOU KNOW I LOVE YOU? by The Clovers
Nugetre (Ahmet Ertegun)

DOWN IN THE SUBWAY by Soft Cell
Jack Hammer (Earl S. Burroughs)

EYE LEVEL by The Simon Park Orchestra
Jack Trombey (Jules Staffaro)

FEVER by Little Willie John/Peggy Lee
John Davenport (Otis Blackwell) and Eddie Cooley

FORGET HIM by Bobby Vee
Mark Anthony (Tony Hatch)

FROM RUSSIA WITH LOVE by Matt Munro
John Barry (John Barry Prendergast) and Lionel Bart (Lionel Begleiter)

GIRL WATCHER by The O'Kaysions
Buck Trail (Ronald B. Killette)

GITARZAN by Ray Stevens
Bill Everette (William E. Justis) and Ray Stevens (Harold Raymond Ragsdale)

HAPPY ORGAN by Dave 'Baby' Cortez
Ken Wood (Walter R. Moody)

HOW DO YOU DO IT? by Gerry & The Pacemakers
Mitch Murray (L. Michael Stitcher)

I AM WOMAN by Helen Reddy
Ray Burton (Raymond Doughty) and Helen Reddy

IF THIS IS LOVE by The Precisions
Marty Coleman (Martin Cohen)

LOVE ME TENDER

Words and Music by ELVIS PRESLEY and VERA MATSON

Sung by ELVIS PRESLEY
In the 20th CENTURY-FOX CINEMASCOPE Production- "Love Me Tender"

As Recorded by
Elvis Presley
on R.C.A.

Aberbach (Aust.) Pty. Ltd.
250 PITT STREET, SYDNEY

ELVIS PRESLEY MUSIC, INC.
AND SOUTHERN BELLE MUSIC

Sole Selling Agents
HILL AND RANGE SONGS INC.
1650 Broadway, New York, 19, N.Y.

Authorised for Sale only in Australia and New Zealand

3/- net

I GOT STUNG by Elvis Presley
David Hill (David Alexander Hess) and Aaron Schroeder

I'LL NEVER FIND ANOTHER YOU by The Seekers
Tom Springfield (Thomas O'Brien)

I THINK WE'RE ALONE NOW by Tommy James & Shondells/Rubinoos/Lene Lovich
Ritchie Cordell (Richard Rosenblatt) and Bo Gentry (Robert Ackoff)

I'VE GOT A LOVELY BUNCH OF COCONUTS by Freddy Martin Orch.
Fred Heatherton (Elton Box, Desmond Cox and Irwin Dash)

KAY by John Wesley Ryles I
Hank Mills (Samuel Garrett)

KIND OF A DRAG by The Buckinghams
Jimmy Harris (James Holvay)

KISSES SWEETER THAN WINE by Jimmie Rodgers #2
Joel Newman (Huddie Ledbetter) and Paul Campbell (The Weavers)

KISSIN' COUSINS by Elvis Presley
Randy Starr (Warren Nadel) and Fred Wise

LAST TRAIN TO CLARKSVILLE by The Monkees
Tommy Boyce (Sidney Thomas Boyce Jnr) and Bobby Hart (Robert Luke Harshman)

LEANING ON THE LAMPOST by Herman's Hermits
Noel Gay (Reginald M. Armitage)

LET IT ROCK by The Rolling Stones
Edward Anderson (Chuck Berry)

LIPSTICK TRACES ON A CIGARETTE by The O'Jays/Amazing Rhythm Aces
Naomi Neville (Allan Toussaint)

LITTLE BROWN JUG by Glenn Miller Orchestra
R. A. Eastburn (J. E. Winner)

LOVE ME TENDER by Elvis Presley
Vera Matson†† (Ken Darby) and Elvis Presley

MAMBO ROCK by Bill Haley & His Comets
M. Phillips (Mildred Pressman) and others

MARCH FROM THE RIVER KWAI (aka COLONEL BOGEY MARCH) By Mitch Miller
Kenneth J. Alford (Frederick J. Ricketts)

MASTER JACK by Four Jacks & A Jill
D. Marks (David Markantonatos)‡

MELODIE D'AMOUR by The Ames Brothers
Leo Johns (Jimmy Phillips and Marcel Stellman) and Henry Salvador

MEXICAN PEARLS by Billy Vaughan & His Orchestra
Don Randi (Donald Schwarz)

NAVY BLUE by Diane Renay
Eddie Rambeau (Edward Fluri) and Bud Rehak (Andrew Racheck)

NOBODY KNOWS WHAT'S GOIN' ON ... by The Chiffons
Brute Force (Arthur Friedlander)

ONLY SIXTEEN/WONDERFUL WORLD by Sam Cooke
Barbara Campbell (Sam Cooke, Herb Alpert and Lou Adler)

PAPER DOLL by The Mills Brothers
Johnny Black (John Huber)

STEPHENWOLF — featuring JOHN KAY (Joachim F. Krauledat), GOLDY McJOHN (John Raymond Goadsby) and JOHN MORGAN (Rushton John Moreve). Their hit Born To Be Wild was written by Dennis Edmonton as Mars Bonfire.

PLAY WITH FIRE by The Rolling Stones
Nanker/Phelge (Mick Jagger and Keith Richards)

RED RIVER ROCK by Johnny & The Hurricanes
Tom King (Irving Micahnik), Ira Mack (Harry Balk) and Fred Mendelsohn

RED SAILS IN THE SUNSET by Fats Domino/The Platters/The Beatles
Hugh Williams (Will Grosz)

ROCK AROUND THE CLOCK by Bill Haley & His Comets
Jimmy DeKnight (James E. Myers) and Max C. Freedman

SALLY GO AROUND THE ROSES by The Jaynettes
Lona Stephens (Lona Spector)

SHAKE RATTLE & ROLL by Bill Haley & His Comets/Elvis Presley
Charles Calhoun (Jesse Stone)

S-H-I-N-E by Frankie Laine
Cecil Mack (Richard C. McPherson)

SIGNED, SEALED AND DELIVERED by James Brown
Lois Mann (Syd Nathan)

STAND BY ME by Ben E. King/John Lennon
Elmo Glick (Jerry Leiber and Mike Stoller) and Ben E. King (Benjamin Earl Nelson)

ST. JAMES INFIRMARY by The Animals
Joe Primrose (Irving Mills)

SUSPICIOUS MINDS by Elvis Presley/Fine Young Cannibals
Mark James (Francis Rodney Zambon)

TAKE ME FOR A LITTLE WHILE by Vanilla Fudge
Trade Martin (John Lione)

TELL ME YOU'RE MINE by The Gaylords
U. Bertini (Ronald Fredianelli), D. Vasin (Nino Ravasini) and Ronnie Vincent

THE FOOL by Sanford Clark
Naomi Ford (Lee Hazlewood)

THE RIVER IS WIDE by The Forum/Grass Roots
Gary Knight††† (Harold P. Tempkin) and Bill Admire

TIME IS ON MY SIDE by The Rolling Stones
Norman Meade (Jerry Ragavoy)

TOSSIN' & TURNIN' by Bobby Lewis
Ritchie Adams (Richard Adam Ziegler)

TOSSIN' & TURNIN' by The Ivy League
John Carter (John Shakespeare), Ken Lewis (Kenneth Hawker) and Perry Ford (Brian Pugh)

TROMBONE CHOLLY by Bessie Smith
George Brooks (James Fletcher Henderson)

UNCHAIN MY HEART by Ray Charles
Agnes Jones (Bobby Sharp) and Freddy James (Teddy Powell)

WALK AWAY RENEE by The Left Banke/Four Tops
Mike Brown (Michael Lookofsky)

WALK OUT OF MY MIND by Waylon Jennings
Red Lane (Hollis DeLaughter)

WHAT A WONDERFUL WORLD by Louis Armstrong
George Douglas (Robert Thiele) and George David Weiss

WILD THING by The Troggs/Jimi Hendrix/Cold Chisel
Chip Taylor (James Wesley Voight)

WOMAN by Peter & Gordon
Bernard Webb (Paul McCartney)

WRITING ON THE WALL by Adam Wade
George Eddy (George Paxton)

WYOMING by Mantovani
Gene Williams (Lawrence Wright)

YOU KNOW HE DID by The Hollies
L. Ransford (Allan Clarke, Tony Hicks and Graham Nash)

† Andy Razaf was the nephew of Queen Ranavalona III of Madagasgar.
†† Vera Matson was the wife of actual writer Ken Darby, who was unable to take credit because he was affiliated with the wrong performance rights society. Elvis had no role whatsoever in writing the song.
††† Harold P. Tempkin also co-wrote *Vacation* for Connie Francis, as Gary Weston.
‡ In fact, this was really written by Bob James, who credited it to Marks.

INDEX

This is intended as a practical working index of the 'stage' names under which we know music identities. For obvious reasons of space limitation, every name in the book has not been indexed. Christian Name and Surname artists are not included as they can be easily alphabetically referred to on pages 82-89. Pseudonyms of prominent performers/writers are included only when those names have achieved consistent prominence in their own right (Ben Colder, Simon Crum etc). In the areas of Blues Trade Names and Aliases, inclusion has been selective on the basis of significant recording prominence. 'Novelty' sections of the book (No Such Animal, Elvis Presley's Film Names etc) have not been indexed.

Elton John's Birth Certificate

CERTIFIED COPY OF AN ENTRY OF BIRTH

	REGISTRATION DISTRICT
1947. BIRTH in the Sub-district of	Harrow

Columns:—	1	2	3	4	5
No.	When and where born	Name, if any	Sex	Name and surname of father	Name, surname, maiden surname of mother
	Twenty fifth March 1947 55 Pinner Hill Road Pinner Harrow	Reginald Kenneth	Boy	Stanley Dwight	Sheila Eileen Dwight formerly ...

CERTIFIED to be a true copy of an entry in the certified copy of a Register of
Given at the GENERAL REGISTER OFFICE, LONDON, under the Seal of the said Offi

BXA 936220

This certificate is issued in pursuance of the Births and Deaths
sealed or stamped with the seal of the General Register Office s
proof of the entry, and no certified copy purporting to have bee

CAUTION:—It is an offence to falsify a certificate or to
accepted as genuine to the prejudice of any person or to po

...ton

....................in the County of Middlesex

6	7	8	9	10*
Occupation of father	Signature, description and residence of informant	When registered	Signature of registrar	Name entered after registration
...tt ...itenant ... VR.	S. Dwight Father 55 Penin Hill Road Pinner	Twenty sixth March 1947	F.W.Denlyfein Indian Registrar	

...e District above mentioned.

3rd   day of April   1984

*See note overleaf

...Act 1953. Section 34 provides that any certified copy of an entry purporting to be
...d as evidence of the birth or death to which it relates without any further or other
...aid Office shall be of any force or effect unless it is sealed or stamped as aforesaid.

...vingly use a false certificate or a copy of a false certificate intending it to be
...ate knowing it to be false without lawful authority.

Form A502M Dd 8264376 100M 6/83 Mcr (301297)

THE AUTHOR

First published in Australia in 1984 (and updated here), this was Glenn's fifth book, his previous titles being *The New Music* and *The New Rock'n'Roll* (with Stuart Coupe), *Rock Lens* (with Bob King) and *The Beatles Down Under*. It has been followed by *Monkeemania – The True Story Of The Monkees*, with *The Beach Party* (with Stuart McParland), *Rock – The Bottom Line* (with Bob King) and *Glenn A. Baker On Music* due for publication in 1987, to be followed by *Monterey – The First Festival*.

Glenn, 34, is one of Australia's most active and highly regarded specialist rock writer/researchers and radio/television presenters. His absorption of musical trivia is recognised throughout the world. On Boxing Day 1984 he became the BBC's inaugural 'Rock Brain Of The Universe' in an international satellite link.

Australian editor of Billboard for the past 7 years, Glenn has written for a large range of international and local publications, including Musician, Music Week, Record World, History of Rock, Goldmine, Rolling Stone, Penthouse, Cosmopolitan, Sydney Morning Herald, Playboy, Music Life (Japan), People, Rock Video and the Australian Encyclopaedia. He was an editorial consultant to the Australian Music Directory and founder/senior editor of Countdown magazine.

Glenn was formerly alternate compere of *After Dark* (ATN7 TV), co-compere of *Music Video* (TEN 10 TV) and *Beat Club* (SBS 28 TV). He has presented his *Rock'n'Roll Trivia Show* on 2JJ and 2WS and for three years has hosted the popular *Music Buff's Show* with Bob Hudson for the Australian Broadcasting Corporation station 2BL. He was creative consultant to the television specials *The Wild One, Australia Now!* and *Australian Music Stars Of The 60s;* co-wrote the theme song to the Australian feature film *The FJ Holden;* was a successful artist manager; and was voted Best Rock Journalist at the 1979 Australian Rock Awards. During 1983 he wrote the acclaimed 36 hour radio documentary *... And The Beat Goes On* and in 1985 created the best-selling *Rock Academy* board game.

Custodian of one of the largest private record and memorabilia collections in the Southern Hemisphere, Glenn operates the Raven and Rivet record labels and the Rhythm'n'Views video label, is special projects consultant to a number of major Australian record companies, and has compiled over 150 specialist anthology albums of rock and audio archives. He lives in Sydney with his wife and four sons and is becoming increasingly active as a travel writer.

Eliciting rare Rolling Stones secrets from bassist Bill Wyman (William Perks).

Backstage with Bob Dylan (Robert Allan Zimmerman), Sydney, 1986.